CONCEAL

A NOVEL

AVA HARRISON

Conceal: A Novel

Published by AH Publishing

Cover Design: Hang Le
Model: Chad Johansson
Line Edit: Lawrence Editing, www.lawrenceediting.com, editing4Indies
Proofreader: Marla Selkow Esposito, My Brother's Editor, Gemma Woolley
Formatting: Champagne Book Design

Dedicated to all the girls who grew up thinking they needed a knight to save them. That sword looks better in your hands.

It is during our darkest moments that we
must focus to see the light.
—Aristotle

CHAPTER ONE

Jaxson

NOTHING LIKE DINNER WITH THE FAMILY. THIS IS definitely not how I typically plan to spend my Friday night, but when Grayson calls, you drop what you're doing and go. Because what my brother wants, my brother gets. This includes, but sure as hell is not limited to, family dinner.

For our starting course, we'll have a lecture about how much Grayson and Addison have done for the family and company. And for the main entrée, a three-hour dissertation on what a fuckup I am.

When you're me, that fate is inevitable.

Since I don't need a reminder from my brother to show up, I head uptown to his and River's apartment.

Traffic is in my favor today, so it doesn't take me long, and before I know it, I'm riding the elevator up to his penthouse apartment that occupies the whole top level of the building we own.

We.

Price Enterprise.

Addison, my sister, has an apartment similar to this one. Not me, though.

I hate this area.

No. I live downtown in a converted loft space in Tribeca. It's a far cry from the view of Central Park my brother has, but it's more my speed. This uptight building is my worst nightmare. I need space, and most of all, I need privacy. It works well for Grayson, though. With its high ceilings and modern feel, it easily reflects his personality. Here in his fortress, he sits on top of the world like the king. Because that's what Grayson Price is . . . a king, and I, a mere jester.

It hasn't always been this way, though. Don't get me wrong, Grayson has always had a stick up his ass, but it's grown since my father died. He feels the need to fill shoes that were never meant to be filled.

What he doesn't realize is that he can never be Dad. The man was a legend, not only in the boardroom but also at home.

He was always there, no matter how many hours he worked, and missed nothing. My biggest regret in life was not appreciating it. As the youngest child by five years, I always had a large chip on my shoulder because no one was around to play with me.

I always thought my father was too busy with my siblings to care about me. But hindsight is twenty-twenty and now that he's gone, I understand I was wrong, and it was just an illusion in a young kid's mind. Unfortunately, this revelation came too late, as I spent the greater part of my youth acting out to get attention, which is why, years later, I'm still trying to prove that I've grown up.

Like now, rushing to get here early to be taken seriously.

Lucky for me, the ride doesn't take long, and the next thing I know, the elevator opens into the modern space of their apartment.

Even by my standards, it's large, which says a lot, seeing as I grew up on a compound. Floor-to-ceiling windows overlook the park. Stainless steel appliances, black cabinets, and dark floors complete the look.

Fuck, this place is sterile.

Surgery could be performed here, and you wouldn't even need to disinfect.

Maybe surgery to remove the stick.

His apartment is killer. Too bad the location sucks. Because as much as it's a beautiful view, it's not worth having to deal with the people who live nearby.

People like my brother.

People who look down their nose at me because I'm more comfortable wearing jeans than a three-piece suit.

"Jax, you're here."

I get out of the elevator and walk into the apartment. My brother is already standing there, arms crossed, head cocked, looking at me with an eyebrow raised.

Perplexed is more like it. I've shocked him.

Because not only am I here at this impromptu dinner, but I'm also early.

Good. I like to shake things up.

Keep them guessing.

"I am," I respond in my typical, smug as shit attitude.

Now with that observation out of the way, I cross the space between us and give him a nod before turning my attention to River sitting on the couch. They are cute together. Where he's hard, she's soft. Two opposing qualities but when put together, they complement each other. I guess the saying is true—opposites attract.

But in this case, River and Grayson as a couple are quite the paradox. She's like sunshine, and he's like rain, but in the end, I guess they make a rainbow.

"So," I start, letting my lip tip up, "when are you getting married already?"

River is by far my favorite sibling, even if she isn't my sister yet. The faster we can fix that, the better. She grounds Grayson. She makes him lighter and easier to deal with. Sure, he's still a bastard sometimes, but he's at least tolerable half the time now.

"We only got engaged a few months ago." She laughs, playing with the blue diamond on her left ring finger. I'm not sure what that's all about, but it's cool and unique. It's different like her. Like River.

"Mom's coming too."

That makes my brow lift, and I turn to my brother. "Does this mean you're planning the wedding? Finally," I add.

"Yes. It does," Grayson says, his voice still tight. It's as if we're talking about a board meeting and not his future nuptials.

How hard would it be for him to smile? Is he this uptight all the time? I wonder if he's like this in the bed—nope. Not going to go there.

"About time," I respond, and as if on cue, the elevator opens again, making me turn my head to see who's arrived now. This time, Addison, Oliver, and my mom make their way into the apartment.

I watch as they walk toward me. Addison looks beautiful as always. She's dressed more casually than I'm used to, wearing black leggings, a sweater dress, and boots, but as she rarely comes into work these days, I shouldn't be that surprised. There's no need for a pantsuit if you're not in the office.

Her hand rests on her rounded belly.

My older sister is starting to show.

Her face glows with happiness.

Grayson stands and walks over to her, wearing a smile on his face.

My brother appears to be excited. I can't help but be a little jealous.

They both look so damn happy, Oliver included. Everyone has moved on with these lives they've made for themselves, and I have nothing to show at this point. Not true. I have a killer binge list for Netflix.

Once Grayson has stepped away, my mom is the first to hug me and then my sister. Oliver greets me with an outstretched hand. Polite like an English gentleman, but seeing as he is an earl, I'm not surprised.

"Dinner will be ready in a minute," Grayson says, gesturing to the dining room.

"You cooked?" I ask my older brother.

"Hardly," he grunts out as we head toward the table.

"River?"

He shakes his head. "Catered." He shrugs like this question is ridiculous. To them, it might be, but to me, it's not. I don't have staff, nor do I have a cook. Yes, I have a large loft space and a private studio, but that's only for my "second job." I need those things to work. But I don't allow anyone in those places. I can't risk it.

Apparently, hacking is frowned upon by the United States Government.

We all settle at the table. It appears they've placed name cards down on it, which seems stuffy for a family dinner, but something tells me this is River's first "dinner," and she wants to impress. That thought makes me smile. As I approach, I spot my seat beside Oliver's, clear across the table from my brother. I wonder if that was on purpose. Grayson said he would try harder with me, but seeing as I never see him and rarely speak to him, I know he's full of shit. And if these seating charts are anything to go by, it only confirms it. My brother hates me. *What a dick.*

Good thing I don't care.

Or that's what I tell myself as I sit down. I'm facing the window with a spectacular view of Central Park. The apartment has an open floor plan, so it's only a few feet from the living room, the way it's tucked away makes it feel intimate regardless.

When we're seated, the waitstaff appears to serve the food, placing plates down in front of each one of us.

I'm not even sure where they were before. It's like they simply materialized, appearing out of thin air to tend to us. I've got to hand it to Grayson and River. They sure know how to entertain.

Even if it's pretentious as fuck.

I lean back in my chair and enjoy the presentation. After they serve the wine, I pick up my glass and take a sip. I'm about to take another one when my brother clears his throat.

"So, I'm sure you can imagine the reason we are here. With Addison pregnant, we were thinking of putting off the wedding until the spring or summer. After the baby is born."

"How thoughtful." She laughs.

"We've also been thinking a lot about it, and we'd like to get married in the Hamptons. Addy, will you be okay traveling with a newborn?" He's facing her now, his eyes soft as he addresses the question.

"Yeah, totally. Depending on when you get married, the baby will be over three months old, so it will be fine. I might be sleep-deprived and exhausted, but I'll be there."

River laughs. "Okay, good."

Grayson then coughs, and I turn my attention back to him.

"I'll probably be working remotely a lot to help with the wedding planning." His gaze is on me. The room feels like it's getting hotter, and the walls are closing in on me. He's about to say something. Something that will affect me. He's about to tell me, there's no Santa, or worse, Mrs. Claus is a mass murderer. I'm not looking forward to it.

He turns to Addison then, who nods.

"I'll be traveling back to England soon. My doctor doesn't want me flying in the third trimester."

Shit. Where is this going?

"That's another reason I have called this meeting. I want to discuss hiring someone to manage some of the work you do, Addy. I won't be around—"

My lungs tighten at his words.

He doesn't trust me.

He wants to bring in someone to do his job. When Addy stepped back, no one ever questioned Grayson's ability to handle both their jobs, yet now that I'm up for it, they doubt me.

They don't think I can do it.

I can.

"I'll do it," I cut in, not just because my pride dictates that I fight for my place but also because I don't want some stranger meddling in my business. Plus, it would be nice to be taken seriously for once.

"Jax—"

The way he says my name makes my blood boil. I lift my hand in the air, stopping him midsentence.

"No. Don't Jax me. Why would you hire someone else when I'm here, able and willing?" I try to keep my voice neutral, but to be honest, it's hard because I'm so pissed. Years of buried resentment rises to the surface, bubbling like a volcano ready to erupt.

"It's a lot of responsibility." He sounds like Dad, scolding me for coming home too late. But he's not my father, so it eggs me on even more.

"And I can't handle it?" I bite back, the anger now clear in my voice.

"Jax." I hear my name from across the table and turn toward the soft voice. "Gray doesn't mean that," Addison says, but it's too late to calm me down. I push up from the chair.

"He does. He never thinks I can handle anything. Yet who do you all call when you need shit?" I stare at Grayson hard, then turn my attention to Addison. "Me. That's who." I shift my gaze to Oliver next, then to River. Although they haven't spoken, they are guilty by association, especially since I've helped them out too. "Who bails you all out when you need help? Me!" I shout. "So what is it? You say you need me, but now . . . I'm not enough." My head shakes, and I let out a breath.

"Jax—" Grayson pushes his hand through his hair. "It's not that I don't appreciate all your help and all you've done for this family, but this is different." He tries to placate me with his hand, but I'm well beyond that point.

"How so?"

"Meetings. Deadlines. Being at the office by six a.m. some days. Working all night."

"All things I've done for you for free in the past."

"That might be true, but you do that remotely, God knows where and when. If you help in the office, you have to be in the office. If you travel, it's not on your time anymore; it's on the company's time."

"I can handle it."

"You might think you—"

"I said I can handle it."

"Grayson," Addison says, and he turns toward her. "Give him the opportunity. I'm okay with it."

"Fine," Gray answers. "But—"

"Enough," I bark because I'm tired of being the clown. I'm tired of no one taking me seriously. No matter how much I do, they keep doubting me, and I'm sick of it. "It's done. I'm doing it." I turn toward my mom, who looks pale at my outburst. Remorse fills me, but I won't back down. I give her a weak and tight smile. She doesn't deserve my malice. "Bye, Mom."

I storm toward the elevator and press the button without bothering to say goodbye to anyone else. No one says another word, and as I step on, I keep my back straight and my head held high.

I said my piece, and now I'll do what I need to do. Because I will prove them all wrong.

CHAPTER TWO

Willow

THUMP.

Thump.

Thump.

The blood rushes inside my veins as the words I heard only moments earlier replay in my ears.

How is this happening? Twenty-six-year-olds should be getting married and starting families, not on the run.

My hands are still shaking as I pull my car out of the driveway.

Don't speed, I tell myself as I watch the speedometer, but I need to get out of here. As much as I want to pump my foot on the gas, I don't.

I can't risk the cops pulling me over. Or anyone knowing I'm leaving.

If I get caught, I don't know what will happen.

Almost there. I've almost made it. The city limit is approaching, but with each mile my car eats up, my body trembles more and more. I swear I might pass out.

My heart is pumping so hard, I fear it will burst from my chest.

I'm not going to make it. I will pass out behind the wheel and crash and probably die. Though with my luck, death seems like a good fate right now.

Breathe.

Inhale. Exhale.

In the distance, I see the turn. Holding my breath, I move the wheel and make the right off the road and merge onto the street that will lead me out of this hellhole. In my rearview mirror, I spot the sign.

The town I'm leaving.

Madison Bay, Michigan.

I'm out, putting distance between me and the demons living there. But those thoughts can't occupy my head right now. No. There is no place for doubt or fear. I have to stay on course.

I keep driving until the words are no longer decipherable in the distance. Until I merge onto another road. And another.

Until the past is behind me, and I can focus on my future. Or at least the foreseeable future.

The road ahead of me is dark with no other light but my headlights illuminating the path I'm taking, which almost feels like an omen. My future is as bleak as this abandoned road.

With a shake of my head, I don't allow myself to think that. Dark or not, I'm safe and free for now.

An hour later, I think I have gained enough distance to stop safely somewhere, so I do. Pulling over at a gas station, I use the pump farthest from the store, and I don't bother going inside to shop. To be honest, I can't risk it. Plus, I need nothing other than what I packed in the duffel I brought with me. I park at the pump and throw my phone in the garbage, and as fast as I'm there, I'm leaving.

I drive for another thirty minutes, taking turns and gaining more distance before I find the destination for my next stop. It feels surreal leaving . . .

It's as if with each mile I drove, the haze of the lie I was living lifted, and the reality of the hell I was living in is no longer hiding behind plain sight.

Hell isn't a place, though; it's a feeling you carry with you, and I fear that no distance will weaken it or make me safe.

Pushing the thought down, I find a spot in the lot and turn off the car. I swing open the door to leave, but not before I grab my small duffel. I know in time they will find my car, so I make sure not to leave anything behind that could lead anyone to my future destination. I don't know where I'll end up. I know the farther away, the better.

With my duffel in hand, I walk to the window.

"Where to?" asks the woman behind the glass. She doesn't even bother to look at me, like my talking to her is a huge inconvenience.

Where should I go?

How far until I'm safe.

It's a loaded question because he'll travel any distance to find me. The more distance I put between me and him, the better chance I have to formulate a plan before I'm found.

"Ohio," I respond.

That's not my destination. No, not at all. But the more locations I go, the better chance I have.

She nods and rings me up, still not looking up as she types away. When she tells me the price, I take out the cash in my pocket and pay.

With the money in front of her, she finally looks up. She looks through me, and I'm thankful for it. The fewer people who notice me, the better. She hands me the ticket, and without another thought, I take it and head for the bus.

At this time of night, the moonlight shines from above me as I wait. It's strange how in one day my life has changed, yet the evening night stars haven't. Everything is different, yet it's all the same.

I can't believe this is happening. I'm running from the only home I've ever known.

Dad.

No. My head shakes back and forth. I can't think about him. I can't think about the truth of what happened.

But still, as much as I try to force the newfound knowledge about my father out of my head, I can't.

How did things go so wrong? I can't stay. The risk is too great even though my fate is unknown.

The decision to run was not an easy one, but I had no choice. I grabbed some money, a few clothes, and one picture frame.

Nothing more. I didn't have enough time.

My chest falls as I let out the oxygen I have been holding since I left.

Almost time, almost safe.

I repeat the mantra, breathing slowly until I hear the bus arrive. It screeches to a halt, and then I step up into the unknown. It will be okay, I think as I trudge to the rear, looking for a place to sit.

I pick one, hoping no one sits next to me. I'm too shaky as it is.

Luckily for me, the bus is practically empty at this time of night, and within a minute, it's already pulling away.

My muscles loosen as we drive farther away from the station. Once it's no longer visible, I allow my eyes to close and force myself to get some rest.

I wake up at my connection in Toledo, then I'm back on a bus, traveling closer and closer. When I arrive in Columbus, I buy another ticket. This time, I don a hat and sunglasses. My hair is also a dark brown. No longer its normal shade of strawberry blond.

A wig.

Plus, I've purchased a bottle of dark brown hair dye for whenever I reach my final destination.

I had stopped at a local grocery store after getting off the bus. If I'm tracked to Columbus, they won't be able to find me. Now I'm unrecognizable.

With my costume on, I head for the next bus and after a few hours of driving, transfer to a new bus to get to my final destination. A destination I hope is large enough that I can blend in. Hide in plain sight. Where I can come up with a plan of what I'll do next.

We travel through the night. It's been over two days since I've slept in a bed, over thirty hours since my life was shaken up, and everything I knew and loved was taken from me.

I allow myself to sleep, and the next time my eyes flutter open, I can hear the sputtering of the bus stopping. I've made it to my final destination.

Groggy and disoriented, I walk toward the exit and make my way outside. I'm in New York City, and I have no idea where to go from here. I have no phone, and I don't know anyone in the city.

Are there even payphones in this city? Probably not.

I head to the local pharmacy and buy a burner phone.

But who can I call?

Who can I trust?

Maybe I should look through my contacts on my phone.

Oh, shit. I threw my phone out.

I scour my brain, trying to remember all the numbers I

had in my phone, but that will never do. I can't call someone who was a contact in my phone.

That's the first way I'll be found. I can't go on social media or any site that can be traced back to me.

Think.

My brain plays through everyone I speak to, and then everyone I don't.

I think back to all my friends, and then a name pops in my head. Maggie.

Maggie. My best friend from elementary school. In middle school, she moved. It's funny how I can't remember any phone numbers, but I'll always remember hers.

Back then, I didn't have a cell phone. She made me sit on her bed, her bag packed, and keep saying the number over and over again.

She had gotten a cell phone to keep in touch. Maggie made me memorize it that day so that when she moved, I'd always remember.

I hope she hasn't changed it.

We haven't spoken in years.

But I know, no matter what, no matter how much time has passed, she wouldn't ever turn me away.

With my duffel and new phone in hand, I walk a few blocks, and then from memory, I dial.

Ring. Ring. Ring.

Fuck. What if she changed her number? What if she doesn't answer?

All the what-ifs play through my brain.

And as the phone continues to ring, my heart rate picks up.

Waiting. Waiting. Waiting.

I'm about to hang up and figure out something else when I hear it.

"Hello." The voice is low and tentative, but I recognize it right away.

I swear my legs go weak.

No part of me realized how badly I needed to hear her voice. But here it is. As the tears of relief fill my eyes, I know I need her. My throat closes as I try to find the words.

"Maggie?" I ask, my voice shaking with nerves.

"Yes. This is she," she responds.

Tears roll down my cheeks. "It's . . . it's . . ."

"Willow?"

She knows. She remembers. It's her.

The liquid collecting in my eyes falls faster.

"Yes," I croak.

"Are you okay?" Even though I haven't spoken to her in years, I can hear her fear and concern. As if no time has passed and we are still best friends, and she will still do anything for me.

"No," I whisper because even now, free from what haunts me and far away from my fears, I'm not okay.

"Where are you?"

"New York City. Do you . . ." I inhale. "Do you still live here?"

My head tips up, and if there were visible stars in the Manhattan sky, I would wish on one.

"I do."

A strangled puff of oxygen I didn't know I was holding leaves my body.

"Tell me where you are, and I'll come get you."

"No. Don't. I'm fine. Can I come to you?" I ask.

"Of course."

She rattles off an address in Stuyvesant.

Since I'm not sure how far it is, I opt for a cab, pulling out a few bucks of cash from my emergency money in the duffel to pay the fare. I have to be careful with how much I spend. I might not be able to take one in the future, but after the day and night I've had, I lean back in the dirty back seat and welcome the ride.

It only takes about fifteen minutes for it to pull up in front of a high-rise building. Leaving the car, I trudge toward it. My bag isn't heavy, but I'm exhausted. All the nerves rushing to the surface make me swear I could pass out.

I don't, though. No, I push through. Holding back all my emotions, I keep my expression stoic up the elevator and down the hall until the door opens, then the tears come. My friend hasn't changed at all over the years. She holds me in her arms, and I cry because for the first time since my nightmare started . . . I'm safe.

No one will find me here.

CHAPTER THREE

Jaxson

Three weeks later . . .

It's Friday afternoon, and yet again, both Addison and Grayson are out of town. I should be used to it, but I'm not. I know I said it was okay, and I know this is a test to see how well I'll handle the company, but I miss them. Something I would never admit out loud.

It's too quiet.

Sure, at Price Enterprise, we have a building full of staff, but on my floor, the top floor, only a few people work here.

Before the added responsibilities, I never came into the office, so it's strange being here all the time. With my "skill set," I can work from anywhere, and I prefer a remote location where I can't be tracked.

Unfortunately, to prove myself and be taken seriously, I have to be at the office. Even when there is nothing for me to do. Be careful of what you wish for . . . look at Midas. I'm sure when he prayed for gold, he never thought about what would happen when he had to take a piss.

I peek at the tiny clock on the right side of my computer. It's four p.m. Almost the end of the day.

Thank fuck. If it were a few months ago, I'd have left already. Since we've canceled the weekly board meeting, there's nothing for me to do. I've finished all my work, and Grayson's and Addison's, too.

I should get out of here. The only problem is, I risk one of my siblings calling me and finding out I went home early. It might not seem like a big deal, however, putting up with them giving me shit and doubting my ability to lead is not something I want right now.

Then they will hire a replacement.

A spy. A liability.

I can trust everyone on this floor with my secret pastime, I can't risk someone else finding out.

That would cause problems. If there is one thing I don't want, it's the FBI knocking on my door. The fewer people up here the better.

Which is why I'm putting on this show. Rather than leaving, I watch the clock, then play on my phone . . .

And when I grow bored with that, I hack into Addison's travel plans, and once I figure out when she'll be back in the States, I hack into Gray's for good measure.

From what I gather, neither will be back for two weeks and then they will rarely be here. Addison has reasons for not being here, being pregnant and all. But Grayson . . .

I'm not sure what Grayson is doing.

Something tells me this is a test, and when I fuck up, he'll pop out of the closet to tell me he knew I could never do it. *Punked style.*

When the clock strikes five p.m. on the dot, I stand, shutting down my computer, then grab my phone and head out the door.

I wave to Jasmine and Nicole as I pass their offices on my way to the elevator. Jasmine used to be Addison's assistant, but now she's working her way up the corporate ladder of Price Enterprise. Nicole is my brother's assistant. I'm thankful they're here with me because I know if I'm gone, they can run the show.

Once I take the ride down, I head out of the lobby and into the city traffic. I didn't drive to work today, so a cab will do. As I lift my right hand up, I pull out my phone with my left hand.

I don't want to go home. I don't want to be by myself, and I'd much rather grab a drink.

Who can I call? Who would go out with me?

I scroll through my contacts, and the first name that pops up that might be up for a cocktail is Pierce Lancaster. Pierce and I have been friends for years. Having both grown up as the youngest sibling to a family legacy impossible to live up to, we bonded from the beginning. I haven't spoken to him in weeks, so I hit his name and fire off a text.

Me: Where you at?

Pierce: With Lindsey.

Of course he is. Why wouldn't he be? If I were a woman, I'd roll my eyes. I forgot how lame Pierce became ever since he fell in love.

Still standing at the corner of the street with my hand up, I continue to look for another option.

The rush of people passing by, all appear eager for the weekend to start. With smiles on their faces, some are talking on the phone as they move around me, making plans I'm sure.

Must be nice, but unfortunately, I have no place to go.

Normally, I'd have a hot date, but I've been too busy with work to set one up. Also, I'm not really feeling like making plans with any of the women I know.

No. I need a change of pace tonight.

Something different.

I rack my brain for someplace, anyplace. But since I can't

think of anything off the top of my head, I look down at my phone and start scrolling again.

When I get to the *T*'s, I see potential.

Trent.

Good old Trent.

Trent and I have been friends since we went to school together. His family's wealth rivals my own.

But unlike me, he doesn't work. Well, that's not true; he works, but only when he wants, and when he doesn't want to, he's been known to take long breaks from his job as a hedge fund manager and live off his trust fund.

How he manages to have any clients at all with his lack of professionalism is beyond me. Guess he has nothing to prove.

Unlike me.

The good thing about him not working all the time is that he always has something going on. We don't hang out as often anymore, not since I claimed I wanted more responsibility, but desperate times and all.

I'm bored.

I hit the call button.

"What's up, man? I was wondering when you would call," he answers.

It's good to hear his voice. Reminds me of better times, when I could fuck around and sleep until noon.

"It hasn't been that long." Lies. It feels like it's been forever since I've gone out.

My free hand reaches up and runs through my hair, tugging on the strands. The mere thought of the shit and hoops I've jumped through to prove myself, and for what?

Nothing.

No one respects me.

"It's been at least a month," he deadpans. "You quit this crazy pursuit to be taken seriously?"

He's right; it is crazy.

Fucking nuts, if I'm being honest. Sometimes, I'm not even sure why I care.

But I do. So, I'm fucked.

"I wish. But . . ." I trail off. "I figure everyone needs a break."

"And that is why you called me." He laughs, and as I chuckle back, a group of people rush by me. They're trying to make the crosswalk, and I'm in their way.

Time to move.

Standing in the middle of the sidewalk on the phone is probably my biggest pet peeve, and here with my desire to find a distraction for the night, I'm everything I hate.

"Exactly. If anyone has plans, I would be interested in, it's you. Obviously." With no cabs in sight, I walk toward the subway. I should probably figure out this shit before my call drops.

"Well, it so happens I do. That is, if you want to spend some money."

That makes my feet halt as I lift my arm once again to grab a cab. The stairs to the subway are only a few feet away, and once I'm inside, I won't be able to hear him, and this I need to hear.

"Now you have me intrigued," I respond.

"Poker game."

My mouth parts as a smile spreads across my face. Poker. One of my favorite pastimes.

This sounds promising.

"Okay," I answer because it's a no-brainer for me.

"But not your typical poker game. This one is high stakes and very exclusive." Now he really has me interested. I'm always one for high risks, but when he says exclusive, I need to know more.

"Details," I ask because as much as I'm all for playing poker, and as much as Trent is cool, he can also be shady as fuck sometimes. As long as it's not some sketchy game, I'll be down. But you never know with him.

"Do you know Cyrus Reed?"

"Cyrus Reed," I respond. "The name rings a bell." I try to remember why. It hits me. Reed. He's related to River. A cousin or something. "I've met him before. Banker, right?"

"Amongst other things." His voice dips lower in that sentence.

"Such as?"

"His portfolio is spread amongst many different business ventures." His answer is vague and raises red flags, but the thing is, I'm bored.

"And one of his many business ventures is hosting an underground poker game?" I'm not saying I won't go, but I like to have my cards on the table.

"Exclusive poker games," he corrects.

"What's the difference?"

"It's not illegal."

He can't see my face over the phone, but if he did, he'd know I wasn't buying it. The thing is, I don't care. It wouldn't be the first time I dabbled in something illegal.

I highly doubt the United States government would feel too favorably about me hacking into their government records, and I do that shit a minimum of five times a week. What's one poker game?

It would give me something to do.

Again . . . bored as fuck.

"I'm in." A cab finally stops at the corner, and I swing open the door. I fire off the address of my loft to the driver, then turn my attention back to Trent. "Where's it at?" I ask him.

"Connecticut."

"No shit? That's annoying," I mutter back. So much for getting shit-faced now. I'll have to drive.

"It's thirty minutes out of the city. Stop being a pussy and stop your bitching."

I hang up and let out a throaty chuckle, he's full of shit. There is no way it will only take that long, regardless of how fast I drive.

Only a second goes by before a text comes in.

Trent: It's a $100,000 buy-in.

Well, fuck.

CHAPTER FOUR

Willow

THE WEEKS SINCE I'VE COME TO THE CITY HAVE GONE BY slowly. I'm at an impasse, and it feels like I'm sitting here biding my time. With each day that passes, I'm waiting for my luck to run out.

So far, though, I've been lucky, and nothing has happened. It's almost as if I'm not in hiding or running for my life. My life is pretty normal; well, unless you take into account the sleepless nights, the nightmares when I do sleep, and looking over my shoulder all the time.

But who's counting?

I've been staying at Maggie's apartment with her. It's not ideal, but it's my only option while I come up with a plan of what to do with the information I've discovered.

A part of me thinks I'm in way over my head . . .

Okay, all of me thinks that.

I need to tell someone. In order for me to come out unscathed, I need help, but right now, I don't trust anyone. Not even Maggie. I know she would never intentionally hurt me, but she could still inadvertently put my life in danger. Worse, she could get hurt, and no part of me could live with myself if that happened. It's bad enough the guilt I already have in my heart for things I can't change, but I can protect her.

So no, every time she looks at me, begging me with her eyes to talk to her, I don't. I won't risk her becoming a casualty in a war I should've never brought her into.

Since I can't tell her the whole truth of why I'm here, I stay silent.

It kills me, but it's the best option.

Luckily, she stopped asking about a week ago, and her pleading stares ended as well. There was a time she would have tried, but now, weeks later, she doesn't bother. Which I am thankful for. If she wants to know more, you could never tell. She treats me like nothing is wrong; as though I'm a friend down on my luck and living on her couch.

She doesn't know how accurate she is. Occasionally, she mentions working and asks what my plans are for making money. She doesn't know about the cash hiding in her closet. No, I withheld that, too, along with the emotional baggage I brought with me.

Today, I'm sitting on her couch. It's Friday afternoon. I should look for a job, but I have limited options.

With no ID and no background, shit, I can't even use my last name for fear—nope, I'm fucked.

Also, what kind of job can I get when I don't know how long I'll be here? I could be here for months or it could be days. It wouldn't be right to start working and then have to up and leave. I'm resigned to the fact I need a plan before I get a job.

Since I can't go to an office like the rest of the world, I'm watching TV alone. Maggie is not home, and I have to assume she is working or preparing for work.

As if summoned by my thoughts of her, the door to the apartment opens, and she walks in. The first thing I notice as she approaches is that her hair is completely disheveled. Her brown hair is thrown in a messy bun and not a cute one at that. No, this wasn't done for style reasons. This one looks like she did it haphazardly.

My eyes travel down from the bird's nest sitting on her head to look at her face. That's the second thing I notice that is off about Maggie. She looks like actual shit.

Her skin is splotchy, and her nose is a shade of red that is typically only found on a certain reindeer during Christmas.

She looks up at me, eyes glassy, and then right there, staring at me, she sneezes. Not once.

Not twice.

Three times.

Jeez. If she keeps that up, I'll need a surgical mask.

"I'm sick," she groans out.

I lift a mocking brow. "Really? I couldn't tell," I retort, and she sniffles again.

"What am I going to do?" She plops down on the couch next to me.

"Try not to get me sick," I feel bad when she doesn't laugh. She's obviously not feeling well at all because she normally laughs at my sarcastic quips.

"Go rest. I'll go down to the store on the corner and get you some soup." I stand from the couch. Reaching down, I straighten my shirt before moving toward the door.

"You're the best. I was going to stop on the way home, but I was so tired and needed to nap. Hopefully, that will make me feel better for tonight," she says as I'm already walking to grab my bag. Her words have me stopping in my tracks and looking over my shoulder as I shake my head at her.

"What's tonight?" I ask her because unless it's dinner with God, she is one hundred percent not going.

"My first solo gig." She coughs, and her face turns red like she's choking and can't find any oxygen to breathe.

"You can't be serious."

"Deadly."

"You can't go, Mag. You are seriously ill right now."

She shakes her head, but from the movement and the way she groans, it's obvious she's even too weak to do that.

"I have to. I have no other option. I can't fuck this up."

I know how important getting her new company up and running is to her. Maggie launched a new party planning business where she facilitates and rents out servers and bar staff for private parties. Maggie had worked for years in the city as the manager of a luxury champagne bar. She started taking private waitressing jobs, and it grew from there until she was asked to bring more help.

The company has been months in the making. I know how important it is for her, but for her to show up looking the way she does would be career suicide.

"Don't worry about it. When I get back with your soup, we'll figure something out."

She nods and grimaces at the same time. I don't think she believes me, but there's no way she's going to work tonight.

The faster I go, the faster I can fight my case, so with nothing more to say now, I give her a little wave and leave.

Before I head out the door, I grab my hat and glasses. Even though I dyed my hair brown permanently when I first got to New York, I still don't feel safe walking around the city without the rest of my gear. If Maggie notices I'm putting on my disguise, she says nothing.

I leave for the store, head down, trying to blend in. I might feel safe in the apartment with Maggie, but when I'm outside in the city, I'm always looking over my shoulders. Afraid someone will recognize me.

The market is only half a block up the road, but it's crisp outside. People walk by, all bundled in large jackets, while my only protection from the chill is my arms at my chest, protectively clutching myself for heat.

In the rush to leave and take my hat, I forgot to grab a coat. I'm not sure when the air temperature dropped, but Lord, did it ever.

The air smells of burning leaves.

The market, however, reeks of all the prepared foods when I step inside.

It's as if I'm at the spice market and not a grocery store. I move quickly to grab a carton and pour some soup into it.

Chicken noodle should do the trick.

When I was growing up, my mother always said that. A smile spreads across my face as I think of her feeding me it as a child, saying it was better than penicillin. Still grinning and lost in my memory, I walk up the aisle with the soup in hand.

Since I'm already here, I scour every aisle to see what else we might need. Passing the paper products, I grab tissues and toilet paper. Then I head over to where they have medicine.

Once I have everything I need, I go to the register and pay the bill and hurry back. When I step back inside Maggie's apartment, I find her passed out on the couch.

"Mags," I say as I stop beside her, and she lets out a long-drawn-out yawn that ends with a wince. "I have your soup."

I grab a spoon and set the soup in front of her on the coffee table. "Mags." This time, I say it louder, and she must hear me because she stretches out her arms, opens her eyes, and gives me a weak smile.

"Thanks," she whispers before sitting up and starting to eat.

I take a seat and turn to face her. "What do you have tonight? Can you have one of your staff cover for you?"

She puts her spoon down at my question and furrows her brow.

"No." She shakes her head. "We are already short."

"I don't understand."

"Technically, I wasn't prepared to open up shop this early, but I got a fantastic break on this, and I couldn't say no."

"What exactly is this job?"

"It's a high-stakes poker game. Very exclusive. But since it popped up so unexpectedly, I haven't had the time to hire enough staff, so it's me and one other girl serving drinks. We also have Josh manning the bar, but that is not enough. This is high-end clientele, and the number of jobs I can pick up from this gig alone could change my life. I can't cancel." Her voice leaves no room for objection. Changing her mind is not in the cards, but there has to be a solution.

"I'm not saying cancel, but there has to be someone else who can cover your spot?" I ask, desperate to help.

"There isn't anyone. Everyone I hired has a commitment already. Legit, I'm not being overdramatic. I have no other options. I either go sick, or I have to cancel."

Before I can think twice about it, I say something I know I'll regret.

"I'll do it." The words slip out of my mouth before I can take them back, and the moment they do, I know I've made a terrible mistake. This is a bad idea. I won't be able to hide my face, and what will I wear? Something tells me my oversized sweats to hide my figure and hat and glasses will not be on the list.

It doesn't matter, though.

I have to do this.

Even if it means I get caught.

No. You won't. She said it was an exclusive game, which also means private . . .

It will be okay.

Maggie must also think my idea is crazy because her eyes widen at my suggestion. She stares at me as if I'm insane or maybe spoke a different language.

"I'll cover your spot."

She tilts her head at me. "Do you even know how to serve? Any experience?"

"Well, no. But—"

Her head shakes, and I stop speaking. "It's not as easy as it looks," she says.

"I know, but what other options do you have?"

Her cheeks pucker in. "None."

I'm running late.

By the time I convinced Maggie to let me cover for her, I barely had time to get ready.

The worst part was I was right.

I feel naked, unprotected, and I'm hoping this isn't the biggest mistake of my life. There is no hat on my head. No glasses protecting my eyes. And certainly not a large sweater to hide my shape.

Nope.

Not at all.

Now, I'm dressed in a skintight black dress that is way too tight to drive a car in and heading toward Connecticut.

If it's not bad enough that these shoes make it impossible to press the brake, the dress is legitimately cutting off the circulation to my stomach.

It's not my dress.

It's Maggie's.

I'm four inches taller than Maggie, this dress is indecent on me.

But apparently, it's the look, and I have no choice. The only thing that saves me, is I no longer have strawberry blond hair. That alone makes me look different. However, in my rush, I forgot my contacts, so my blue eyes are visible.

Shit.

This is bad.

I'd like to bitch but I can't.

I'm driving Maggie's car to Maggie's gig, in Maggie's dress, pretending to be Maggie, basically. *This is freaking great.* What could go wrong? Everything. I'm the poster child for Murphy's Law. If it can go wrong, you bet your ass it will.

However, in the grand scheme of life, pretending to be Maggie is better than being Willow these days.

The GPS on my phone tells me I'm now only fifteen miles away. The game is being played in the middle of nowhere on some billionaire's compound.

Should be interesting.

I've got no clue how Maggie got this break, but by the way she described it, if she does a good job, this could open doors for her business. She just wasn't prepared for the event to be so soon.

I'm only ten miles away when the low gas light comes on in Maggie's car.

In my own car, or in the car I had before I left, I'd know that the light means I have thirty miles before I'm empty, but

Maggie's car is older than I am, so I'm not exactly sure what that light means. Is it thirty miles? Or five?

I can't afford to break down and not show up, and I can't afford to run out of gas on the way home.

I'll look for a gas station as soon as I get off the highway. Hopefully, I'll find one because it would suck if I didn't. When the GPS indicates it's time for me to turn off, I'm rewarded right away.

There on the corner of the street before I take the turn is a station.

Having no clue what the next ten miles will bring, I enter and pull the car up to a pump. When I get out, I notice a car right across from me, but other than that, the station is empty. No one is around, and it's dark. Very, very dark.

Are there cameras?

I pull my coat tighter around my body and walk to the pump with my head down.

Grabbing my wallet out of my bag, I look for money.

Shit.

Shit.

Shit.

I can't use my credit card, and I forgot to ask Maggie for hers.

The amount of cash in my bag . . .

One dollar.

Wow.

This is pathetic.

In my rush, I also forgot to grab some cash. Since I had spent what I had in my wallet earlier on tissues and soup and medicine, I have no more money on me.

This is bad.

There is no way I can drive to the party and make it home. Maybe I'll get lucky, and I'll get tips, but what if I don't? What would I do then to get back home?

I pull my bag apart and try to find some spare change but come up empty-handed. What am I going to do? I look around. Maybe the car next door will be someone who can help me.

Reluctantly, I look up, and I'm met with the clearest green eyes I have ever seen. They are a color I imagine is only present in the tropics.

Endless depths.

But it's the whole picture that does me in. This man is gorgeous and dangerously so. With tousled dark brown hair and a sharp jaw that looks like it was molded from granite, he could have stepped off the cover of a magazine.

"Like what you see?" a voice asks, and I shake my head and right myself.

That's when I realize I was not *just* staring at this stranger but gawking. And not only did he notice, but he called me out on it, too.

Ass.

Who does that?

If someone is caught staring—maybe drooling is more like it—you say nothing. You pretend you didn't notice.

Jeez.

Common courtesy.

My cheeks begin to warm, and I know they are turning crimson.

I lower my gaze, but before I can fully pull away from him, I notice the smirk. A damn smirk with a dimple and all. This guy's head is so big, it probably has its own zip code.

My back goes ramrod straight.

Old Willow would have told him she'd seen better. A lie, but she never passed up an opportunity for a good comeback.

New Willow mutters a comeback under her breath. "Not particularly."

I turn away from him. I'd rather walk home from the city than ask this prick for money for gas.

"Shame," I hear, but I refuse to look. I peer down at the ground and watch his footsteps. Staring awkwardly at the asphalt has my other senses heightened.

I can smell the faint waft of cologne as he passes. I can hear him rummaging in his pocket.

Then I hear him answer his phone. He's distracted as he walks toward the convenience store attached to the gas station. He's so distracted that he doesn't even realize he dropped his wallet while he was fumbling in his pocket for his phone.

I open my mouth to speak, to get his attention and tell him what happened, but I don't say anything.

Fuck that.

The dick doesn't deserve it.

He deserves to have it stolen.

I grab it off the ground before anyone notices and pocket it. The wallet is much heavier than I would have thought. Ducking behind my car, I open it. I see a bunch of credit cards first, and then I see some cash. I wonder if he'll even notice if I take a bill.

That's stealing. But you're desperate, so what's the harm in taking a few bucks? It's the same as if he dropped cash on the ground. That's not stealing. If I saw a bill on the floor, I would take it. Because anything left behind on the ground is no better than trash.

At least that's what I tell myself as I pocket the money and return the wallet back to where he dropped it.

With the money safely in my bag, I head into the convenience store as he walks out. I know he's looking at me, but I never lift my gaze from the ground. I can't risk a camera getting a clear picture of my face.

"Twenty dollars on pump three," I say, bringing the money up and handing it over.

The cashier takes my money, and from the corner of my eye, I can see him reaching into the register and placing the bill my friendly douche at the neighboring pump provided for me inside, then he grabs my change. He dangles it in front of me, but when I refuse to look up, he drops it on the counter. My hand reaches for it, all while I never lift my head up.

The man must think I'm rude or strange, but I don't care; it's not worth the risk.

"You're all set," he says, and I nod, turning on my heel and walking out.

Now that I've paid, I head over to the pump and fill my tank. I don't have a lot of time, so as soon as it's done, I jump back into the car and head in the direction of the house.

Thank God that idiot dropped his wallet because as I weave through the dark streets lined by trees and nothing else, I realize getting stranded here would have been awful.

I'd most certainly be in trouble. A large part of me knows I should feel bad about stealing, but since I'll never see that man again, I don't dwell on it.

With everything going on in my life, stealing—or "finding"—money is the least of my problems.

CHAPTER FIVE

Jaxson

I'm early, *again*. Not something that happens often, but since I'm trying to be taken seriously, it's becoming an annoying habit of mine.

Now I'm here at what I'm sure is Cyrus Reed's place, or one of his properties, ready to play poker.

With my work taking over my whole life and whatnot, I haven't played in a while. It's been even longer since I've been in a game with a one-hundred-thousand-dollar buy-in. It's a hefty price to pay, but poker is a game of skill, and I have that in spades.

As I sit in a chair in the corner of the room, waiting for the rest of the players to show up, I see a woman with dark hair walk by.

She reminds me of the gorgeous woman at the gas station. The one I caught staring at me.

I was a complete dick . . . but usually that works for me.

Apparently, she didn't agree. The woman in front of me can't be her, though. She's wearing a skintight black dress that shows off her every curve. She's also holding a drink in her hand and walking up to Cyrus.

When she turns, our gazes lock, and she stumbles. Actually, she almost falls forward in her heels.

She's quick to right herself.

It is her.

I'm one hundred percent positive she's the girl from the gas station, and when she notices me, she looks as if she's seen a ghost. I'm about to stand and go up to her, another waitress appears in front of me. The same one who previously took my drink order.

Don Julio 1942. I accept the drink and pull out my wallet. I remove the cash and start thumbing through it, looking for the fifty to give her.

Drinks might be free, but I tip well. Since I don't have chips yet, cash will have to do for this round.

I move to stand and reach into my pocket.

That's odd.

I could have sworn I broke a hundred and had a fifty.

But now it's gone.

Grabbing two twenties, I place the bills on her tray. It's not exactly what I wanted to give her, but it will have to do.

Sitting back down, I lift the tequila to my mouth. The liquid pours down my throat while I try to remember where I put it. I had it when I left the city.

I didn't go anywhere but here.

No.

That's not true.

I went to the gas station. I dropped my wallet, but all my shit was in it when I found it next to my pump. I had my money, dropped my wallet, and now it's gone . . .

A crazy thought pops in my brain. More like a look, or rather a lack thereof. The way the waitress refused to look at me in the convenience store.

It almost appeared as if she was caught.

Because she was.

Not only did she find my wallet but . . . she also took money from it. Then she returned it and tried to pretend it never happened.

That's why she was scared when she saw me again. Because she stole from me . . .

Interesting.

A million things that I want to say to her play out in my mind. First, I want to call her out on it, and then . . . what then?

Before I approach her, I need to think. I need to formulate my plan. But before I can, Cyrus Reed is standing in front of me along with my buddy Trent.

The Devil came out to play, bargaining lives for a price, sending those to hell who crossed him.

I stand from my seat to greet him.

"Jax, this is Cyrus Reed. He's the host of tonight's game," Trent introduces.

I extend my hand, and we shake.

"Thank you for having me," I respond.

"Pleasure is all mine." His voice holds no warmth or sincerity. It's ice water on a snowy day.

"We have a mutual acquaintance. My brother, Grayson, is marrying your cousin's daughter," I say.

"That she is." He doesn't say more, just nods before he looks down at his phone that must be ringing. "Gentlemen. Enjoy the game. I have to take this." And then he walks away.

"A man of many words," I say to Trent.

"Scary as fuck, if you ask me." He laughs.

"Then why play in his game?" Other than the obvious fact, Trent loves trouble.

"Because it's the best. Not only for money but for

connections. Everyone who is anyone plays. I'm surprised I haven't seen you or your brother here before at a game."

"I've been too busy to hear anything, and Grayson has too big of a stick up his ass to play poker."

At that, Trent laughs. "I'm telling you, man, I've picked up half of my best clients here."

"Oh . . ." I lift an eyebrow in speculation. "You're working again?"

"Believe it or not, I am. Not as much as you, but now and then, I go into the office, and when I do, if it's after a game, I have an extra mil to put into the fund." He sounds all smug and proud. If he could pull out his dick, I'm sure he'd do that too.

If what Trent says is true, and he is, in fact, working, then the amount of money here is probably Trent's wet dream. I'm sure chumming up to some of these guys has made him the highest earner.

"Sorry, man, if you invited me to get my business, Grayson handles that."

"Nah. I just missed your ass." He chuckles.

"I'll try not to stay away again." This will not be my last time here, not after knowing the waitress stole my money or that she might be here again.

I'm not sure what about her intrigues me, but it does.

After I finish my drink, I see that most of the players have arrived. I stand and head over to the table. Cyrus isn't present, and I imagine he probably doesn't play at all. It's the smart move. Gather intel and clients, but keep yourself above reproach.

Smart.

Yet, as smart as he is, there is still something shady as fuck about him.

From the corner of my eye, I see the game is about to begin.

Trent settles in beside me, but I don't know the rest of the guys at the table.

With a few more minutes before we start, I turn my gaze away from them. These men aren't my focus.

No, my focus is on a certain thief.

I find her in the crowd, and then lift my hand to signal for her to approach me.

She glances around the room, and it appears she is looking for another server to help me. I want to laugh out loud as she tries to pawn me off on someone else. But, unfortunately for her, there is no one else here. I let my lips split into a grin as I shake my head.

Her shoulders rise and fall as she inhales deeply before she squares them and heads in my direction.

She takes each step as if it's her last. As if she is in the French Revolution and I'm the guillotine ready to chop off her head.

Which, in fact, is the truth right now. To her, I am. One word from me, and she'll probably lose her job here. Fuck, I could press charges. She can be arrested. I don't have proof, but that would be easy to find. All I would have to do is check out the video surveillance cameras at the gas station and show her pocketing my money.

I'm not sure why she stole it, though, and the mystery of that keeps me from doing any of these things.

I always need to know the why.

Does she need the money? Or was it her way of paying me back for being a dick? I study her face as she comes closer. The way her jaw is tight and her cheek is pinched in. It's her eyes that haunt me, though. As if she is concealing a world of pain.

I'm not sure what plagues her, but I have every intention of finding out.

CHAPTER SIX

Willow

ONLY ME.

This would only happen to me.

He would be here. The first time I borrow—okay, steal—money from a stranger, and he's here.

The worst part is he can ruin this.

A million scenarios play through my mind, starting with ruining Maggie's business and ending up in jail.

Then the worst thought hits me in the stomach . . .

What if this is how I'm found?

A mug shot over stealing a fifty-dollar bill hardly seems worth it.

Hopefully, he won't notice. Maybe he won't remember how much money he had. Or better yet, maybe he won't remember me.

That hope or prayer is quickly lost the moment our eyes meet. His facial expression tells me there is no way he forgot me. I almost fell over when he looked at me, and now I'm trying to regain my footing.

Yet there he is, sitting at the table, cool as a cucumber, and I'm falling all over myself like an idiot. Why does he have to keep looking at me? Why can't he let me be? Isn't he supposed to be playing the hand?

Those crystal green eyes stare at me, waiting for the moment to pounce. I don't want to go over to him, but when he waves his hand at me, I have no choice.

There is only one thing to do, so squaring my shoulders, I head over.

He's not looking at me when I approach. He's focused on the game. The sound of the chips echoing as he fiddles with them scratches at my nerves. I know he's doing it to toy with me. I'm not sure how I know this because I don't know him, but I can tell. The chips rattle over and over again, making the hairs on my arm stand up. The sound reminds me of nails dragging down a chalkboard.

Scratch.

Scratch.

Scratch.

It's almost as though it's a nervous tic.

I take a deep, long inhale and summon up all the strength in my body not to yank the annoying chips from his hand and throw them at him.

No.

There will be none of that.

Only smiles and a sugary sweet voice that would give me a cavity. A grin so deep, he'll never think I would have the audacity to steal a fifty from him.

"Can I get you something to drink, sir?" I ask.

Sweet. Sweet. Sweet. Sugar. Sugar. Sugar.

At the sound of my voice, the chips stop moving, and I wait for him to look up, but I'm not prepared when he does. I'm not at all prepared for the look he gives me. Nor am I ready for how green his eyes are from this vantage point. These are the eyes of trouble. Eyes you get lost in.

Scratch that . . .

They are eyes you drown in.

But not me.

Not now.

Not after everything I've been through. Maybe a few years ago. Maybe before.

Now I am long since jaded.

No. Those emerald orbs hold no power over me.

"Sir?" I say again, and this time, I know without a measure of a doubt, if I were any other woman, I would melt on the floor because as I stare down at him, the right side of his lip curls up into what I could only call his signature smirk.

This is the kind of smirk that a man like him has perfected. Its goal is to cause permanent damage to the recipient.

This is a smirk that is only fit for a god.

The worst part about it is that he knows it.

Bastard.

The thing, though, is he doesn't know I am immune to smirks like this and even more immune to men like him.

After what I've been through, I know you can't trust anyone but yourself.

"A drink?" I ask.

"In a rush?"

"Not at all, sir."

He leans forward in his chair, arms resting on the felt of the table beneath him. His head is cocked, and he's arched his right eyebrow.

Jeez.

Does he have to look at me like that?

I straighten my back, fusing my spine so tightly it could easily snap.

A gust of wind would be the culprit or another smile from him.

Either way, my facade of indifference has dropped into place. I'm a fortress, impenetrable to this man. No matter how handsome he is.

I'm not in the right frame of mind for men or distractions. Only one thing can take up space in my mind right now . . .

What I'm going to do about the news I found out about my father.

If someone had told me how far off the path my life would drift in the past year, I'd never believe them, but here, serving drinks to this arrogant jerk, I can't recognize myself, and that's not because my hair is dyed and I'm wearing contacts. Strike that, I forgot my contacts. It's because my life is an episode of *America's Most Wanted.*

"No need to call me sir. My name is Jaxson Price."

Thankfully, I keep steady and show no reaction to his name. My walls are up and strong, but I'm no idiot. I might not be from New York, and I might not go out much, but I know exactly who this man is, and if I thought his looks were deadly before, now I know this man is bad for my health. Jaxson Price is Manhattan elite.

Fuck that, Jaxson Price is so much more than that. He's an American god.

I need to get out of here.

Of all the games for him to show up at, of all the gas stations for him to stop at, and of all the people for me to fuck with, it had to be Jaxson Price.

"What can I get you, Mr. Price?"

I should know what he's drinking, but I don't. Maggie would know. But I'm not Maggie, so I have absolutely no clue. I have to hope that whoever is behind the bar does.

He tilts his chin up, and his grin broadens, and then on a

faint whisper as if he can read my mind, he says, "Don Julio, 1942. Extra chilled." And then as if he never said it, as if he didn't throw me a life raft on this job, he looks back down at his chips and the sound of the rattling starts again. He's back to playing.

I turn on my heel. The sound of my stiletto echoing against the marble as I leave. My steps are fast because I need to get far away from him. Even though I'm immune to his charms, I don't like to be close to him. Because I might not be that immune at all. He was an ass. And I don't have time for another hot rich boy. Especially one who's so obviously a player.

No.

No time at all.

I make my way over to the bar. "What can I get you, Willow?" asks Josh, the bartender.

"Don Julio," I grit out, and his forehead scrunches at the sound of my voice. I know he'll ask me why I'm pissed because it is obvious from my tone, but I can't be that girl. I might know Josh, but I don't know him well enough, so I shrug my shoulders and grimace. "My feet hurt," I offer as my excuse for my sour mood, and he nods before setting off to make the drink.

With him now gone, I look around the room. It's a large wood panel library that's been converted in order to play cards. Tables are set up in the middle and the bar is placed in the corner. As grand as the room is, it's intimate, with sconces and candlelight giving a warm glow.

This is not the first poker game I've been to. It's just my first time being on the other side. Watching others play without the excitement of taking part in the game. It's different from this viewpoint.

From this angle, I can see the stress and, for some, the boredom. I like the observation, though. It's fascinating. You can take in the whole scene, reading each person, understanding the wins. The only one I can't pinpoint is Jaxson Price. Unlike the rest, he doesn't look to be at all into the game. It's more like he's bored and has nothing better to do, so he plays. Or at least he wants the players to believe that.

What does that mean for me tonight? Will I leave here unscathed, or will I be another casualty or attempted conquest for Price?

"Here," Josh says, pulling me out of my thoughts.

"Thanks."

I grab the drink and head back over to Jaxson Price. Like a lamb being led to the slaughter, I wait to see my fate, highly certain my life or more aptly my sanity is in peril.

I place the glass down on the table, on top of a napkin, and as I do, his hand reaches out and touches my skin.

My breath hitches. I'm frozen in place at the contact.

"I would tip you," he says, and I look at where our hands touch, "but it seems I *lost* my fifty . . ."

My heart pounds, and my palms grow sweaty.

I couldn't have heard that right.

I lift my gaze. His eyes gleam at me with mischief.

But he stressed the word lost.

A nauseous sensation churns inside me as I realize what that means.

Fuck.

He knows.

CHAPTER SEVEN

Jaxson

THE WAY HER EYES WIDEN IN ABSOLUTE TERROR AT MY WORDS has my back going straight. Yes, I wanted to call her out for stealing my money, but I didn't want to scare her. Because that's how she looks. She looks petrified.

I don't like it.

Not at all.

I'm a sarcastic prick, but I'm not a bad guy. Before I can say another word, she's turned and walked away. I don't even know this girl, but I can tell by looking at her, she has baggage.

Baggage I don't want any part of, but I don't want her to be concerned about me.

Even if she took the money, there was obviously a reason. It's not like it makes or breaks me, but maybe, it did her.

With the game still going on, I can't stand and go after her, but what I can do is concentrate on what I'm doing and play my hand this round.

By the time this hand is over, I'm itching to find her.

I stand from the chair which scratches against the floor as I push it back, and I turn to face the room.

She hasn't come over in a while, but I need to see if she's okay.

I head out into the hall and down the corridor that leads to the bathroom. The house is dimly lit. I assume that's to add to the ambiance and all, but it makes it hard to see. I'm almost by the door when I finally make out a form in front of me. Her back is to me as she faces the wall.

Although it's dark, I know it has to be her. She stands out regardless of the dim lighting, the same way she stood out when I first got here. I would recognize her anywhere.

I step up behind her and lift my hand.

Before I even connect with her, she is jumping forward and then turning around.

She's facing me now, and her eyes look wild. She resembles a caged animal, trapped against its will.

I hold my hands up, trying to pacify her. "It's me," I coo, lowering my voice so as not to spook her. She narrows her gaze but doesn't speak, so I try again. "Are you okay?" I ask softly, my concern clear in my tone, and to show I am no threat, I keep my hands lifted in the air as I step backward, letting the distance between us grow.

"Of course, I'm okay," she fires back. Her posture becomes rigid, her arms crossing in front of her chest in defiance, but I see how her body trembled before she noticed. She's anything but okay, but she's too strong to let me know that.

To allow me to see her weakness.

I respect her strength and her determination, but I'm not just anyone. I'm well equipped in reading people, and I know something is up with her. But like any caged animal, I proceed with caution, not wanting to anger her anymore.

"I'm sorry if I upset you," I say.

"You didn't upset me."

"Startled you then. It wasn't my intention."

"Walking up behind someone will do that," she quips. She doesn't like me, that much is obvious. That, however, won't stop me from trying to understand her.

"I wanted to use the bathroom," I say as an excuse. She narrows her eyes, obviously not buying what I'm selling.

"No, you didn't."

"No." I smile because she reads right through me, and I like it. "I didn't. But I wanted to find you."

"Why?" she asks.

"To say I'm sorry." I shrug.

"Sorry for what? You didn't do anything wrong." She's looking at me like I'm crazy, and the truth is, if I were in her position, I would think I'm crazy too.

Here I am apologizing when she stole my money.

Maybe she's right. Maybe I am insane.

"My brother would say otherwise." I grin. "I like to tease people, but I'm trying to be more serious. I'm sorry if—" I stop, and I'm not sure what to say at this point because I'm sorry for upsetting her, but after what she did, who am I to apologize.

"Again, you did nothing wrong, so you don't have to say anything. It's me—"

I lift my hand and shake my head.

"Here," I say as I reach into my pocket. I pull out my card and hold it toward her. Her forehead scrunches, and her cheeks pucker in. She looks down at my hand as if I'm holding a weapon. Something I'd wield to kill her. How wrong she is.

"What's this for?"

"Well, this is a business card."

Her gaze lifts to meet mine, a question there. She wants more information before she takes it.

"My business card," I clarify.

"Why are you giving me this?"

"It's obvious you had your reasons." I don't specify what

I'm talking about, but we both know. It's the giant elephant in the hallway. "So I'm giving you this."

"For what reason?" she asks.

I think about telling her not to pay me back, that the money doesn't matter to me.

I respond, "If you ever need anything."

"You don't know me. Why would you want to have anything to do with me?"

I'm not sure why either. I'm mystified by my reaction to her as well. "Everyone needs help sometimes."

"I won't be taking help from you. But I will take this. And I will pay you back. I'm not the type to steal."

"I'm sure you're not."

"My car ran out of gas, and I forgot my money at home."

"Honestly, you don't have to explain. Let's call it paying it forward. I paid it forward, and now it's your turn. I don't want you to pay me back. I want you to one day help someone, and we'll be square."

"Okay. I don't need this." She lifts her hand and holds out the card for me to take.

I shoo her hand away. "No. I don't want it. Keep it."

"I won't use it."

"Then don't." I smirk, and before she can object or throw the card back in my face, I return to the main room, my smile growing with each step I take.

Maybe she'll use it or maybe she won't, but I sure hope she does. Because something about her intrigues me.

But as I take a seat at the table, I realize I never asked her name. Nor do I know anything at all about her.

The ball is now in her court.

Something I hate.

I've never let that happen before, and the knowledge that I don't have control over this girl makes this even more enticing.

It makes me want to know everything, and I plan on finding it all out.

Something tells me, though, it will be harder than I expect.

She's a fortress I won't be able to penetrate.

I can't wait.

CHAPTER EIGHT

Willow

ONCE THE NIGHT IS OVER, I DRIVE HOME AND DRAG myself in the door. My feet are killing me, and I'm so tired I'm surprised I can walk.

But I survived, virtually unscathed.

When I walked into Cyrus Reed's house, or should I say compound, he and his staff made it very clear that this was a private affair. They even took our phones, telling the waitstaff that some patrons were very important people. No pictures. No comments. No interacting at all. Other than to grab drinks.

It annoyed the other girl, the no-phone rule, but relief crashed through me. For the first time in a month, I could let out my breath. This job might not have been ideal, but at least I didn't have to hide my appearance to feel safe.

I push the door open, and as soon as I step in, I hear her voice.

"So . . ." Maggie trails off. "How was it?"

I'm surprised to see her awake. But there she is, lying on the couch, looking like she's knocking on death's door.

"Fine," I respond, stepping farther into the room and dropping my coat on the chair. My heels click as I walk to the couch and throw myself dramatically down onto it. "Exhausting." I smile. "How are you feeling?" I lean forward, placing my elbows on my thighs. She looks beat. She rubs her eyes, and I know I woke her when I entered the apartment.

"A little better," she mutters, but it's obvious she's lying. I'm surprised her nose isn't growing at this point. Pinocchio will be jealous.

"Is there something I can get you?" I suck in my cheeks because I know how bad it is to be sick, and I hate that she is. Maggie has done so much for me, and I want to help her.

"You already did enough." She coughs, and I reach forward to grab her water and hand it to her.

"Here. And no. Not when you consider everything you've done for me." The least I can do at this point is make her life easier. Lord knows, me being here, living on her couch, has to be a burden.

"That's nothing."

"You've done so much for me. Let me help you."

She nods, takes the water from me, and then swallows with a grimace. Once she's done, she places it down, turning her head back to me with a small smile.

"What was it like being around all that money? I heard the buy-in was a hundred grand."

When Maggie and I were friends in elementary school, we were too young to know about money, so she probably doesn't realize I'm from money. I don't correct her, though. I laugh. Even I have to admit that that buy-in is absurd.

For rich boys with too much money, Cyrus Reed's home was the Devil's playground.

"It was crazy," I say dramatically. "The stacks of chips. Lord, it was unlike anything I have ever seen before. Insane. Truly."

"Did you make any tips?"

"I did." It wasn't until after everyone had left that I realized how much money I made. Had I known earlier, I would have paid Jaxson Price back, but now I'm indebted to him. Sometime this week, I'll send him cash. I can't write checks, that much is for sure.

"Did you love it so much that you want to do it again?"

"Maybe." I shrug, and her face falls at my words. "If you need me, I will for sure. But I have a few other things I'm looking into."

"You don't have to explain. I understand."

Maggie is too good to me. She doesn't ask or pry. She knows what I'm not saying without me even having to tell her. I'm not sure how long I'll be here. I don't want her to rely on me because if I have to move fast, I will.

A gazelle will always run when a lion approaches.

Hopefully, that won't be the case.

Hopefully, I'll have enough time to put a solid plan together before I go back to where I came from. But as of right now, I have nothing—no plan and no place to be—but I still can't make false promises.

"How about for now, if you need extra help, you ask? If I'm around, it would be my pleasure."

To that, she smiles, and I stand and so does she. Because technically, since I'm home now, she's sleeping in my bedroom, *the pullout couch* in the living room.

Maybe I should take her up on the offer. If I do, I could probably make enough money that I can spend the little I have on a hotel, so I don't have to put her out anymore.

Hotels need identification and a credit card to book a room.

I have neither.

The couch it is.

I let out a large yawn, and she walks to her room. "Thanks again for tonight."

"Anytime."

As soon as she leaves, I pull the couch bed out and then walk over to my duffel to grab my PJs. I might have been here for weeks so far, but I'm still living out of a duffel.

One can never tell.

Better to be prepared than not.

Once I'm dressed and wash my face and brush my teeth, I lie down in bed and fall right to sleep. Tomorrow, I'll think about sending the money back.

With each step I take, the darkness pulls me in. Engulfing me into the abyss like two strong arms grasping and holding me prisoner.

No matter how much I try to see, I can't, and I know where I am. I'm stuck in this nightmare.

This isn't real, the voice inside my head screams, but no matter how hard I tell myself to wake up from the hell, I can't.

I find myself walking the familiar hallway toward the light in the distance.

Closer.

Closer.

I know what I'll find. I know what I'll hear. The hardwood floor beneath my feet squeaks as I make my way toward the light. Again, I'm standing in front of it, and again, the door is slightly ajar. I can't see who is inside, but I can hear his voice. Clear as day.

And I know exactly what he's going to say . . .

Desperately, I let out a strangled cry. Anything to push it away. I don't want to hear.

Wake up!

With a jolt, I awake in my bed, shaking my head to push the nightmare away. Early morning sunshine streams in through the windows. I went to bed way too late for the bright light peeking in through my lids.

That's one problem with staying in a living room—well, besides the nightmares, and I'm certain I'd be getting those even if I was sleeping on twenty mattresses, princess and the pea style—and that's the fact there are no curtains.

I probably should spring for some and hang them myself, but seeing as it's not my place, and money is tight, I don't want to impose. Sure, I have cash saved up for an emergency, but I'm certain no one considers sleeping an emergency.

Lifting my hand, I rub the sleep from my eyes, and then I stretch my arms above me.

Once every bit of the nightmare has left my body, I stand and pad into the bathroom to do my morning business.

A few minutes later, I'm making coffee, and decide that once it's done, I'll head over to the post office. As I wait for it to brew, I open the cabinet and look for an envelope. Lucky for me, not only do I find envelopes but also stamps. I grab a piece of paper and fold it in half, and then pull out a fifty from my tips and tuck it into the paper for safety.

I don't leave a note. I'm sure he'll know exactly who it's from. I address and stamp it and then wait for my coffee to finish.

When it is, I grab a to-go cup, pour the hot liquid in it, and head out the door, money and drink in hand.

Today is colder than yesterday. Strands of my hair that have escaped my hat whip against my face as I walk. It's not far to the mailbox, but far enough that even the short distance is too long in this weather. I probably could have left it with the mail in the building, but I don't like the idea that it could be stamped from Maggie's address as the pickup spot. I can't take the chance that someone could track me. Not that I think anyone would consider looking for me at Maggie's place, but you can never be too careful.

That's what I tell myself as I'm freezing my ass off on my trek to the post office.

With eyes watering and hair flying, I make it to my location and drop the envelope in the bin, then I set off to go back home.

CHAPTER NINE

Jaxson

THE WEEKEND IS FINALLY OVER, AND THE WORKWEEK IS IN full swing, which also means I'm back in my office, unfortunately. When I told my siblings I wanted to do this, I didn't really think this through. I'm tired after a long weekend and want nothing more than to hang in my apartment and work from my couch.

But I guess there is one thing I want more. Respect. Which is why at the ungodly hour of five a.m., I'm waking up and not going to bed.

Because let's be honest, in my former life—a month ago before the gauntlet was dropped—I'd be strolling into my apartment right now, girl for the night in tow, as opposed to throwing on sweats to hit the gym, then showering and going to work like an adult.

My arm raises, and my fingers scrub at my eyes, willing them to open. Adulting sucks.

Once I can finally see, I get up from my bed, head to the bathroom, and do all the shit I need to start my day. Then I hit my gym. I live in a sick building in Tribeca. And not just an apartment. I own the whole building and downstairs is the gym. Upstairs is where I live. With exposed brick and metal beams, it's perfect for me.

There's only one spot probably more perfect, but that's behind a locked door and blocks away.

If I have to work on something private, that's where I do it.

Work I can't have traced back to me. This place is home. Heading down the elevator, I make it into my gym and jump on the treadmill.

An hour later, I'm in the shower. The hot water relaxes my tight muscles as I think about all the work I need to do today. It's not long before I'm driving uptown to Price Enterprise.

Traffic isn't bad as it's early. Hell, the sky is pitch-black, and headlights and buildings are what illuminate the sky. There are no stars in the city. But it doesn't matter when this is your playground.

Unfortunately, other than the poker game, which was, in fact, not in the city, I haven't been able to appreciate much. When I make it to the building, I park and head to the elevator that leads to my floor. I assume I'm the only one here, and I am. Most of the employees aren't here until eight a.m. at the earliest, but I'm not an idiot. At seven a.m. on the dot, Grayson will call to check-in.

Not trusting me. It's getting old. He's been doing this for weeks. And right on the dot, the phone rings.

"Morning, Grayson," I groan through the phone line.

"Jaxson." His voice is short as always.

How does River put up with his attitude?

"And what can I do for you this fine morning? Is there a reason for your call? Or are you trying to drive me insane? Because if that's your intention, you're about to win a medal."

"Can't I just be calling to say—"

"Nope."

He lets out a chuckle, a sound I'm still not used to. But ever since he got together with River, he's been doing it more and more often.

"Fine, you got me. I was checking in."

"No shit," I jest. Does he think I'm stupid? Obviously, he's checking in. He never called me before I was in charge. Now I'm gifted with one call a day. Do the math.

"But can you really blame me?"

"I couldn't blame you the first time, but like, dude, this is getting ridiculous. We're going on like twenty calls. Yes. I'm here. Surprise, surprise. I'm working."

"Very well."

"Other than that, is there anything you want?" *Say, my soul, or maybe my resignation . . .*

"Umm. No."

I tap my fingers on my desk and wait for him to say more, and when he doesn't, I do.

"Well, I have nothing to tell you either, so I guess we're good to go."

Grayson is silent for a minute, and then he sighs. "Talk to you later."

"You mean tomorrow," I deadpan.

"Yep."

"Fine. Gray, I'll talk to you tomorrow. Tell River I said hi."

"Will do."

I hang up the phone and open my computer to look over correspondence.

A few hours later, I hear the clicking before I see Nicole, walking into my office. I've never had an assistant before. Usually because I worked from home. Also, I'm private as fuck. I know everything about everyone, but that comes with some problems. It means I can't let very many people have access to my shit.

There is an abundance of skeletons in the closet, especially the closets I have hacked over the years.

"Hey, Nic," I say. "Don't you look lovely today." She is significantly older than I am, but she still blushes at my greeting.

"Stop flattering me, Mr. Price." She laughs.

"Jax."

"Mr. Price." She looks like a mother scolding her children.

"Mr. Price isn't here right now. Just me." I smile back at her, and she shakes her head at me.

"And you're doing a fine job." Her compliment makes me smile. At least someone thinks so.

"What can I do for you?" I ask.

"You have mail."

Inclining my head, I raise my eyebrow, "Don't I always? Or better yet, don't my siblings?"

"That they do, but this time, so do you."

"I do?" Most people wouldn't find that odd, but I'm not most. I'm fully digital. No snail mail for me . . . ever. Except for today, obviously. I take the pile from her hand and leaf through anything not addressed to me until I find the envelope with my name on it. Ripping it open, I see a folded-up paper. Unfolding it, I look to see what it says.

Nothing.

I can't help the laughter that bursts through my lips because tucked inside the envelope is a folded up fifty-dollar bill. It doesn't take a rocket scientist for me to figure out who sent it. With a smile lining my face, I look on both sides of the paper and then the envelope. Other than my name, there is nothing there. Nothing to tell me who she is. Or even her name. Well played, mystery woman.

Well played.

I always like a challenge.

After work today, I headed out but decided not to go home. Instead, I'm at my favorite place on earth.

My workspace.

My highly illegal workspace situated in a converted warehouse.

I bought this building with money from my trust that I placed in a shell company.

For all intents and purposes, I don't own this building. Nor does anyone reside or work here. From the outside, it's condemned. Fancy computer work on my part.

My mouth curves into a smile. Coffee in hand, I stare at my monitor. A retinal scan opens up the screens. I don't just have one, though.

What fun would that be?

Grayson makes fun that I hack every girl I'm interested in, but there is truth to the jest. I won't approach a woman who doesn't want me. But on the off chance that she does, I always research my conquests or even potential ones at that.

I do it to protect my family fortune.

But also, because I'm good at it.

As my fingers start to tap on the keyboard, I stop.

Nope.

I fight the temptation to look because unlike other women, she's given no indication that she's into me. I won't be finding out anything. Instead, I type in Cyrus Reed. The host of the poker game.

The sketchy as fuck banker definitely has hordes of skeletons in his closet. Now he's a man I can look into. At first, I wasn't going to, but since I had every intention of going back to the poker game this weekend, I need to see who I'm dealing with. The first thing that pulls up is his driver's license. I stare at him.

He looks angry as fuck. Delving a little deeper, I pull up the finances of his business and go down the rabbit hole.

Hours later, I come up for air. I didn't find too much. A few offshore accounts. Some less than reputable clients. I wonder why he hosts the poker game. Leverage, money, to get more clients? Is he using it to bring in new clients, or is the poker game used solely to clean the money?

Knowing he's shady as fuck should put me off from attending another game. It shouldn't make me want to go, but like all things in life, the things that should push me away the most intrigue me.

For the rest of the afternoon and well into the evening, I find out more about my host. Then when I feel satisfied that he's not a human trafficker, I pick up my phone and fire off a text.

Me: Poker game on this weekend?

Trent: You know it. You in?

Me: Yep.

Trent: Fan-fucking-tastic.

I drop the phone back on my desk and then look toward the center of the room. From where I'm sitting, I stare out the window to a perfect view of the Hudson River.

The street is usually empty when I'm here, but today people pass by, so it must be the time of day. Walking with purpose to get to where they need to go. They can't see me; they can't even see in my building, but I can see out. Through the frosted and dirty glass, I have a perfect view of them.

I like to watch them. One of my favorite pastimes is imagining what they are thinking. Sometimes, I imagine I'm one of them. Going about my business, melding with the crowd.

I'm not, though.

I've been privy to too much bad to ever be like most.

These people are ignorant to the world. They don't know what I have found with a click of a mouse. I know the evils most people hold, and I don't trust anyone because of that.

Only my siblings. When you've seen what I have, you wouldn't either. That's why I built this place in this building off the beaten path. This secret sanctuary. Because behind that wall is so much more than meets the eye.

Like me.

CHAPTER TEN

Willow

Today is frustrating. There is no way for me to find out what I need. Not from here, at least. A sobering and scary thought pops into my head.

Go back. It's the only way.

I shake my head back and forth because that can't happen. If I go back . . .

No.

Sweat beads line my skin. Goose bumps form, standing tall on my arms.

No.

I won't think about what will happen to me if I do.

I'll have to find a different way. There must be someone I can ask to help me. I would ask Maggie, and I know she would if she could, but this is too much to drag her into.

I sit on the couch, lift out the picture I brought with me, and stare at the girl in the picture. How young and innocent to the world she was. Now, years later, I'm not that girl. I'm older and jaded.

And most of all, that girl in the picture wasn't alone.

"Willow, you in for today? You want to work?" Maggie asks as she walks out of her bedroom and into the living room.

"Poker game again?"

Her head bobs up and down. "Apparently, you all did such

a good job. Mr. Reed called me back and hired me for every Friday."

My eyes go wide at what she says. "Wow," is all I can muster because I was sure I sucked but guess not.

I also was sure Jaxson Price would rat me out, but I guess I was wrong about him too.

"So, you in?"

Her voice is hopeful, but I shoot her down quickly. "Nope."

"Ahhh, come on. You were good. What else do you have to do tonight?"

"Rearranging my socks." I smile.

"Where? In your duffel or while they are still on your feet?" she chides.

"Har. Har." I fake laugh.

"You know I could give you a drawer for your stuff."

"You know I can't."

"Because that would mean you're staying, and you can't say that yet. The same way you can't commit to a job," she responds for me. She knows me too well, and her answer is spot-on.

"Maggie."

"I know. I know." She lifts her hands in surrender.

"I'm not ready." A long sigh escapes me. I'm not ready to admit defeat, but the longer I stay on Maggie's couch, the more I have to admit that failure is appearing to be the only option at this point.

I don't have anyone to turn to. The thought has me worrying my lip.

At the movement, Maggie gives me a weak smile. "I'm sorry. I didn't want to make you uncomfortable."

"It's not that."

"Then what?"

I bury my hands in my hair. "I don't know," I admit.

"You know you can talk to me." Her eyes plead with me to believe her, and I do. Truly, but I won't. Maggie is a good person, the best really, but I'd do nothing more to put her in danger. Being here puts her in danger, but at least if she's left in the dark . . .

Selfish.

You're being selfish.

She deserves to know.

I wish I could. To unload my issues on her would feel so good, but it would also be selfish. The less she knows, the better.

"I do know, but I can't." I let out a sigh. "At least not yet."

"I understand." With that, she walks to the bathroom to get ready for tonight. I think about what she offered. A job working for her company serving at parties.

Giving drinks to men playing poker.

The tips were excellent last time, and I'm sure they would be even better tonight. I could use the extra cash. Because although I took some money with me when I left my home, it won't last me indefinitely. Maybe I should take her up on her offer.

It would be the smart move. Especially since I know how tight security is. At least at Cyrus Reed's, I know I'll be safe. As crazy as that sounds, working at his home is my best option.

Just as I've decided, another thought pops into my head—a reason I shouldn't work at the poker game—but I shake my head, not allowing myself to think about Jaxson Price. Yes, I might see him, but I'll be working. He won't be able to speak to me if I'm working. It's a sound logic, I tell myself as I stand from the couch and knock on the bathroom door.

"Mags!" I holler over the sound of the water.

"What's up?" Her voice is louder than usual, the words muffled. "You can open it."

I crack the door, and the warm steam of the water pounds my face.

"I'm going to take you up on that offer," I say, and when she hears me, I swear there's a yelp of excitement, followed by the sound of the curtain screeching against the metal rod as she pulls it back to look at me.

Maggie's face pops out from behind it, hair wet, water streaming down her face.

"Really?" Her eyes narrow as though she heard me wrong, and I'll be changing my mind any second now.

"Yep."

"Omg. This will be great." She gushes with excitement, and I lift my hand to stop her. "I know. I know. This is a temporary gig, and you don't know how long you'll be working with me."

I nod at her assessment. She's right. All of it. If all goes well and I can think of a plan that might work, I might not be in the city for long. At least that's what I hope.

If only I were so lucky.

I'm lost in that train of thought when I hear her speak again.

"Well, I'll hurry up then so you can shower."

I step back and close the door. I realize I will have to wear Maggie's dress again. If I'm going to be working more often, I need to buy a dress of my own.

Forty minutes later, I'm dressed. Maggie and I are now twins. Well, not really. Because her dress doesn't appear as short on her. Mine is basically a napkin on me. I'm that much taller than she is.

We head out onto the city streets to find her car so we can

drive to Mr. Reed's house again. I'm not sure where she parked, but it's cold enough that I'm shivering, so I hope it's not far.

Maggie keeps her car parked on the street instead of a parking lot. Apparently, city parking lots cost an arm and a leg, so she parks on the street, rotating spots depending on the days and the parking rules.

It sounds exhausting to have to move your car every few hours, but she needs a car for work. In heels and dressed like I'm working the streets, we finally get to her car and climb in. Then we set off out of the city again. The only difference is we have gas this time. There will be no gas station. No arrogant, gorgeous stranger and, more importantly, no stealing from said arrogant, gorgeous stranger.

I wonder if he'll be there. Or maybe I'll get lucky and won't have to face him.

We're already square, seeing as I sent back the money, but being face-to-face with him again still makes my stomach nervous.

I'm not sure why.

It's not because I want him. Sure, he's handsome, but I'm not in the right frame of mind for a relationship, let alone a one-night stand. But he still does crazy things to me. Maybe it's because he shows me how far from grace I have fallen in the past few months.

Before my recent turn of events, I'd never thought I'd steal. But I guess you never know what you'll do when you're desperate enough.

I was desperate, and I made a bad decision.

He has seen the ugliest side of me, and I'm not proud of that. I hope he doesn't tell Maggie.

That would be awful.

It's bad enough I'm ashamed of my actions, but to have anyone else know would be too much. I couldn't handle that.

Not now.

Not after everything.

She already looks at me with eyes full of pity. This would be downright awful. I'm not sure I could ever look at her again if she knew. Fuck, I'm not sure I could look at myself again.

With a lot on my mind tonight, the weight of my decision to work again hanging over me, I don't speak.

We ride out of the city in silence. She weaves in and out of traffic while I stare out the window, lost in space.

Even though I'm not ready to see Jaxson Price, I'm happy to have left the apartment. Hiding out was getting old. It's the only place I feel safe.

It's not like anyone will find me here. It will be okay.

It doesn't take us long to get out of the city, and the trip flies by from the moment we cross over the bridge.

Traffic at this time of night is minimal.

Soon, we are turning onto the sprawling property. Darkness is all around us as we pull in through the back driveway, the one reserved for the help.

I'm not used to entering this way.

But things have changed, and if there is one thing I have learned these past few months, it's adapt or die.

Since I'm not ready to die . . .

I'm willing to do anything to survive.

Including and not limited to putting up with drunk men for tips.

Maggie parks the car, and then we head inside through the servant's entry.

One woman I recognize from last week, and another one I

don't. Today there are four servers and a bartender, so I assume tonight will be busier than last time.

I'm okay with that.

Even if it's more work, it means that if Jax is here, there is less of a chance that he'll blindside me.

One can hope at least.

That man is way too good-looking and arrogant. He's the type of man who could distract me from my purpose here, and I don't need any distractions.

The guests filter in not long after we get there. I don't see him at first. Then from the corner of the room, a familiar smirk meets my stare. We lock eyes for a beat, and I'm not sure if he'll approach or what I'll do if he does.

He turns and walks in the opposite direction. For some unknown reason, I'm disappointed.

I shake off the feeling. There is no room for it here.

My life right now is like choosing to fly into the Bermuda Triangle. A bad idea. I will not concern myself with him.

I head over to a group of men mingling on the other side of the room. When one looks at me, I open my mouth to speak, but the arrogant jerk cuts me off. "Scotch for us all, doll."

My back goes stiff, and I'm left staring at him like a gawking fool. It's hard for me to bite my tongue. Old Willow wouldn't have.

"Now, that's no way to talk to a lady," I hear from beside me.

I'd know that voice anywhere . . .

It's him, and ironically, after the way he first spoke to me, he's now knocking this guy. I won't say I'm not happy he has, but still . . . ironic.

A part of me wants to call him out, but I can't get my mouth to work not just because of shock but also because this gig means a lot to Maggie and I don't want to fuck it up for her. So instead, I turn slowly to my side and meet the green eyes of Jaxson Price. I lift a brow at him, silently calling him out, and he rewards me with that damn smile of his.

The one I don't want to admit does crazy things to my insides. Dimple and all this time.

Jeez, this man.

He opens his mouth, and without a sound leaving his lips, he says, "I know."

Good. He should know he sounds like a huge hypocrite.

"Lady?" dickwad says. "She's *just* the help."

Jaxson steps forward then and leans in toward him. He says something. I'm not sure what because I can't hear him. But the jerk's face goes pale. All the color has left his cheeks, and it's as if he's seen a ghost.

He lifts his hand in surrender. "You don't need to do that, Price. I was joking." Then he turns to me. "You know I was joking, right?"

I allow the largest fake smile to line my face. Maybe in the past, I would have fought. But here, I can't, so I smile and tilt my head.

"Of course, sir. I'll go get you that scotch." Then, before I can say anything else, I leave. I hate being meek and holding my tongue. I hate weakness, which has been increasingly hard for me. Because in the past few weeks, I have been so weak, and it kills me to be that way.

I was never overly strong, per se, but this person is not me.

No . . .

Fear has made me weak, and I hate it.

Unfortunately, I can't do anything about it, so I square my shoulders and head across the room to grab him and his friends their drinks.

They will all be sitting down soon, so there shouldn't be any more run-ins with him or Price. I can keep busy, mind my business, and then leave here unscathed.

Once I have two drinks in hand, I head back. I'll have to make two trips to get the rest of the men their scotch, but at least it keeps me busy. Jaxson is still there, but this time, I don't make eye contact. I place the drinks down and walk away before Jaxson can say anything to me.

I need to stay far away from him. That's what I know I should do, but it doesn't stop me from watching him, wondering, and worse . . . thinking about him.

About an hour later, while I'm walking toward the bar, I feel a presence behind me. I don't need to turn around to know it's him. The familiar scent wafts up to my nose.

I wish it didn't send shivers up my spine. The way I feel when I'm near him is not okay.

First, I know nothing about him. He could be crazy. He could be a stalker. Hell, he could be a serial killer for all I know.

Or he could be a nice guy, a pesky voice says in my head, but I shake it off. It doesn't matter. He could be these things. But the one thing I know for sure is—regardless if he's an asshole or not—he is bad for my health.

With everything going on, I shouldn't be interested or attracted to him.

I tell myself I'm not, but I've been robbed of companionship for so long that now I'm desperate for anything. Even something this small, the little attention he has shown me, makes me feel normal.

I'm anything but normal, and if this man was smart, he'd run far away from me. I have enough baggage to sink a ship.

"Are you avoiding me?" his raspy voice asks from behind. I keep walking because I one hundred percent am. "I'll take that as a yes. But why?"

That halts my steps. I turn around to face him while placing both my arms beside my hips and glare at him. "There is no why. I'm not avoiding you." Lies. "Hell, I didn't even know you'd be here." Lies. I can sense him anywhere. "I am here to work. To serve"—I pause for emphasis—"the likes of you. Is there anything I can get you, sir?" My voice is sugary sweet. I might get diabetes from how sweet it is. I let my lips split into a ginormous and utterly fake smile, to put the icing on the kiss-ass cake. The bastard rewards me with his signature sexy look. The one I'm sure he holds a patent for. Collecting money every time it's replicated.

A real renaissance man.

"The usual," he responds as if I've known him for years and have been serving him for that long. As if I have memorized his order. Which I have, and he knows it.

I nod and then turn back around. The less time I spend in front of him, the better. There's something in his eyes. Well past the color, there's a depth. There is an understanding there. Like I can't fool him. Like he'd see past everything I throw at him, and I don't like it.

Jaxson Price has that look . . . the look that says he's smarter than everyone else. The look that says he knows more than everyone else. It's scary, but, it's almost invigorating.

No one has ever looked at me as though they know all my secrets. It makes me want to hide, but—and I'm not sure why—it makes me want to confess. It makes me want to tell him everything.

Yes. This man will be a problem.

CHAPTER ELEVEN

Jaxson

It's been a week and a half since I've gone out. Work has me by the balls. When I think I can have a life, something happens, and I realize, yet again, I'll be working late.

That coupled with the fact I have to be here well before seven a.m. to intercept the morning Grayson Price check-in means I'm beat and itching to spend the night drowning my sorrows in booze.

It has become very clear to me that I have bitten off more than I can chew regarding taking over Grayson's and Addison's workload. The days of me having a cushy as fuck job are done, and I'm beat.

However, I would never admit that to anyone. Least of all anyone who shares my last name.

Today, though, has promise.

I wasn't expecting the phone call I got earlier when my phone rang. It was from an unknown number, so I answered it, obviously.

Curiosity killed the cat and all.

Cyrus Reed.

Apparently, he was calling me personally to see if I wanted or had any desire to attend a fundraiser he was hosting tonight at his estate.

I said yes, obviously. Even though I should probably steer clear of him. There's something off about this man, but I've yet to put my finger on it.

It shouldn't take me long to find his secrets. I've been too busy to delve deeper. Plus, his cousin is River.

Out of respect, I contemplate not doing my due diligence. The truth of the matter is I never go to a fundraiser without figuring out where the funds are going. However, I'll make an exception for River's family.

Straight from work, I head home to change. I dress in casual attire all the time, my usual choice being a thermal and ripped jeans, but now I'm in a three-piece suit.

Have to dress the part.

Grayson mentioned earlier today when I spoke to him, he would be there. So technically, I don't have to go. However, a personal invitation from Cyrus Reed is enough to raise an eyebrow. That and the fact I'm curious to see if a certain waitress will be there.

I don't know if she only works poker games. Maybe she doesn't work the fundraisers too, but that doesn't stop me from wondering, and it didn't keep me from accepting the invitation.

I pull up to the circular drive, and a valet waits to park my car. It was stupid of me to drive. But unlike Grayson, I don't like to have a driver. I'm not pretentious like that. I prefer to blend.

I've always been like this. Sure, I have a fabulous car, and yes, I have the best computers and toys money can buy, but I don't like to flaunt my wealth like him. I hop out of my Range Rover, irony not lost on me that I'm a hypocrite, and then head toward the door.

The party is not being held where we play poker. No, it appears the party is being held clear across the mansion. This room is the polar opposite, resembling a ballroom. Decorated with high-top tables, low tops as well, and bars everywhere.

The place is already packed even though I'm right on time. There are a lot more people here than I assumed. It's almost as though I'm late.

If she's here, I might never see her. There are at least fifty servers walking around, and that's only the ones on the floor. She could be in the back helping. I continue to scan the vast room for a sign of her, but as I peer around, I doubt she'll be here.

I don't see her anywhere, but I do see someone I know. My brother and River.

Figures.

The familiar face is my judgmental older brother, who is looking me up and down. Since I know they have seen me, I stroll over to where they're standing and smile.

"I'm surprised to see you here," Grayson says.

"I told you I'd be here."

"Yes, but you never know with you. Although, come to think of it, it is a party with booze, so maybe I'm not surprised at all."

River cringes at his words while shaking her head and leaning up on her tiptoes to give me a kiss hello.

"Ahh, there he is, the dick. I almost forgot you were alive. Couldn't keep him hidden for long," I jest.

"What are you doing here? You hate these things. You prefer to drink when there isn't a cause."

"Oh, come now, brother, I like to drink and party any way I can." The verbal sparring between my brother and me is getting old. He'd said he was done, but I guess the habit is too hard to break because here he is, being an ass again. My stance is, if he fires at me first, I will always fire back. So here we are, in front of hundreds of guests, going at it.

"This is true," he retorts.

"Oh, stop, you two," River pipes up, and I turn to face her. She looks as gorgeous as ever. Young and full of life.

"You look gorgeous, sis." I lean in and give my brother's fiancée a second kiss on the cheek.

"I'm not your sister yet."

"Semantics."

"I prefer him to call you sis. Maybe then he'll remember his place and stop ogling you," Grayson adds.

"Down, boy. It's not my fault your fiancée is stunning." I swear Grayson looks like he's about to murder me. River reaches her hand out and touches his arm. I watch as all the anger leaves his body with the one touch.

"Well trained." I laugh at them, and River rolls her eyes at me.

"Don't you ever stop?" Grayson asks.

I shake my head. "Nope. And on that note, as amazing as it is to see you, I'm going to the bar to get a drink."

"Did you drive?" he asks, knowing full well I did.

"Yes, Dad."

He raises a brow. "Don't drink too much."

His condescending tone makes me ball my fists, but I do nothing. I won't lose my cool here. That would prove him right.

"As you wish," I mock, using humor and sarcasm to mask the pain I feel inside for how little he thinks of me.

"Seriously, Jax."

"Jeez, Gray, I'm not a complete idiot. Even though you treat me like I am." I cross my arms at my chest and wait for his next insult. I'm prepared to spar.

"Start acting like an adult and I'll treat you like an adult," he finally says. I open my mouth to send back a witty reply, but he cuts me off. "You're Icarus. You think you're indestructible, but eventually, you'll fly too close to the sun and burn."

"Fuck you, Grayson."

River steps forward. "You guys have to stop fighting. We're in public." River, the voice of reason.

"Fine."

"If you need us to drive you home, don't be too proud to ask."

"Good to know. Now, I'm going to get that drink unless there's anything else you want to add."

"No."

"Great." I don't bother with formalities like saying goodbye and whatnot.

I turn and walk toward the bar. When the bartender looks at me, I order my usual. Tequila. Might not be the drink of choice at one of these events, as most are drinking champagne and scotch, but I'd rather have tequila any day of the week.

With my drink now in hand, I wander around the room. There's only one person I'm looking for, and it only takes me one lap before I see her.

She's dressed in the normal skintight black dress that hugs every inch of her body. This must be the uniform, and I want to thank whoever suggested it.

She's gorgeous.

Even with drinks in hand, she's more stunning than anyone else in this room. There are plenty of women here, dripping with diamonds, makeup done, gowns that are the highest couture, yet they don't hold a candle to her. Seconds go by, becoming minutes, as I watch her. I'm a voyeur, studying her every move. I watch as she hands off the drinks to the patrons; I watch as she takes orders from another group of men, and I watch as they look at her the way I look at her, and I don't like it. Yet as we all stare, she doesn't have a care in the world. Until she hears a sound. I hear it too. It's the shutter of a camera taking pictures. The sound echoes through the air.

Flick.

Flick.

The group of men standing next to her is the primary focus of the photographer. She takes a step back from the crowd. Her face has turned a pale, ghostly white. She tries to stay calm, but I watch as her chest rises and falls, and then she hands off the last drink before turning and walking faster toward where I assume the kitchen is. What's that all about?

CHAPTER TWELVE

Willow

THE SOUND OF THE CAMERAS MAKES MY BODY FREEZE.

Ice spreads through my veins.

I'm stuck in a trance, and I don't know what to do.

Move.

Goddammit, why can't I get my legs to move?

Fear knots inside me as my heart thumps, beating frantically behind my breastbone. It beats so hard I'm sure it will explode. The ringing in my ears starts next, making the room sway beneath my feet.

I'm sure I will pass out.

I can't breathe. I can't breathe. I can't breathe.

Panic like I've never known before wells in my throat.

My picture is being taken.

He will find me.

And when he finds me . . . the thought of what he'll do tears at my insides until I'm sure I'm going to fall down underneath the weight of my fears, but as my knees buckle under the weight of my panic, I feel two hands grab me.

I'm so lost in my thoughts that I barely recognize the movement of my body as I'm ushered out of the room and brought down a hallway. Only when we push through the doors of the kitchen, can I finally breathe.

That's when I see who's holding me. It's him. It's Jaxson

Price who's not letting me fall. He pulls me farther to where the door exits to the outside of the house and opens it.

The cold air slaps across my face. The smells of nature infiltrate me, the burning leaves filtering through my nostrils. It helps to calm me. It helps to bring me back to the here and now.

It takes a minute of inhaling to understand where I am and how I got here. I'm now sitting on the back stoop of the kitchen.

"You're okay," I hear him say.

My eyes blink rapidly. I open my mouth, but it's hard to get the words out. It feels like I'm choking on my breath. I reach my hand up to my throat, trying to clear it.

"Let me get you water." Jaxson stands, leaving me alone here in the dark, lonely night. Here in Connecticut, where the stars are brightly illuminating the sky.

There isn't much light out here, but the stars are so bright I can see them. I wait for him to return and wonder what's wrong with me. It must have been the sound of the cameras because when I heard them, the all-encompassing fear I had was unlike anything I've ever felt before.

That's not true.

I felt that fear before . . .

The night I left.

My brain hurts from trying to understand what happened, and the only thing I can come up with is that I was afraid someone would take a picture of me.

Images had paraded through my head of my picture being seen by him.

My imagination ran wild. I was sure someone would find me, and that I would be in danger.

On a large exhale, my head drops. The sounds around me calm me as I wait for him to return with my water.

It doesn't take much longer before he does, but this time as he makes his approach, I can hear clicking heels behind him. I look up over my shoulder, and I see Maggie is with him. Her eyes are wide, and her jaw is tight as she looks down at me.

"Are you okay?" Maggie asks.

I stare blankly at her. I'm not sure what to say. How to explain that I was so scared of my picture being taken. Of being found.

My pulse speeds up again. My breathing comes out in strangled bursts as I fight for oxygen. I feel as though I'm a balloon, floating up with nothing tethering me to the ground.

"Are you okay?" It's his voice now, and even though he's a complete stranger, I float back down to earth. He is the rope that tethers me. "I got you," he whispers as I breathe normally. "Welcome back."

"Why are you here? Why are you helping me?"

"Why shouldn't I be?"

"You're supposed to be like every other asshole," I whisper more to myself than to him.

"I'm not like anyone. I'm me." With that said, an unwelcome tension stretches between us. It's as if it's just him and me in this world, it's unnerving. The silence now looming around us like a heavy mist.

Making myself look around, I'm now aware of my surroundings and feel my cheeks warm. Maggie is still there, and I had forgotten her. I try to stand, but the movement is too fast, and I fall forward. Yet again, he catches me.

Warm. Protected. Safe. This stranger makes me safe, which makes no sense.

"Where do you think you're going?" He pulls me in tighter to his body to support my weight.

"Back to work?" I say in question, and then I look up at Maggie, who is shaking her head. "You need me," I tell her.

"I don't."

"But who will—" I say before Maggie lifts her hand to silence me.

"We'll be fine." She moves to go back inside. "You stay here. I'll be back soon."

"I can take her home," Jaxson pipes in, and Maggie looks shocked by his suggestion, her eyes wide.

"No, go, Romeo. How do we know you're not a serial killer?"

I almost choke at her words. Figures that I'd feel comfortable with him if he was one. I'm apparently not a good judge of character.

"I'm Jaxson Price." He says this like it means something. As if his name excludes him from being crazy. But I know better. It doesn't matter how good you look on paper; you never know who a person is behind closed doors.

"And that means you're not insane? Plenty of pretty boys are serial killers," I say before I can stop myself.

The only problem with my verbal diarrhea is that Jaxson caught the one word I didn't mean to say. His lips tip up into a gigantic smile. I want to wipe it right off his face.

"Soooo," he drags out, and the urge to roll my eyes at him runs through me because I know what he is about to say. "You think I'm pretty?"

I turn to look at Maggie. "I'll be fine. Regardless of the fact he's an ass"—I point over to him— "he won't hurt me." I might not know him well, but I trust him.

Which should probably sound off blaring alarms, but it doesn't.

Guess I'll never learn. Maybe he'll prove me wrong or, in this case, right.

"Fine," she huffs. "But you can't leave her alone." Maggie turns to me, her face awash with sorrow. "Also, when she's like this . . . she likes chocolate." I lift a brow. "You do. Don't think I don't see you eating Kit Kats in your bed." A small laugh escapes my mouth.

"You sure you'll be okay?" she asks again.

"I'll be fine," I promise.

"We'll stay right here or, better yet, in the kitchen. I'll watch over her. She'll be well taken care of," Jaxson says.

Maggie looks at me, and I nod. "Go."

"You sure?" She must see the answer in my eyes because she hurries back in to work.

Jaxson is then reaching his hand out, but I don't take it. "Come on, let's go inside so your friend doesn't have a heart attack."

"I'd like to stay here for a bit if that's okay?"

"Whatever makes you happy."

"I'm happy outside." I tilt my head up and look toward the sky. From my peripheral, I can see him sitting beside me.

"The stars are pretty sick tonight."

"They are. I didn't realize how much I missed them until now," I say. My voice is low amongst the backdrop of the quiet night. The evening sky is now black and silent. You would never think a party is going on behind us.

"Yeah, I feel you. No stars in the city."

"Nope."

"So that's where you live?" And I realize I walked right into that. A desire to talk weaves its way through me. It feels as if no one can hurt me here cloaked by the night sky, and I can say things in the dark of the night. At least that's what I tell myself as I open my mouth. A little information won't hurt.

"I live with Maggie."

"And do you have a name?" he asks.

I think about what to say. Should I give him the name Willow . . . or another name altogether? It's not like he can find me with it. It's not like it's real anyway.

Both options are fake.

"Willow," I respond before I can second-guess myself.

"And is there a last name, Willow?" He sits forward, his curiosity oozing out of him as he stares at me.

The thing is, it doesn't matter how curious he is, I can't offer him more than my first name.

"Nope, just Willow. Or at least that's all you're getting."

"Ah. You're like a celebrity." He smiles as he nods in approval, as if he thinks my reason is part of some act to entertain him.

If only that were the case, my life would be much easier.

"Something like that," I retort playfully, playing up the game he thinks I'm playing.

"You're a tough crowd."

"Sorry."

"No worries. I like it." Even in this light, I can see his dimple peeking through, and I realize by going along with this game, he thinks I'm flirting.

"I'm not trying to play hard to get," I clarify.

"I know, that's why I like it."

I look back at the sky to distance myself from this conversation, and this time, I close my eyes and let out a deep breath because now that the moment is over, all my troubles drift back into my mind.

"Do you want to talk about it?"

"Not particularly."

I can feel the shaking of his body as he must nod to himself. Then I feel him stand, and my lids jut open.

"Where are you going?"

"Inside to grab some supplies." He smirks.

"Supplies?"

"Well, obviously. If you don't want to talk, then we at least have to drink . . . and eat. I'm starved."

It's only a few minutes before Jax returns. I look over my shoulder and find him carrying a bunch of stuff. In the dark of the night, I can't make out what's in his hand.

He hands over what he's carrying and then drapes a coat over my shoulders. "I thought you might be cold."

"Thank you." Now that he mentioned it, I realize I am, "What is all this stuff?"

"I brought some booze. Some food." He hands me the bottle. "And some chocolate. Not a Kit Kat, but I hope cake will do."

I lift the bottle up to look at it before taking a sip.

"Seriously? You swiped a bottle of Don Julio?"

"Actually . . . I swiped a bottle of Don Julio 1942."

"Is there really a difference?" I ask.

His eyes go wide and he feigns shock. If I wasn't so high-strung, the look on his face would send me into a belly laugh. It might not make me giggle, but it loosens the tension in my shoulders nonetheless.

"The fact you have to ask that proves to me you don't drink tequila."

"Sorry, I don't have your refined palate."

"It's not about my palate. This shit is better than everything else."

"You're a snob."

"I very well might be, but until you try it, don't knock it."

"Fine. Whatever you say."

"So . . . Willow . . ." he says my name slowly, letting it drip off his tongue like a spoon full of molasses.

Decadent and sweet, and one hundred percent bad for my health.

"Yes?" The word comes out short, probably because I'm frustrated by how much hearing my name from his mouth does to me. You would think I'm a lovesick schoolgirl rather than a woman on the run. One who doesn't have time for crushes.

"Nothing." He's still staring at me, and I cross my arms.

"Then why did you say my name?"

"I like hearing it roll off my tongue," he retorts in his smug and cocky voice.

If cocky bastard had a picture in the dictionary, Jaxson Price would be in it.

"Lord. Does that work?"

"Does what work?"

My head lowers. "Your cheesy pickup line."

"That wasn't a pickup line, and if you think it was, you need to get hit on by someone else. Because if I was hitting on you, you'd know, and cheesy wouldn't be the word you'd use."

"What else do you have?" I ask, changing the subject.

"Food."

"Vague much? What type of food did you get?"

"I really have no idea."

"What do you mean?"

"It's the fancy food they always serve at these types of parties."

"Canapés," I answer for him.

"If you say so."

"It's not me who says so. It's everyone." He nods, and I shake my head. "No, really. It's even in the dictionary and shit."

That's when his lip tips up. "You were messing with me."

Full smirk.

"I was."

"You're so annoying. You can leave now," I say.

"And miss the canapés or hors d'oeuvre or whatever you want to call it . . . small meal?"

"Has anyone ever told you you're an ass?" I grab the platter from him to look at what he has.

"Why yes, actually, on a daily basis."

"Only once a day?"

"Sometimes twice, but that's when I'm in a good mood." And then he winks, and a part of me melts. That's right. Right there on the cold stoop of the back door, I melt.

Pathetic.

"Do you go to a lot of fancy parties?" I ask, and I want to know more about this guy. Sure, I have heard about him. He's usually dissed on all the gossip sites, but he's not at all like I expect. Sure, he is playful and flirty, but there's more to him. How many other rich billionaires would leave a party to sit outside with a server even if it was only to get into their pants?

None.

At least no one I know would put this much work into getting laid. But he's not even about that. He's playful, but I don't feel unsafe with him.

Not at all, actually, and I don't trust anyone.

Not anymore at least.

"What about you? Is this your first party?"

"No." I stop myself. He means as a server and not as a guest. "I mean yes."

His eyes narrow as if he's trying to understand me.

"I have never worked a party like this."

"You normally do . . . ?" he leads.

"I've never worked serving before. The poker game was my first time," I admit. I'm not sure why I tell him this, but it comes out naturally. Maybe it's where we are, or maybe it's the adrenaline coursing through my veins, but it's easy to speak to Jaxson.

"If you're not a server, what is it you do?"

"Pass."

"Pass? Seriously."

"Yep. Have a problem with that?" I lift a brow and he gives me a look I can't place.

"No problem at all. Just trying to get to know you better, Willow. What was that last name again?"

"No last names, remember?"

"As if I could forget. You're a famous celebrity and whatnot. Too cool for a last name. Although I'm a little surprised that your first has two syllables."

"Hey, there're quite a few two-syllable celebs, I'll have you know."

He takes the tray back from me and lifts it, picking up a piece of something. I can't tell what it is, but I can see him lift it to his nose as if to smell it. Then his arm is reaching toward me.

"What is this?" he asks.

The smell of the small food wafts up into the air and hits my nose. I can't tell what it is, but my mouth waters.

Then my stomach growls loud enough for him to hear.

"I have no clue."

"But it appears your stomach wants it. Here, have it."

"I'll take a pass since you touched it already. Don't know where your hands have been."

"Seriously? I save you from passing out, and you are going to discriminate against my clean hands? I'll have you know, they are probably the cleanest hands of anyone you ever met."

"Yes, probably because you disinfect them in tequila every day," I retort.

That brings a chuckle. A full body chuckle that makes me laugh too. I'm not sure what it is about Jaxson Price, but it's easy to be around him and smile. To forget all the shit hovering in the back of my mind.

"How about this. I'll clean them again—fuck, maybe I'll just dip this in tequila again, and then it will be sanitized for you."

"Oh, jeez. Give me the damn food."

He laughs again and hands it to me. I take a bite, and the moment it hits my taste buds, I moan.

"Seriously, that good? Did you at least save a bite for me?"

"My mouth touched it."

"Like I care." He grabs it out of my hand and pops it into his own mouth. "Fuck, that's good."

"Right."

"But what is it?" he moans as he takes another bite.

"No clue."

"I can take chef off the potential lists of things to know about you," he says, and I pull my gaze away from the food and to him.

"You have a list?" I ask.

"I do."

"And what, pray tell, is on this list?"

"Well, as of right now, nothing. It says . . . Willow. No last name," he chides.

"That's a pretty good list."

"It's a work in progress."

His words have my stomach tightening again because I can't have him looking into me. I can't be anyone's work in progress. I'm too much of a mess to complicate things more with having Jaxson Price around.

We both continue to eat, and neither of us speak. From the corner of my eye, I see Jaxson lean forward, balancing the weight of his arms on his knees.

"What happened before?" he finally asks, bringing up the giant elephant I was hoping he would ignore.

"It was nothing," I say a little too forcefully.

He turns his head in my direction, and as much as I want to ignore the movement, I don't. It's like there is a gravitational pull making me want to look at him.

"I don't like crowds."

He studies me, and I can tell he isn't buying it. But really, how could he? I had a major panic attack in the middle of the party.

"The sound. It scared me." Although my answer isn't completely true, it's the closest I will get.

"Were you scared someone might hurt you?" he whispers, and I nod. Under the dark sky, where he can't really see my face, it feels good to be honest about something for once. "You should take a self-defense class. I know a lot of friends who live in the city who swear by them. Makes them feel safer."

I nod my head again.

Because as much as I don't want to admit it, he's right.

I need to.

CHAPTER THIRTEEN

Willow

BLOOD.

So much blood.

It drips off my hands, pooling onto the floor.

His blood is on my hands.

My body jerks awake. My heart pounding in my chest like a freight train. Looking down, I see my hands.

They're fine.

Untouched. Unblemished.

His blood is not on my hands.

At least not literally. His blood will always be on my hands. It's my fault, after all.

I rub my eyes, trying to wipe the images away. Trying to wipe the fear. The same dream over and over again has haunted me for weeks. Sometimes, I go in the room, and sometimes, I don't.

The images flash like the flicker of a camera.

Flick.

Flick.

Flick.

Still frames replay. If only I could scrub them from my brain.

He's looking for me, and I'm running.

He's supposed to protect me.

Dad.

There's blood on my hands.

No. I can't think about this now. It's already been a few days since the fundraiser, and I have spent them trying and failing to figure out how I will deal with all the issues I have piling up in my life.

With each day that passes, my nightmares get worse.

I know the reason too. It's because it's been over a month, and I still have nothing. I'm still living my life in limbo and fear. There has to be something I can do.

I need information.

And I need it now.

Without the information, my life will be in a permanent holding pattern. The first thing I have to do is buy a laptop. Then I can start trying to figure out who from back home I can talk to or even trust.

It's a risk, but I'm running out of solutions.

Go to the cops?

I shake off the thought.

I can't.

I have no proof. I have nothing.

I stand from the kitchen table and head to the bathroom to shower.

Thankfully, Maggie is no longer here. Another thing I need to do is look for a place to stay. I know she said it was fine, but I feel like I've overstayed my welcome. If I continue to work with her on the weekends, it could cover the rent at a hotel. Not a nice one, but beggars can't be choosers. Lack of ID is still a problem, but maybe I can find a sublet, off the books of course.

Turning on the shower, I step under the warm water. It feels heavenly. It washes away all the thoughts clouding my brain. I close my eyes and allow myself to relax, allowing my muscles to loosen. After a few seconds, I grab the shampoo and lather it, then wash my body. When I'm finally ready, I shut it off, step out of the shower, and go to buy a laptop.

I think about going to the Apple store. I even make it all the way there, but I stop before I enter. If I have a computer, I'll be tempted to look at my old social media accounts. I'll want to look up people from my past. I can get caught.

No. I can't have the temptation of a laptop. At least not yet. I continue to walk, needing the air to clear my brain, and I make it to the library. There, Jaxson's words ring in my ear from the other night. I go to a computer and do a Google search.

Jaxson's words have stayed with me for days.

Every time I thought about what he said about taking a self-defense class, I brushed it off. But today is the day I make a change.

I can't be afraid.

If I'm going to be stuck in New York for the unforeseeable future, I can't be afraid of my shadow.

It took me a full four days to work up the courage to be here. But I'm here, and that's half of the battle. The only problem as I look around the room is that a part of me thinks I shouldn't be here.

Don't make excuses.

Don't make excuses to hide and not be here. Don't be scared. You are not some little mouse.

He might not have laid a hand on you yet . . .

Yet.

He wants you dead.

You need to be strong.

You need to protect yourself.

You need to find your strength.

"Hi, can I help you?" a woman asks. She looks at me with sadness and compassion in her eyes.

Looking at me, she can see through my facade.

Through the disguise I present to the world.

Because up close, you can see my roots. My false eyes, my baggie clothes. She might not ask, but she can see it.

Most of all, as she peers into my eyes, I know she can see my fear.

"I want to train," I whisper. "I want to learn self-defense."

I want to scream that I don't want to hide anymore, but I don't. Instead, my teeth nibble on my lower lip. I'm a work in progress, a story unwritten, coming here merely the prologue.

She nods and gives me a smile.

"Come, follow me. I'll get you up and running."

I follow her as she walks over to the desk, but when she pulls out a form, my heart rattles in my chest.

The air in my lungs dries up.

If I have to use my name . . .

No. I can't.

I can't show my ID. I can't have anyone find me.

"This was a mistake," I say, and I watch as her eyes dart toward a man who's facing away from us.

She scribbles on the form.

Then hands it back to me. "Here, *Sarah*, your form looks good." When she says the fake name she's provided me for the papers, I feel the tears welling in my eyes.

"Thank you," I whisper.

"Now that we have that taken care of, join my class." At

her words, I finally look at her. She's dressed in tight-fitting leggings, a sports bra, and gloves.

"You're one of the teachers here?"

She smiles. "Yes, I teach self-defense." She gives me a knowing look, and now I understand. We might not be the same. My story might be different, but she saw my fear and understood it as if it was her own.

I move closer to her. "My name is really Willow," I whisper.

"And I'm Shay." She extends her hand, and this time, I take it. "*Sarah*," she says to me again, and I nod in approval. "You ready?"

"I am."

Together we walk into the main room. I see a few people practicing already.

"I'll start with the basics one on one, but we will build up. And fast."

"Let's do this."

A train has hit me . . .

Or at least that's how I feel today.

My body and my mind are exhausted, but there is nothing I can do to fix it.

Once again, I couldn't sleep.

Once again, I woke up in a cold sweat.

This time in my dream, I was living my life, back in my town, in my house . . .

This time I never got away.

The uncertainty of my life is getting to me. All the questions I have and not knowing what to do.

I have to talk to someone. I need help, but how?

There is no one who can help me.

No one who can help me prove my claims.

I can't trust the local police. They are bought and paid for. I remember his words . . .

"Don't bother going to them, they're on my payroll." Friends with the mayor, largest donor to the sheriff's department, has my options limited.

Maybe the FBI?

But I have no evidence.

There is nothing to prove my beliefs.

A voice inside of me screams you have to try.

That there is no way I can sit in this room for another week without trying.

It's already been too long.

Does anyone even know I'm gone?

Are they searching for me? What if he finds me first?

My dad's face pops into my head, and I shake my head back and forth.

The icy tendrils of fear spreading in my veins.

No.

I can't think about him.

Throwing my feet over the side of the pull-out couch, I pad over to the bathroom. The floor is cold beneath my feet, and I shiver.

Everything inside me is cold, and I know I'm fooling myself when I say it's from the floor.

It's not. It's him.

It's what will happen if I go to the police and am caught. They won't help me. Maybe, though, I can make an anonymous tip. Maybe then they will look into it.

One can hope.

It makes what I'm doing worth it because the way my body shakes and the empty feeling inside as I walk, bundled up with a hat and glasses, outside is hard enough.

I gather my strength from the knowledge that it could help me go home sooner. As I hop in a cab and head into Jersey, tipping the driver to wait, I tell myself I have to do this. No matter how much I try, terror creeps its way into my head, but I can't stop what I'm doing.

Walking over to the payphone, I drop the money in before dialing the number I gathered on my last trip to the library.

Then call the Major Case Contact Center of the FBI.

I have to keep the call short.

When it's time to talk, I do. My voice is clear and concise, but it's also not my own. No, instead I give myself a Southern accent and pray this doesn't backfire.

"I'd like to report a murder." Thump. "You need to exhume the body of." Thump. "Henry Craft."

CHAPTER FOURTEEN

Willow

Days pass, and then a week. There has been nothing new since I've called the FBI, but I guess I'm actually not sure since I have no way of knowing.

I keep my days and mind occupied with the self-defense classes. At first, it was every other day. But I realize how much stronger I'm getting and how much I like it, so now I go every day.

In the beginning, it was only Shay and I. She taught me how to box. Nothing I wouldn't learn at a gym if I was taking a kickboxing class.

But today is different.

I can feel the shift in the air. Today, there is a man in the room with Shay and me.

"Sarah, this is Beau, and he's going to help us train." My eyes go wide, and she lifts her hand. "It will be okay. Beau is here for the height factor." She laughs. "I'm just as tough as him, so if you can fight me, you can take him down. But I need to show you."

I nod my head and walk over to where they are. I stand in front of Beau.

I'm still wearing my baggie sweats, and I know that I shouldn't. That this is a liability he can use in his favor.

"Remember . . ." Shay says. "No one can hurt you here. It's just us."

I know I'm shaking. I know I'm scared. This. Fighting with a man feels too real. It reminds me of the nightmares I have.

The one with blood on my hands.

My eyes close as the pounding in my heart intensifies.

"Breathe." I hear. "Relax."

It's Shay talking, and her voice helps calm me.

My eyes flutter open. I know he's not here. He hasn't found me. And no one can hurt me.

I move to the position that Shay taught me last week with my legs hip-width apart. My arms and hands in position.

Beau moves in.

"Are you ready?" I nod.

"You attack," Shay says, and I do.

Punch. It's like a dance. I punch; he blocks. It's different from when practicing on Shay. The height and the speed. I know this is what I need, but the fear of how real this feels is too much for me to handle. My breathing is becoming labored.

I'm not sure if I need to fight that I'll be able to. I can only hope that I'll be able to find out the information I need to catch him before he finds me, but this will help.

We continue to spar, and then we change it up. I'm on the defensive now. I'm the mouse.

I don't like the feeling. It reminds me of running all over again.

I hate that I wasn't strong enough back then to face what I heard and stand my ground.

But next time, I will be.

After a few more blocks and hits, my body aches. I throw my hands up in the air.

"I can't," I murmur. "He's too strong."

"Even if he's stronger, that doesn't mean he can hurt you.

Your strength is your will," Shay says. "Even if you are on your last breath, you are not down. You fight."

"I can't." Tears sting my eyes. "I can't."

"Is there someone you can bring with you that you trust?"

I slump forward, and Beau steps back, giving me time to calm my frazzled nerves. I fight the nauseous feeling churning in my stomach.

No.

That's the problem.

CHAPTER FIFTEEN

Willow

Every day since I've started my self-defense class, I have been pushing myself to feel comfortable again. One thing I've been forcing myself to do is walk around the city.

Sure, I'm still dressed in baggie clothes, and my hair is still dark, but at least I'm trying.

Baby steps.

I'm walking down the street on the way home from one of my attempts to find my strength, when I look up at the sign to see where I am. The address looks familiar, but I'm not sure why. It reminds me of the address where I sent Jaxson his money. I wonder if his office is close to here.

I reach into my pocket and pull out the card he gave me a few weeks ago. I should thank him. What he did for me the other day, he didn't have to.

At first, I thought he had ulterior motives. But he didn't even ask for my number at the end of the night. I didn't ask for his either, but I guess I have it on the business card he gave me.

At the corner of the street, I see the familiar cupcake station. I know he loves sweets. He said as much that night at the fundraiser.

Nodding, I cross and then head inside. I order and then check the address one more time. Maybe I shouldn't do this. Maybe I should leave well enough alone. But something makes my feet move toward his office. Before long, I'm standing in front of the oppressive building, and with reluctance, I walk in.

Any air that is in my body leaves as I step into the lobby. If I thought it was oppressive from the outside, the inside is even worse. Security is everywhere, and cameras riddle the ceiling. These are the things I notice. There is no way I'm getting upstairs without showing identification, but that's something I can't do.

Shit.

I hadn't thought this through.

I don't know what to do.

You can do this.

"Excuse me, miss. Is there something I can help you with?" With my head still down, I turn to the security guard. Even from my vantage point, I can see that he's looking right at me and I feel like a deer stuck in headlights.

I'm not sure how I should respond, so I hold the box up as if that's the answer, as if the box full of cupcakes will talk. My eyes might still be downcast, but his head bobs down as if he looks down at what I'm holding and then it moves back up. Even though I refuse to make eye contact with him, I can hear him tap his foot impatiently and I know he wants me to explain.

"I'm dropping this off."

He nods, his chin pointing down to the box. "Who would you like to leave the box for, miss?"

I have to answer because if I wasn't suspicious enough, I'm very suspicious now. The level of security in this place would make the White House envious, so I'm sure red flags have gone up and a SWAT team will walk in soon.

"It's for Jaxson Price. The cupcakes." I open the box and show them to the security guard. "See. The cupcakes are for Jaxson Price."

"Can you please follow me, miss?"

"Umm. Okay."

Officially, this is the worst idea I've ever had, and now I will be arrested. They probably think I've poisoned him.

"And who shall I tell him the cupcakes are from?" he asks when he leads me to a desk and picks up the phone.

"Willow. Just Willow." I can hear him talking, and then he places the phone down.

"If you can, please wait here for a minute."

My heart pounds rapidly in my chest. Here I am, trying to be careful. Trying to keep a low, untraceable profile, and I'm doing the opposite. I should have called him from my burner phone.

I could have said thank you and gone about my life. I'm lost in my own inner crazy when I hear his voice.

"Willow."

I turn and see him standing there. Tall and lean, and devastatingly handsome.

He's not wearing the typical attire I would expect in an office such as this.

A white thermal and ripped jeans. He has a leather bracelet around his wrist, and unlike at the fundraiser, he's no longer clean-shaven. No, he now has a dusting of hair on his face. His green eyes are clear and focused on me, and his brown locks are tousled.

No. He doesn't look like a Park Avenue prince at all.

"Is everything okay?" There is concern in his voice, and I don't want to look back up, but I know I have to. When I do,

I'm met with crystal green eyes wide with shock. His gaze is on my oversized outfit, then he lifts it up and looks me in my eyes. He squints as if he's trying to remember something, and that's when I realize my mistake. The impulsive decision to come here is sending off red flags to him because today my eyes are brown.

I lift the box and hand it to him. "I wanted to say thank you."

"Thank you?"

"Yeah. For the other day . . . staying with me. I brought you cupcakes." I ramble when I'm nervous. He takes the box and then gestures to the door.

"Do you want to grab a bite and talk?"

I don't know if I should go with him, the thought of standing awkwardly in the lobby is too much to handle, so I nod.

"Great, come with me."

I follow him out of the building. Then he turns left. He walks faster than I do, but I'm wearing Converse. It's not like I'm in heels, so it's easy to pick up my pace. He must realize my strides are longer to keep up because he slows down.

It's about a ten-minute walk before I realize where he's taken me.

I don't like that we're here.

I don't like that we walked this way . . . but what am I going to do?

I have my hat on, so I don't feel as naked as I did the last time I saw him, but I don't feel like myself, and the fact that he's taking me to Times Square is hell. Actual hell.

I'm not at all prepared for this. Sure, I have my cover. But Times fucking Square.

There are more people here than anywhere on earth.

I already am jumpy . . . but this.

Not a good idea.

We continue to walk, but I'm not sure where he's leading me. Something about grabbing a hot dog, but I have no clue. He walks, and I follow. We're at the corner of probably the busiest intersection in the city when he stops.

My feet come to a halt, eyes still trained down. Looking at the concrete beneath my feet. Garbage littered, remnants of gum.

It's gross, but I don't want to look up. It's something I have trained myself to do ever since I left. Never look up.

You never know where a camera is. You never know who will see.

"Willow."

"Yep."

"Look," he says, "we're on." Out of habit, I do. I shouldn't, but I do.

There, on the large screen, are tourists waving. I watch for a second, not realizing, not seeing. But that's because sometimes I forget what I look like now. But what I don't miss is Jaxson, waving at himself as if he were a tourist too.

Beside him is a girl. She has a hat on, but from this angle, her face is clear to see.

It's me.

Because from this angle, you can't see the freshly dyed hair, you cannot see the new clothes that are too big, and there are no glasses.

It's obvious that it's my face is on the screen.

I have to go.

Before I know what I'm doing, I'm off.

Running away . . . running down the block out of the crowd. The sound of a horn blaring as the car nearly hits me rings through my ears, but it doesn't stop me. Not even when the yellow blinds my eyes, a cab.

I almost got hit by a cab.

My head looks up, and I notice I have run out of Times Square, and I'm now on a side street.

Heavy footsteps batter the ground like the sound of artillery fire during a war. I know it's him, but I can't look back. My heart is beating too fast. Terror engulfs my conscience, and as much as I've tried to put distance between me and my fears, even running hasn't pushed it down.

My movements halt, and through my haze, I can feel my nails digging into my palm. Leaning forward, I unclench my fists and place my hands on my hips as I try to catch my breath. My body shakes from the force of my pants.

I'm still looking toward the ground, trying to catch my breath when Jaxson's shoes are in front of me.

He doesn't speak at first, and the anticipation of what he will say has my stomach churning.

"What was that about?" he finally asks, his voice sad and resigned.

Inhale.

Exhale.

"Are you okay?"

I continue to breathe.

Inhale.

Exhale.

When my breath regulates, I finally look up. The look of concern on his face has my face heating with mortification.

I've never felt more stupid. Not once but twice, I have completely lost my cool in front of him. Having a panic attack in the middle of Times Square takes the cake.

This man must think I'm nuts.

"I told you I don't like crowds . . ." I say lamely. He nods and moves closer to place his hand on my back as I'm still leaning forward, trying to catch my breath.

I step back and almost fall over . . .

"I'm not going to hurt you."

"I-I . . ."

"I know you don't trust me, but you can." His voice is steady as if he's trying to be strong for me. "Let me get you . . ."

"No," I respond too forcefully. "I'm okay."

Why does this keep happening?

Shouldn't the self-defense classes be helping me? Maybe my body is stronger, but the fear is still there, trapped in my brain.

The nightmares . . .

Still there.

I might be stronger, but I'm still weak.

"You're not okay," he says, and he bites his lip. He wants to say more, but he continues to watch me, and it's unnerving.

I hate it.

"I'm not really hungry anymore," I finally say as I distance myself away from him, turning to walk toward the street to hail a cab.

"If you need anything—"

"I'm fine."

After the incident with Jaxson, I got into a cab and crawled into my bed. Today, the feeling I had yesterday is still there.

I'm mortified by my behavior, and the embarrassment is making me think twice about what I know I should do. I think about everything I have learned in my self-defense class.

Strength isn't just about kicking ass and punching. It's not only about being able to escape danger. It's also about facing your fear.

I'm afraid, and that means I need to push past it. So today, I stand in his lobby once again. This time, I have both my hat and glasses on, and yet again, I'm wearing a ridiculous outfit. I'm surprised he has said nothing. But what I can tell is that Jaxson Price is way too nice to ask.

The same security guard stops me, and again, I have him call up to Jax to bring him down.

When Jaxson is standing in front of me, he smiles.

"And to what do I owe this unexpected visit? Two days in a row."

"We never got to have lunch. Would you like to eat with me today?" As if he's not giving me a moment to change my mind, he heads toward the lobby door. When I don't immediately follow, he looks over his shoulder. "Let's go." That makes me move my body to catch up to him.

Together, we walk out of the building. He's walking fast as if he thinks I will freak and run away again, but he looks back at me. I let my lips tip up into a smile.

"What would you like to eat?" he asks as we walk.

"Oh, I don't really care," I say.

"Sushi? Or what about diner food?"

My mouth waters at the idea of a chocolate milkshake.

"Definitely diner."

"A girl after my own heart. I love greasy food. Honestly, I just love food. The greasier the food the better."

"I would never have guessed." I laugh. "Remember, I was with you at the party, tequila and food."

"Life's simple pleasures."

"If only it was that easy."

"It can be."

I don't know what he means or why he says that to me. He doesn't know me. He has no idea the shit I've been through, let alone the shit that brought me to the here and now.

"Come on, one more block. Best diner in NYC."

"Promises. Promises."

"If I'm wrong, I buy lunch. Actually, I'm buying lunch anyway. I'll think of something else."

"No bets."

We keep walking the rest of the block, and when we arrive at what looks like a beat-up and dirty diner, he stops.

"Here?"

"Yep." He opens the door and leads me in.

The place looks like it's failed over ten health code violations for the décor alone.

"Trust me," he says. And I do. I let him usher me to a seat.

It doesn't take long for a waitress to walk over to us and place two glasses of water down. She has a gigantic smile on her face as she looks at Jax. Then she looks me over.

"Jaxson, I haven't seen you in so long. Are you cheating on me?" the old waitress says.

"Nope, just working, Mabel."

"Is that grumpy old brother of yours still giving you a hard time?"

"Not that bad. He's actually out of town most of the time, so I'm running the show. Mabel"—he looks over at me and then signals to her—"this is Willow." Mabel's lips lift into a mischievous smile. "Not like that, Mabel. We're *friends*." The fact he has to clarify that doesn't sit well in my stomach.

"Very well. You can't judge a girl for trying. It's nice to

meet you, Willow. Jaxson has been coming here for years, and he's never brought a lady friend."

"It's nice to meet you too, Mabel. But we're *just* friends. Jaxson tells me you're the best diner in New York City."

"That Jaxson," she coos. "He sure knows how to spoil a girl."

I smile at her and catalog all this info into my Jax memory box.

"What can I get for you kids?"

"After the lady." Jaxson points at me. "And we're hardly kids."

"When you're as old as I am, anyone under fifty is a kid, especially since you've been coming to eat here since you were in diapers."

"This is true," Jax says wistfully, and it makes me smile.

Mabel turns to me. Her face is weathered with age, and I wonder how long she's known Jaxson.

"I'll have a chocolate milkshake, and what's your specialty?"

"They make a mean grilled cheese," Jax cuts in.

"I asked Mabel, not you," I chide.

"I like this girl. Keep her around." Mabel laughs and her forehead crinkles further. "Our specialty is the barbecue brisket sandwich."

"I'll have that."

"I'll have my usual."

"I didn't ask," she says while rolling her eyes.

"I like you too," I say, and I do. Even without Jax in tow, I plan to come back here.

After Mabel takes our order, she leaves. We both reach our hand out to grab a straw sitting in the middle of the table, fingers touching. I try to keep a neutral expression on my face. But the contact burns through me. Lighting my skin on fire. Making me hyper-aware of the growing need inside me.

Shit.

I pull away, severing the feelings that swirl inside me.

Feelings I can't have.

A stilled silence settles around us, I'm tempted to flip the cup of sugar packets and make shapes with them like I used to do with Maggie when we were kids. But that's something Old Willow would do. I can't be her.

Jaxson leans on the table, placing his forearms on the surface. A move my mother would have hated. My mother was very ladylike. My father humored her, but they raised me to be a lady too. She would roll over in her grave if she saw my current outfit. With sweats two sizes too big, I don't look like the debutant she raised me to be, rather a homeless woman. Which isn't that far from the truth, seeing as I am homeless and living on a couch.

"It was a nice surprise to have you stop by the office . . . two days in a row," he says, breaking the silence.

"As I said before, I wanted to thank you. I figured you loved to eat cupcakes." I grow silent. "And I wanted to apologize for my behavior yesterday."

"One: no apologizing. Two: You made a superb choice. Those cupcakes were my favorites."

I nod. Because what is there to say? The surrounding room goes quiet. Although we have been together before, it's still awkward and stilted.

"Willow. Just Willow. Tell me something about yourself." His husky voice cuts through the silence.

Biting my lip, I turn my head away from him to look out the

window. I watch as people walk by with smiles on their faces. People with seemingly easy lives.

I was that person once. Before my life got too complicated to answer a simple question.

"I'd prefer not to," I say, still looking out at the street.

"Shame."

That makes me turn back toward him. "Shame?"

"Well, I want to get to know you. Be your friend." He says the word friend playfully.

"It takes a long time to get to know someone. I'm not sure I'll be in New York for that long," I admit.

"You don't live here?"

"No."

"Where are you from?"

I shake my head. "Nice try."

"Wow, you really are a closed book." I shrug at his words because I am, no need to pretend otherwise. "I like it that way. Makes you all the more intriguing, a puzzle I need to crack."

"I'm not a puzzle, and I certainly don't need to be cracked, so please don't try. I won't budge."

"You see, but now you're dangling the forbidden fruit in front of me. Finding out information is my drug of choice. You've basically dropped a bag of candy on the table and told me not to take a bite. Impossible."

"What do you mean?"

"It's in my nature to find out everything."

I shake my head, not understanding what he is saying, and when I still can't figure it out, I finally open my mouth and ask.

"I don't know what the heck you're talking about."

"Finding out information. Well, it's my thing."

"What?" I croak.

"Don't worry, though, I won't be looking you up. You're lucky." He laughs when he says this, but while he is laughing, my spine is growing tight.

"How do you mean?"

"Well, apparently my brother, Grayson, says that it's creepy to hack girls I like . . . So since I like you, Willow, I'll refrain from looking you up. I'll find out all your dark secrets the old-fashioned way."

He keeps talking, but I am no longer listening. All I hear over and over again in my brain is the word hack.

Hack.

Did he say hack?

The muscles in my back pull tightly, I almost can't breathe as I try to make sense of everything.

"I—"

"Don't worry, I won't. And I know we're *just* friends."

"I don't understand. What do you mean when you say hack?" I mutter.

"Can you keep a secret?" His voice lowers. I can still hear him, but no one else in the restaurant would be able to.

"Why would you want to tell me a secret? You don't know me."

"This is true, I don't. But what I know is how to read people, and I already know I like you. So yeah, I'll trust you even though you haven't agreed yet." When he pauses, I nod my head so I can find out more about what he's saying. I would sign my name in blood to hear more at this point. "I like to find out things about people. And I use any way necessary even if it's not okay. Lucky for you, I will not do this. I will do this the old-fashioned way."

"And what is the old-fashioned way?"

"I'm going to guess, and you'll tell me if I'm right."

"And if I don't tell you?"

"I have a lot of skills in my arsenal. I'll be able to tell when you're lying. It'll be fun."

I should tell him not to do what he wants to do, but I'm still too hung up on what he said. Could this be exactly what I need?

I need to find out information, and he's offered the solution on a silver platter. Jax likes to find out things about people, and I need to find out things.

But can I trust him? He trusted me. But this is a little different.

A plan pops in my brain. Just because I want information from him doesn't mean I have to ask him now. If I spend some time with him . . . What if I wait to see if I can trust him? And when I know I can, I can ask him for help.

Jaxson Price may be exactly what I need to fix my problem.

CHAPTER SIXTEEN

Jaxson

MY NEW TACTIC TO GET TO KNOW HER IS GETTING HER TO trust me, and the best way to get her to trust me is by being honest and open about myself. That and asking her dumb questions about herself.

In a joking nature, of course.

The ball is in her court with how she will answer these questions.

I won't lie and say I'm not completely intrigued by her.

Running facial recognition on her off the lobby camera consumes me.

But every single time I think of looking into her, Grayson's words from only months ago play out in my head. Apparently, stalking someone you are interested in, as he said, is not okay.

The thing is most people assume I'm good at finding out things because of my skills on computers. But that's not the only reason. I let them believe that. What they don't know is, after years of doing this, after years of confronting people, after years of digging deep into the dark web and analyzing pictures, voices, and the way they breathe, I don't need them to tell me anything. I can find out the whole truth by looking at someone long enough. I can deduce the truth by watching. My ability to read people makes me a good poker player. That doesn't mean I know everything right off the bat, but with the right questions,

I'll find out everything even if she doesn't tell me. That's my truth. I can read people.

I sit back in my chair, leg stretched forward and reclined back as if I don't have a care in the world.

I care, though. I care deeply. I let my lip tip into a smile.

"So . . . ?" She narrows her eyes at me, but when she doesn't object outright, I quirk a brow. "What can you tell me? Other than nothing. I need to know a place to start the game."

"There is no game," she finally says.

"There is always a game. You just don't always know you're playing it."

"Fine. Start your damn game. But you won't find out anything."

I decide not to start with serious questions. I want her to let down her guard.

"What's your favorite color?" I ask, my voice dead serious.

"Wow. That's your question?" she responds.

"I didn't really think you'd tell me your full name or your Social Security number."

Her eyes go wide like two large saucers. Almost as if she fears the question.

I lift my hand in surrender. "I'm kidding. But yes, my first question is, what's your favorite color? You can learn a lot about a person by their favorite color."

"Such as?"

"Well, I really can't tell you. That ruins the fun."

"I won't answer unless you tell me."

"Fine. Example. Yellow. If you say yellow, I know you are a cheerful person, happy and always looking on the bright side."

"And if I say black?"

"Well, then obviously, you are dark and morbid."

"Black." But the thing is, her answer doesn't match her eyes. Plus, she looks to the right. She's lying. I smile brighter.

"You're lying."

"How can you tell?"

I have no intention of telling her. If I do, then she won't let me play this game. I smile bigger.

"Isn't it obvious?"

"And how is it obvious?"

"The three times I've met you, you've been wearing black. But now underneath your coat, I can see a hint of color peeking out. You might wear black often, but that's not your favorite color because you're not wearing black under that coat. Whatever you're wearing underneath is your favorite color."

She looks down and notices that I'm right. The color is peeking out through her coat. A coat that is charcoal gray, so the color is bright and vibrant behind it.

"Fine. You're right. Red is my favorite. Fun game." She rolls her eyes.

"This is the easy stuff."

"Bring it."

"I know your favorite food is not grilled cheese."

"That's because I'm not ten."

"Again, don't knock it until you try Mabel's." And as if summoned, Mabel appears beside our table with two plates in hand.

"Here's your food, guys." She places the plates down. "I'll be right back with your milkshake."

Mabel steps back and walks away, so I return my attention back to Willow.

"You know I'm going to make you try this."

"As long as you don't make me try it out of your hands again."

"Fine, I'll use a knife and fork."

"Here's mine."

I shake my head at her but take it anyway, then cut a piece of my grilled cheese off and place it on her plate, handing her back the fork.

I sit back and wait. She lifts the piece and places it in her mouth, her eyes closing, her chest rising and falling. Watching this woman eat could be a religious experience.

She swallows, and I know from the way her eyes dilate that she loves it. But she's way too proud to tell me. She stifles her moan. The sound might not come out of her mouth, but I don't have to hear it to see it.

"Admit it's the best thing you've ever eaten."

"It's good, but I wouldn't say the best."

I look over her features, noticing the tic in her cheek. The tell. She's lying again. I smirk at her.

"If that's so, go ahead and eat your sandwich."

"I will, thank you," she retorts. She lifts her own sandwich to her mouth, takes a bite, and swallows. "This is so good," she groans. It's the same as when she ate mine, so I believe her. Mabel wouldn't make anything that wasn't good, but it's no grilled cheese. And even though she won't admit it, I see the tic in her cheek.

"Whatever you say."

We continue to eat, and I can see her glancing at my grilled cheese.

"What?" She lifts a brow at me.

"I see you looking at my sandwich."

Still staring, she nods. "It reminds me of my mom's." Her voice is low, and then she reaches her hand out to grab a napkin.

"What about you, you grow up on Mabel's?" She leans

forward in her chair, and I can tell she genuinely is interested in my life. I welcome the feeling it brings. Like I matter.

"I did," I respond. "I used to go all the time."

Willow smiles. "Who took you?"

"I went alone . . ." My words trail off as I remember all the times I would go straight to Mabel's after school. How she would help me with my homework.

"You went to dinner alone? As a kid?"

"My parents were busy with my brother and sister."

"But you were a kid."

I shrug and then lift my sandwich and take a bite. Finishing the conversation. As we eat, we don't discuss anything more. We really don't talk at all. But when we are both done, and finally when the quiet got stifling, I start to ask my dumb questions again.

She thinks I'm annoying. Maybe I am, but what I'm really doing is gauging her.

I need to measure her reactions, see the way her pulse in her neck jumps, watch how her cheeks tuck in and study the furrow of her brow. Because one day, these tells will give me all the information I need to know about Willow.

When lunch is finally over, I pay the bill, and we stand, walking outside together. Her coat tight around her, and she looks cold, but I need to say one more thing.

"I got it."

"You got what?" she asks, a small line forming between her brows. Her chin trembles and I know as we stand here that it's too cold to keep her any longer. Winter has officially taken hold of New York City.

Cars drive by and horns honk, but I pay them no mind.

"I know who you are."

Now the rattling jaw stops, and instead, it tightens. I look into her eyes. They look glassy. A normal person would think her eyes were glassy from the cold, but I can see the way her chest rises and falls.

I can see everything.

I make sure I smile. Big and bright.

Playful.

"You, my friend Willow, are a preschool teacher."

She lets out an exhale. Relief.

I go on. "Who realized, after a few years of teaching, that you, in fact, hate little kids and prefer to spend your time with drunk men."

She laughs, her whole body relaxing. She thought I learned something about her.

I did. Just not what she thought. What I learned is Willow is the farthest thing from a preschool teacher.

But I also learned . . .

Willow . . . is scared.

CHAPTER SEVENTEEN

Jaxson

I can't get my lunch with Willow out of my head. It's been days but still, every comment lingers in my brain. Something is off about her. She's jumpy. The first few times I saw her, I knew something was off. But this last time it was obvious.

I told her I wouldn't hack her, but it's killing me to keep that promise.

She's scared.

The way she walks and looks down was the first tell. At the gas station, I noticed it when she was at the store. She looked down and away from the cameras. Her hair is not naturally that color either. Also, when she worked at the poker game, I swear she had blue eyes, but at my office, they were brown, which makes no sense unless she's disguising her appearance because she's worried about public places. The phone number, though, was the kicker.

Right before I left her, she gave me her number. Most wouldn't have known there was something wrong with it, but I knew right away that it was a burner phone. To the average person, maybe these things wouldn't stand out, but I'm not the average person.

Each clue proves it. The fear of the cameras, looking down, changing her appearance. Wearing glasses all the time that I'm sure are fake.

Even her clothes are too big. If I hadn't been at the poker game, I might have missed it, but I was. I know what's behind the large clothes she wore the other day.

Who is she hiding from?

I pick up the phone and dial the number she gave me.

Pressing send. I wait for her to answer.

"Hello," she says.

"Hi, it's Jax," I say.

Through the line, I can hear her sudden inhale of breath.

"Is everything okay?"

"Of course, it's okay. Why would you ask that?" I say.

"Well, you've never called before . . ."

"I just wanted to see what you were up to."

"Umm. I'm working."

That makes me laugh. I pivot my chair and face the city. It's a beautiful day. Cold, but it's still beautiful. The sun is shining bright. No rain and still no snow.

It's the perfect day to lure the prey out to play.

I know she's lying.

Although it would normally drive me crazy to know she's lying, especially since I can't do my usual stalking, I find it's even more intriguing to figure her out. It feels like this is becoming my new favorite pastime.

"You're lying." I chuckle.

"How do you know?"

"Well . . . you told me you only work for your friend's catering company. Since I'm sure there is no party at"—I lift my wrist and check the time on my watch—"at ten thirty-five a.m., I know you're lying."

"I'm busy," she says again, but it only makes me smile broader.

"Too busy to eat lunch?"

"I'm skipping today," she mutters. She knows I've got her there.

That makes me sit forward in my office chair. "And why is that?"

"I have a class at the gym."

"Oh, you don't say. So you plan to skip lunch and work out? That's not very smart, Willow," I playfully scold.

"Jeez. You're like a dog with a bone."

"I am, aren't I? My brother says I'm annoying. But I like the way you say it better."

When she doesn't answer, I continue to press. "Come on. We'll grab a quick bite, and then you can go to the gym."

"Fine. But only because I'm hungry."

"Great. Meet me at Fifty-Fourth and Lex. It's called Estia."

"What's there?"

"The best Greek restaurant in the city. Noon."

After we hang up, I go back to work on finding intel on a contractor Addison wants to hire. She needs to know if he's mixed up in anything shady before she gives him the contract. The job is straightforward, and it doesn't take long for me to realize she will have to find someone else.

The guy is shady as fuck with direct ties to the underworld. I can turn a blind eye to a lot, but this guy takes the cake. Drugs, women, there isn't much he doesn't have his hands in. No way will I allow Price Enterprise to become involved with this man's company.

Once I'm done drafting an email and then sending it to my sister, I stand from my desk and head over to the restaurant.

When I see Willow standing in front of the door, she's in her usual attire. Clothes that are too big for her slender frame, glasses I'm ninety percent sure have fake lenses, and brown contacts. Every time I've seen her in public, other than the poker game, she looks the same. She looks different from how she does at work. I wonder if she looks this way in front of Maggie, or if Maggie even understands why she does it.

When I walk over, she gives me a small smile, and then we walk inside. I don't let her order when the waitress comes. Instead, I order everything in Greek.

"You know Greek." It's a statement more than a question, and the surprise is evident in her voice when she says it.

"I do."

"Are you Greek?" She leans forward in her seat, placing her elbows on the table.

"I'm not."

Her eyes go wide. "Wait, seriously . . . so then why do you know Greek?"

"I lived in Greece for a few years. College was never really for me. While everyone was studying, I traveled. I loved Greece and settled there for a bit."

Her eyes are watching me intently. It's as if she is truly interested in what I have to say, and I realize this is my in. By telling her about myself, she might open up to me. She might tell me something about herself too.

She's obviously not going to come out and talk to me. I need her to trust me, so I'll open up to her first.

Talking about myself is not something that comes naturally to me.

Usually, I make jokes and keep things on a superficial level. Normally, I don't allow people to see the man behind the mask, but if this is what I need to do to get her to, I will.

CHAPTER EIGHTEEN

Willow

ANOTHER DAY.

Another nightmare.

With each day that passes, my patience wears.

Growing up with an absent dad, I took care of myself. I've never been the type of person to sit and wait. I can't be trapped in this house. This isn't me. I don't recognize this scared girl.

This isn't living, it's a cage.

He hasn't found you yet . . .

So why are you so damn scared?

In order for me to get my life back on track, I need to rid myself of this fear that someone is looking for me.

The only way to do that is by pushing myself.

By stepping outside my comfort zone and leaving the safe confines of this apartment and neighborhood.

You have no comfort zones, Willow.

Remember when you and Maggie used to give each other dares? Nothing was off limits.

You mixed every soda on the machine and handed it to Maggie's dad when he asked for a refill.

You placed Whoopie Cushions under all the seats in Mrs. Cromwell's classroom.

You snuck into the haunted house and fell asleep on the master bed.

You are not a wimp.

I've left a few times. Working for one. But that doesn't really count seeing as Cyrus Reed does have more security than the White House. I've also left to see Jaxson. The first time was an utter failure, but since then, I've been okay.

Maybe I can convince him to be my chaperone and keep me safe while I explore the city and get my bearings. We won't be able to do much, seeing as I have no social security card and no ID, but I'm sure we can see some of the sites. The more I explore, the more comfortable I'll be. The more comfortable I am, the less afraid.

At least that's what I hope.

A plan forms in my brain, one that checks off many boxes in the things I need to accomplish.

If I invite Jaxson, I'll feel safe and I can see if I can trust him.

Now, I need to figure out how to ask.

CHAPTER NINETEEN

Jaxson

THIS IS HELL.

Absolute hell.

I'm not one to wait around for a girl I'm interested in to call me, but I'm trying to, and it sucks.

No matter how much I tell myself I'm hanging out with Willow as friends, I'm full of shit.

She's a gorgeous and intriguing girl, so obviously, I want more. Whatever she's dealing with, she's not ready. I'm okay with that, I'll wait, but I want her to get to know me, trust me, in the meantime, which doesn't make it easier for me.

Deciding not to look into her is much harder than I thought it would be. She's entered my office building twice now . . . which means with only a click of my finger, I could pull up her biometrics.

I could run facial recognition . . . and know everything about her. But I don't do that, I hold true to what I promised myself. I will not be that guy with her.

It's obvious she's hiding something. Something big. Something she doesn't want me to know. And she's terrified I will find out.

I will find out.

Eventually.

It's inevitable.

But for now, I'll take it slow and wait. Bide my time. Even if it kills me.

So instead of doing research on her, I'm doing a project for Price Enterprise.

We've had an offer on a piece of land, and I need to find out all perspectives on the company looking to buy.

Apparently, this is all I'm good for. I don't know why I bother coming in. I'm supposed to be working on new projects, proving myself, and the only requests I get are to hack someone.

The irony isn't lost on me.

First, I was worked too hard. Now, I'm not worked enough.

I shouldn't complain. It's easy work, and I'm miserable doing the other shit, but still. There is another benefit—it's a lot more enjoyable than going over numbers and figures with Grayson.

It takes no time to find a correlation with the buyer and his shady practices.

Money laundering.

To be honest, it's so easy I wonder what the catch is.

I shake my head as I realize there is no catch. I'm good. And this guy is an idiot.

I then send an encrypted email to my siblings. They know how I work, and I know they will understand what I found.

Once all the information is sent, I stand from my desk, stretch my arms over my head, and look at the clock.

It's already five p.m. on Thursday, and I know I should go home, but I don't want to. I'd rather go out for drinks. Grabbing my phone, I'm about to call Trent when it rings.

I see the number.

Willow.

I swipe the screen.

"Hello," I answer as I walk toward the elevator.

"Jaxson."

"Willow," I respond.

When she says nothing, I continue. "Is everything okay?" I ask as I enter the elevator and head toward the basement to my car.

"Oh, yeah, of course. I was thinking . . ."

"You were thinking . . . ?" I trail off, urging her to go on.

"Well, I'm new to the city, and I don't know a lot. You seemed to know all the good places to eat, and I imagine you would know all the places I would want to see . . ." She trails off, her voice sounding nervous.

"And you wanted a tour guide."

"I mean, if you aren't too busy."

"Never too busy for you," I drawl out automatically, and as soon as it comes out, I cringe at my mistake.

"Really?"

"Yes. When were you thinking?"

She doesn't answer right away, probably trying to decide when she's free.

"Well, I work tomorrow, but I'm free Saturday," she finally says.

"Saturday it is, then. I'll show you all my favorites. Dress warm, wear comfy shoes, and be prepared for a full day."

"Okay. Thanks."

"Bye, Willow." I hang up as the elevator door opens, happy that my weekend plans are looking up already. I had considered going to the poker game again tomorrow, but now that I'm seeing her on Saturday, I opt out. But I will see what Trent is doing today.

I pull my contacts up and hit the button when I get to Trent's name.

"What's up, bro?"

"Not much, just wanted to know where you're at today."

"Looking to go out?" He chuckles.

"I am." I laugh back.

"Excellent. I'm hitting a club downtown, but first sushi. Interested?"

"Always."

"Okay, be at my apartment at eight."

I hang up and head to the car. A drink and a night out are exactly what I need. I've been working myself too hard, trying to prove myself.

Yeah, this, and then Willow, are exactly what the doctor ordered.

CHAPTER TWENTY

Jaxson

LAST NIGHT, I WENT OUT TO THE CLUB AGAIN, TWO NIGHTS in a row, but yesterday while Trent was becoming obliterated, I was nursing a glass of water.

Sure, I had a tequila first but only enough to take the edge off, not enough to get me drunk. Knowing I made plans with Willow had me going to bed early because typically after a heavy night of drinking, I'm feeling it the next morning.

But today is different. Because today I am not hung over. One of the many things I have tried to change in my life. In the past, even if I had plans, I'd show up half drunk. But since I'm keeping to the straight and narrow for work, it's filtered its way into all aspects of my life. Including the weekend.

The sad part is I shouldn't have to prove myself. I really shouldn't, but since I do, I probably should compile a list.

The list that will get Grayson Price off my back one day when he bitches about something he deems I have done wrong. No longer getting drunk and missing work would be on that list.

Instead of all that, though, I'm up on Saturday morning at a reasonable hour.

Reasonable hour, my ass. I'm up at eight a.m. No. Normally—well, before Grayson's rules—I wouldn't wake up until ten a.m. Then Grayson started micromanaging me.

Today, I have a plan, or at least, I have to come up with a plan, and it starts at nine. That will be when we meet. The first place I intend to take her is to get a bagel.

Then pizza, donuts, and after that, we'll work our way to Chinatown for some dumplings. By the time we're done for the day, she will know all the best joints in the city.

I could call her and tell her I'll pick her up, but she's still standoffish, so I don't want to rattle her. *Stick with the original plan and don't change it.* Nine a.m. at H&H.

When I arrive, she's standing outside with her coat pulled tightly around her body and a scarf wrapped around her neck. Her hands entwined in front of her, and I'm surprised to see her wearing gloves. It's not that cold yet, so why the gloves?

The weather is hit or miss in the city, but I warned her we would do a lot of walking, so she took my advice. As I take a step closer, she finally sees me. Her hand lifts with a small wave.

"You're here," she says.

"I said I would come."

"That you did."

"And did you doubt me?" I smirk.

"Maybe a little." She smiles. She pretends to pinch her finger in measurements. "This much."

"Well, it could be worse. I'll take it."

"Good."

"Now that we have that settled . . . bagels," I say, opening the door and letting her pass before I join her.

"Bagels." She steps farther into the shop, and once I'm in, I close the door behind me. It's relatively busy, and I don't see many empty seats. None actually.

"Let's grab bagels and walk," she says.

"We could. If you don't think you'll be too cold."

"Nope, I'm good."

"I imagine if you were an icicle, you still wouldn't admit you were cold, anyway."

She's playful this morning, a lot more so than any previous time we've met. I'm not sure what that's about, but I'll take it.

When we get to the counter to order, I turn to her, and she shrugs. "I don't know what to order," she says.

I often forget that she's not from here. I'm not sure where she's from and what type of bagels they eat there, but here in the city, we don't do fancy-ass bagels. It's just cream cheese. Maybe we get fancy and do sesame or everything, but after that, I draw the line at asiago.

"You like everything bagels? They have the best here."

"Sure," she answers, and I turn back to the woman behind the counter.

"Two everything bagels toasted with cream cheese."

"Anything else?"

I turn back to Willow. "Coffee?" I ask.

"I'm good," she replies.

"Nothing else, thank you."

Together, we wait, and while we wait, I pay. Seeing as we only got cream cheese, it doesn't take long. Only a mere minute or two later, we are walking out the door and heading downtown.

"It's a long walk to our next location, but I figured we'll work up an appetite for it."

Her mouth is full of a bite of bagel as we continue to walk.

"Jeez," she says after swallowing. "That's the best bagel ever."

"Told you." My voice is proud as if I had something to do with the greatness of the bagel.

She takes another bite. "How is it so good?"

"We have better water."

"What does that even mean?"

"Oh, come on, everyone knows New York has the best water, hence the pizza and bagels are better than anywhere else on earth."

"I didn't know that."

"Where are you from, Mars?" She lifts an unamused eyebrow at my comment. "Speaking of, where are you from?"

"No comment."

"No name. No job. No location. You're not making this easy for me, Casper."

"Casper?"

"Like the ghost."

"Wow. Is that supposed to be a nickname or something?"

"Or something," I chide. "I got it. Not only do I know your job, but now your location."

This time, no terror appears in her eyes at my joke. She must know me well enough to see my sense of humor. She stops walking, tapping her foot impatiently on the black pavement beneath us, so I stop too.

"You, my dear Casper, are no ghost. No. You are the daughter of a missionary raised in the wild. With no bagels and no knowledge of New York." I grin and watch for any truth. Her eyes roll.

"That's the best you can do?" She laughs.

"Nope, I have plenty up my sleeve."

"Well, you'll need that because you aren't even close."

"Good. It means more time with you." I wink and then turn and start walking.

"How much longer?"

"With you?" I say over my shoulder playfully. "Or until we are there?"

"What do you think?" I love how sarcastic she is; it makes me chuckle.

"Fifteen blocks. Work up your appetite."

She stops moving again. Glancing over my shoulder, I look at what's taking so long. Her hand is on her stomach, and she's puffed out her cheeks.

"I can't possibly eat again," she groans.

"Wait till you see what I'm feeding you, and you might disagree."

"That didn't come out dirty at all." She laughs.

It's a sound I can get used to. I've heard it a few times, but the more I hear it, the more I like it. The more I want to hear it again.

Great, just great.

CHAPTER TWENTY-ONE

Willow

I HAD WAY TOO MUCH FUN WITH JAXSON. SO MUCH FUN, I'M thinking twice about calling him again because this could get complicated. Who am I kidding? It already is.

I know what I need from him, but I'm not sure I can do this without my feelings getting confused. One thing I can't do is catch feelings.

The last time I did that, it was catastrophic. But Jax is different. He's someone I want to be friends with. He's someone I want to see if I can trust—if he can help me—because as much as I want to do this alone, I need help.

Desperately. If I'm being honest with myself, Jaxson Price might be my only hope.

Instinct tells me I can trust him. Being near Jax is like reading a book from my favorite author. I don't know what happens next, but I know I'll like it.

A few days have passed since the last time I've seen him. My searches so far haven't turned up anything. I can't think of any allies, no one back home to talk to, and I can't go back home until I find the information I need. The thing is, just because I had one good night with Jaxson doesn't mean he'll help me.

I need to make him want to be there for me. I need us to be friends. And the only way to do that is to pick up the damn phone.

The idea of using him, however, doesn't sit well in my stomach. It makes it churn with repulsion. When did I become the girl to use someone?

But is it really using him if I want to be with him? That's the thing, sure I need his help, but I also like spending time with him. He makes me feel things I haven't felt in a long time.

He makes me feel normal.

I should call him.

Bite the bullet already.

He hasn't called me since the first time. I know what he's doing. He's putting the ball in my court, and I respect him even more for that. Since time is not on my side, I pick up my phone and hit his contact.

"Took you long enough," he answers.

"If you wanted to speak to me so badly, you could have called me," I respond, standing from the couch and pacing the small apartment.

I'm nervous, and I'm not sure why.

"What fun would that have been?"

"What does that mean?"

"It means now I know you miss me."

That stops my movements. I'm happy he isn't here to see me because I'm sure my mouth is hanging open as I try to think of something witty to cover up for the fact that he's right. I did. But since I can't think of anything, I lie.

"I hardly miss you. I just—"

"Missed me."

"No."

"Then what?" His voice rings with humor.

"I'm bored."

"And?"

"Jeez, you're impossible. Has anybody ever mentioned that to you?"

"Yeah, maybe one or two times."

"Probably more like one hundred in the last week," I deadpan.

"You were about to tell me how much you missed me."

"I was actually going to tell you . . . you suck." At this point, admitting that I want to hang out with him seems like torture.

"I'm playing. Tell me, what's up." When I don't speak right away, he continues. "I'm done. Promise."

I let out a long sigh. "You sure?"

"Yep."

"Very well, ummm." I pause, mulling over the strength to open myself up to his teasing. "I kind of was planning to see more of the city . . ." I don't say I need to see the city, but that's the truth. I need to get over my fear, and he's the only person I want with me when I do.

"And you need a kick-ass tour guide *again*?"

"Pretty much."

"When were you thinking?"

"I'm free, pretty much always," I admit. Because it's true. Other than Friday nights, I don't do much.

"I've got nothing today if you want to meet me?"

"Really?" I'm shocked that he doesn't have plans. I would expect Jaxson to have plans every minute of the day.

"No. I'm lying." Sarcasm drips off his voice, and even though he's not here, I know he's smirking. I can hear it as his voice taunts me. "When can you meet me?"

"Whenever."

"I can pick you up at your apartment," he says.

"Nope, I'm good. I'll meet you." No way can I tell him I live on my friend's couch. Too many questions will arise, and I'm not prepared for an inquisition. Because that's, for sure, what it would be. I know I'll get grilled today, but this little sidestep could very well protect me from the brunt of it.

"Fine. Let's meet. Say in one hour at Chelsea Piers."

"Okay." Interesting choice, but since I've never been there, I look forward to it.

"Dress warm, in layers." It's funny how he never wears a coat but always insists that I do.

"Got it, boss."

"And Casper."

"Casper?"

"Yeah, remember the ghost?"

I shake my head, but again, he can't see me, so the movement was pointless. "I'm not a ghost . . ."

"No name, no apartment . . . you're a ghost. But you're a damn cute one, and I want to spend my day showing you the city, so don't get pissy about the nickname. It works. Now as I was saying, see you soon." He hangs up, leaving me with a quiet phone and my mouth hanging open. Casper. The first time he called me that, I ignored him. But this time . . . I'm not sure if I should laugh at his sense of humor or cry at the pathetic turn my life has taken. He has no idea how accurate he is.

I am a ghost.

No one back home knows where I am. I have no name. No job. No identity. And most of all, like a ghost, I wander the earth not even knowing or feeling alive anymore.

By the time I get to our meetup location, he's already standing by the entrance of Chelsea Piers. He doesn't see me at first because his back is against the wall and he's looking down at his phone. Surprise, surprise, he's not wearing a coat. Which I still find funny as he once again stressed how badly I needed one.

Nope.

He's wearing a white thermal, ripped jeans, and Adidas shoes.

He looks younger today, donning a well-worked baseball hat. He doesn't look like the billionaire I know him to be. No, he looks like the boy next door. The boy who would have climbed up your window when your parents were sleeping.

But knowing he's Jaxson Price, I doubt there were any windows to climb. But I can still imagine it. His devastatingly handsome face, smirk and all. Brimming with the promise of a nighttime of fun. One where your parents would surely wake.

As if he can hear my rampant thoughts, his head lifts.

One . . . two . . . three . . .

And there it is.

Cue the smile.

Cue the incessant butterflies that form when he smiles at me.

I push them down. Because that is not why I'm here. I'm not here to let this man in my pants. I'm not here for a relationship.

I'm here for a friendship. For someone I can trust, and someone who can help me. And every time I see him again, I believe he might be that person.

It's an added benefit that I like him, his funny and playful personality, and it doesn't hurt that he's easy on the eyes.

I watch as he places the phone in his pocket as I make my approach.

"You're late." He smirks.

"I'm exactly on time."

"Well, then I guess I must be early . . ."

"Ah, is that a first for you?"

"No comment," he quips back.

"Must be your excitement to be my tour guide."

"Definitely that. I'm beaming. Can't you tell?" It comes out sarcastic, but I can see the mischief in his beautiful green eyes. The way the emerald orbs sparkle and gleam.

He is excited to show me around. And that notion does dangerous and treacherous things to my body.

"I can." Now I let my lip tip up. "So where to first?"

"Well, obviously, the market," he says flippantly.

"Oh yes, obviously."

"You wanted to see my New York. So . . . let's go."

"Lead the way." I salute.

That earns me a laugh. Rich and hardy. One I could get used to hearing.

Down, girl. No men for you. No distractions. Maybe this is a bad idea. Maybe I can ask him for help now. A thought pops in my brain . . . what if it's like before? What if you think you can trust him, but you can't?

Then where will you be?

Running again.

No. This plan is better.

When we step inside Chelsea Piers, I'm not entirely sure why we're here. Jaxson keeps walking, and I pick up my pace to follow. Although tall, my legs are not nearly as long as his, so it's difficult to keep up.

He must know this because his movements stop, and he waits. He has a boyish grin on his face as I make my way toward him.

"Sorry." He laughs.

"It's fine. I didn't work out today." I shrug. "Now I've broken a sweat, so we're all good." I roll my eyes. Chuckling, he reaches out and takes my arm in his. I'm taken aback by the movement. My gaze drifts down to our entwined arms.

Despite the drafty chill, I'm warm all over.

"This way, I won't lose you."

"I'm not a kid."

"No." He looks me up and down, his gaze skating over me, and even though I'm fully clothed, I feel naked. For the first time in a long time, I like it.

The attention.

The way he makes me feel.

All of it.

Even though I won't do anything about it, I'll allow myself to bask in it for the time being. To bask in the glow that radiates off Jaxson and soak up the heat that penetrates me.

He's like the sun. His presence brings me warmth, but if I allow it, it will set me ablaze. Burn me.

That's what I've learned recently. I step back from the heat. Distance myself. It's safer this way.

"What's the plan?" I say as he pulls me forward until we are standing under the clock.

"This," he says as he pulls out a list of questions.

"I'm not sure what this is." I point at the paper. "Should I?"

"It's a scavenger hunt."

"Seriously?"

"I wouldn't joke about a scavenger hunt."

His voice is somber, but I know him well enough to know this again is his lighthearted sarcasm peeking through.

He's so playful, so witty, yet I've seen glimpses of a more

serious side. That's the real Jax. That's the one that scares me. Because that's the one I could fall for.

He's the man you fall in love with, if you allow it.

I welcome the charming, funny, mischievous man who puts a front up that nothing bothers or scares him because at least when that facade is up, there's no fear he'll steal my heart.

CHAPTER TWENTY-TWO

Jaxson

THE LIST WASN'T HARD TO CREATE. A SEARCH ON THE Internet, a printer, plus a few questions.

These scavenger hunts are meant for team building. But seeing as it's only us taking part, I have made the aim to gather information on her.

Handing the piece of paper to Willow, I watch as she reads each item on the list. I can tell she's unsure of this, but the thing I like about her is even if she is reluctant, she doesn't allow fear to push her down. She pushes through.

Sure, there have been setbacks, but I believe she's waiting to size me up. So as much as this is about her finding out about me, this is also about her learning about me.

Seeing if she can trust me.

My hope is the more I let her in, the more she opens up to me in return.

Not something I always do. Rarely, actually. But this girl speaks to me. At first, it started as the need to solve an unsolved mystery, but that's bullshit.

It's more than that.

With her, I'm able to let down my guard for a second and show her a side I don't show anyone. Show her she can let me care for her. That she can lean on me.

That's a role I've never played before. Most don't take me seriously enough for that.

Take my family . . .

I'm good enough to get the information, but that's where it ends. Once I find out what they need, they don't need me again and barely call for any other reason.

But with Willow, I think she sees me.

"Where do you want to start? Since we're not competing per se, it's mainly a way to learn facts and see some sights."

"Sights? But this is only Chelsea Piers."

"There's more."

"There is? How much time did you spend on this?" Her eyes are wide.

"It only took me a bit."

"Thank you." Her voice drops. "You didn't have to."

"I know I didn't."

"What's on the city list?" she asks, and I hand it to her. Instantly, she laughs; a soft sound that makes me chuckle too. "This is a food hunt."

"Yes, I know." I shrug, not seeing the problem with this.

"Is this supposed to be done in one day?" She holds up the list.

I read what she's pointing at: Eat 1 slice of New York pizza, add 5 points.

"Yes. One day."

"Can I count previous days?"

"No, that would be cheating now, wouldn't it?"

"Not cheating as much as stretching the rules," she jokes.

"Nope. All or nothing."

She nods her head, then lets it tip up. "All or nothing." We lock eyes. It feels like she's saying more, but before I can delve deeper, she turns and walks away.

"Where are you going?" I ask.

"Item five . . ." I can't remember what item five is, so I stare at her. "Eat a street vendor pretzel. There was a stand right outside." Again, she heads back to where we came from.

"Or we can do that later." I raise an eyebrow.

"I'm starving. You stay here."

"Kill two birds with one stone."

"That really is a horrible expression."

I nod. "It is."

Willow turns and walks off. I look back down at the list. The first one is simple. The second could take more time. I'm not sure if she realizes that by committing to that list, she's also committed to seeing me again, because she's right. No way we are finishing this in one day. But since I know she's attracted to me, I don't think she'll mind.

It only takes a few minutes before she's back with one large pretzel in her hand. She smiles when she sees me waiting and holds it up.

"We can share," she says and then rips a piece off, handing the other end to me.

"I feel like we should make a toast or something."

She giggles.

"What do you have in mind?"

"To new friendships."

She says the word friendship differently as if she's trying to stress what this is. I'm not who she's trying to convince, but I'm okay with that toast. I'd be lying if I said I didn't want to fuck her. But for me, the chase for knowledge is almost as enticing.

Finding out what she's concealing is almost better than sex.

Almost.

"That works. To new friendships." I take my pretzel and tap it to hers. Then we both take a bite, sealing the deal.

"Next on the list. We have to find a vintage timepiece that hangs in the middle of the market."

"Do you know where it is?" she asks.

"Maybe." I smirk.

"Are you going to help me?"

"Nope."

"So much for being friends."

"Casper, we'll always be friends."

"And there's that nickname again," she chides.

"Well, to me, you're still a ghost. The cutest ghost I've ever seen. But maybe one day . . ."

"Maybe," she whispers.

And I smile. "Come on, I'll point you in the right direction."

Feeling bad for sobering the mood, I throw her a bone. I won't tell her where it is, but I'll lead her to it.

A few minutes later, she's waving and pointing like a lunatic.

"Found it. Didn't need your help." She puffs out her chest in pride resembling a little kid who won a board game.

"I showed you where it was."

"Not true."

"I actually took you here."

"Shut up. I found it. What's next?"

"Now, we search for remnants of when this place was a bank."

We spend the next hour doing this. We talk throughout, but she still hasn't told me much. I know a few mundane facts. I tell my own stupid facts. Like how I don't eat dark chocolate, a fact that she thought was blasphemy. And I love whipped cream.

That one she agreed with.

I learned she has a mild obsession with peanut butter and would marry it if that were possible.

I told her about how I never learned to ride a bike until I was an adult. And she looked at me as though I was crazy.

"I don't get it. How could you not have ridden a bike?"

"By the time I was born, I don't know, I guess you know what they say about the youngest."

"I wouldn't know."

"Only child?"

She nods. But she looks sad as she does.

"Do you miss home?" I don't ask where home is because I know she won't tell me.

"Not so much home." Her gaze drops to the floor.

"But the people?" I assume. "You can visit."

She worries her bottom lip but won't look up at me. "I can't."

"They can visit you . . . ?" I lead, and she finally meets my stare.

"Now that is not possible."

"Why?"

"Jeez, you ask a lot of questions. I don't talk to my parents. Good? You can file that in your mental scrapbook." I watch as her arms cross protectively in front of her.

"Willow . . ."

"Not Casper anymore?"

I shake my head. "I'm sorry. Not that it's any consolation, but I didn't know, and now that I do, I'll stop."

Normally, I'd throw in a funny quip to lighten the mood, but there isn't any for this. And I don't want to hide from her. So, I step closer to her, taking her hand in mine.

"My father died . . . and although I have my mom, she wasn't emotionally there for a while." I inhale. "I know it's not the same, but if you ever want to talk about it . . ."

"I'm good. I'd rather stay here. What's your next guess?"

"My next guess?" I ask.

"Yeah. I gave you a big clue about my life, so you must have a guess."

We continue to walk, and I keep thinking. She gave me some information about herself that is useful, so I don't want to push too hard.

"So are you going to try?"

"Hmm. Let me think about this," I say. We stop walking, and she turns in my direction. I make a straight face, knowing my next guess is so stupid that I might not be able to control my laughter.

"Spit it out," she says with a straight face.

"You're secretly Oliver Twist. An orphan trying to make it in the big city."

"That is officially the worst guess I've ever heard. I told you all of those things."

"But you didn't tell me your name, Casper."

"Willow. My name is Willow. You don't need to know my last name . . . at least not yet."

"The plot thickens."

She nods, then lets out a sigh. I can tell she plans on telling me. Not today and maybe not even tomorrow, but whatever it is, it's big.

She wants to trust me. I won't give her a reason not to.

CHAPTER TWENTY-THREE

Willow

AFTER AN HOUR OF WANDERING ALMOST AIMLESSLY around Chelsea Market, crossing off check marks on the scavenger hunt, we finally parted ways, him with a grin, and me feeling lighter than I had in months.

A day has passed, and it's now Sunday. Once again, Jaxson is my tour guide. We meet on the corner of a random block in the city, shivering in the cold air. The temperature continues to drop. When I exhale, I can almost see my breath. I pull my coat tight around my body, tucking my scarf in to cover the exposed skin. I look over at Jax, who's now finally donning a coat. It's odd to see him in one. Every other time I've met him, he's always in a thermal and jeans. Well, except the time at the fundraiser. Today, he's in his normal attire. He has a hat on his head, which is funny because for the first time in weeks, I'm in public, during the day, and I don't have a hat on. He looks handsome, his face has a light dusting of scruff. Underneath his jacket is a thermal, but today there are no holes in his jeans. Sneakers on his feet. If his face wasn't so recognizable, no one would know he's a billionaire.

But looks can be deceiving. Take me, for example. No one would know. I know my time is running out, and I've already decided to tell him. I just don't know when. To be honest, I've enjoyed living in this bubble—since I know once I tell him, it will pop. I tell myself I'm waiting to make sure I trust him, but there's no measure of doubt I do. I'm not ready.

Together, we walk to the street. He lifts an arm to hail a cab. From where I'm standing, I admire him.

He looks so natural on the streets of Manhattan. Like a college boy. I know he's older and well out of school, but here on the street, he looks more like an NYU student than the COO of a company.

I have only ever seen him twice at his office, and even then, he didn't appear to fit in. I wonder where he feels like himself. I wonder if he's like me and doesn't.

Cars rush by as we stand and wait. Eventually, a yellow cab stops in front of us. His light is on, ready to take us where we need to go. Jax opens the door for me, and I slide in until I'm sitting behind the driver. Jax slips in next and closes the door. He fires off an address, and I'm not one to pay attention, but it's downtown.

"Where are we going?"

"It's a surprise," he says.

"Do I get any hints?"

He shakes his head. Pain in the ass. Telling me where we're going would be too easy for Jax. I think he enjoys getting a rile out of me.

A little part of me thinks I enjoy it too. The banter makes me feel young as if I don't have a care in the world. It makes me feel how I used to feel before the curtain of lies was lifted.

But now that I see everything, I appreciate this feeling even more, which is why I don't want to talk to him about who I really am.

I'd much rather hear his ridiculous guesses because each time he does, each time he tells me some off-the-wall story of who I am and how I made it to New York City, he makes me laugh.

Both of us are quiet as the cab leads us downtown. We keep going all the way past China Town, past Tribeca, until we get to Battery Park.

"Are we going to Wall Street?" I ask as we weave in and out of traffic. I don't know the city well enough to know the address.

He shakes his head.

"Are you planning to ever speak on this cab ride?"

With a smirk, he shakes his head again. I roll my eyes at him and watch as a muscle in his cheek twitches.

Soon, we're pulling over, and that's when it finally dawns on me what we are doing here.

"So . . . the next place is . . ." He rolls his hands for me to continue. "Ellis Island," I add.

"You said you wanted to see New York. Figure what's more New York than this?" He smirks.

"From hole-in-the-wall diners to Chelsea Piers, to Ellis Island. What's next, the Statue of Liberty? You sure do know how to show a girl a good time."

He puffs his chest out. "I do, don't I?" A smirk forms across his face.

As I'm about to open my mouth and make idle conversation, the car rolls to a halt. Jax moves his hand to his pocket.

"Can I pay?"

"Nope. My city. My treat," he says as he fishes bills out and hands them to the taxi driver.

"Fine," I say with mock annoyance and put my wallet away.

Jax gets out first. He stands on the side of the street, his arm outstretched, and reaches his hand toward me. I let him take my hand and step out of the cab.

"So now what?"

"So now we go to the pier and get on our boat."

"I seriously can't believe you're taking me to see Ellis Island."

"I still can't believe I am either." He laughs.

"Have you ever been?" I ask.

"Believe it or not, no."

"Isn't it crazy how no matter how long you live somewhere, you might not see the sights?"

"It truly is. Say for . . . where did you say you were from?"

"Har. Har. Har."

"Nebraska?"

"I'm from New York." I wink. "Couldn't you tell?"

"Yes. Totally. Born and raised, right?"

"Is that your next guess?"

"Yep. I got it. You're actually from a famous New York family, the Astors, and you were switched at birth and raised in a humble upbringing."

"You got me." I roll my eyes.

"I knew it."

"Not even close."

"I'll get it next time."

"I'm sure you won't."

I continue to walk and smile. But the truth is, I'm doing anything but smiling inside. Every guess he makes means he's closer, and I know I need to find my words and tell him everything. I need an ally. I need to turn Jax into one.

So why haven't you done it yet?

Because powerful people would kill for information on you.

And . . .

I want to say I can't trust him yet, but I know I can. I'm

just not sure I'm ready to let this carefree fantasy end. I'm not sure I'm ready to deal with all the shit in my life that I'm hiding from.

A few more days.

A few more days of pretending to be a tourist, to see the sights and enjoy myself.

That's all I want.

We walk another block until we reach the ferry. I can't believe he planned this.

Once on the water, I stare at him. The wind batters against us, but he doesn't seem cold at all. I, on the other hand, am freezing. I pull my arms around myself tighter, and he must notice.

His forehead creases. "I didn't really think this through," he says as he steps in front of me. His large frame blocks the wind, but it doesn't remove the chill from my body as the cold winter air seeps into my bones.

"I'm fine. Don't worry about me."

"Do you mind?" he asks as he stretches out his arms. I'm not sure what he's going to do. He reaches around me and pulls my body toward his. His warmth instantly engulfs me.

A sudden urge to kiss him grips me.

Old Willow would have. She was fearless, always taking what she wanted.

New Willow doesn't. She lets Jaxson hold her and settles into him.

I feel hot with his hands on me. But something deep inside tells me it's not from the heat radiating off his body, but rather what his proximity does to me.

From where I'm tucked into him, I can smell his cologne, or maybe it's his deodorant. But whatever it is, it smells crisp and clean, and I have a strong desire to tuck in closer to him and bask in his scent.

It's almost primitive how I feel now tucked in his arms as though he's protecting me. I let out a small sigh, my body loosening within his grasp.

A part of me knows I should pull away. But I feel so comfortable I can't. What's the harm in enjoying this moment even if it only lasts for a second? I know it's fleeting, and I know it will end, so I let myself savor it.

Something's so comforting about him it's almost scary. In the past, I've made bad choices and trusted people I shouldn't have, so it makes me worry about the future. I don't let myself dwell on it.

I stay there and let him hold me even though I shouldn't. I let him comfort me even though it's a bad idea. I stay there tucked inside his arms until the boat docks and it's time to leave.

When it's time to move, he lightly pushes off me, but he takes my arm in his, cradling my elbow in the crook of his arm. To someone who didn't know us, it would seem we were together, but nothing could be further from the truth.

We are not.

But knowing that I might be leading him on doesn't stop me. He hasn't made a pass at me. Not since the beginning. He's respected that all I can give him is friendship, so who cares what anyone else thinks.

Together, we walk off the boat and on to Ellis Island.

The ground is hard beneath our feet, surely starting to freeze from the winter cold.

As we walk toward the building, I look across the water, and in the distance, I can see the Statue of Liberty. I wonder if he will take me there.

The freedom she symbolizes. A pang in my heart captures me, and I feel like my oxygen is becoming depleted.

"Are you okay?" he asks as I stop moving.

"Sorry, I . . ." I try to think of something to say. Something to make sense of the emotions being forced from the depth of my chest. But I can't think of a plausible reason for why I stopped.

"My foot."

"Your foot?" he asks.

"Yeah. Umm. It got caught on a rock."

Goddammit.

Is that really the best I can do? Even I know that was a pathetic excuse.

He looks down at the ground and then back up. He stares right into my eyes, and I wait for him to say something. To make a witty comment and call me out on my bullshit. But he doesn't, and I'm profoundly thankful for that. Because I don't know what I would say if he did. I'm not even sure I know what's wrong with me, so how can I explain it to him?

"I hate when that happens," he says. He continues to walk, and I follow him. We step inside, and he lets go of my hands. He stops his movements and turns to face me.

"My family came through here," he offers with a smile. "It's kind of cool to see."

"It is."

"How many generations are you in America?" I ask.

"To be honest, I don't really know." He laughs.

"You don't?" I say, lifting my eyebrow. "How's that possible?"

"To be frank, I'm kind of a selfish dick." He chuckles. "Or at least that's what my brother says."

A line in his forehead appears as he furrows his brow. I can tell that his brother is a sore topic for him. On instinct and without wanting to, my hand reaches out and takes his. He's warm to the touch, which is surprising because of the cold.

"I don't think you are a selfish prick."

"I said dick." He chuckles.

"Same difference." I shrug. "But I really don't think that. If anything, I think you're quite the opposite. I think you're the least selfish prick I know."

"You don't know me that well."

"I know you well enough. I know you helped me that night. I know you have gone out of your way to make me feel not alone in this city. I know a dick wouldn't do that. So yes. I might not know you well. But I know assholes, real assholes, and you are not one of them."

"If you say so."

"I do. Deal with it."

I'm rewarded with a smile, his lips tipping up and a small sexy dimple forming on his right cheek.

Shit.

Did I refer to Jaxson as sexy?

Yes. I did.

This is bad.

"Come on, show me this place and tell me the little information you know about your family history." I laugh.

He nods and walks, keeping my hand in his. I keep pace and allow him to lead me in to hear the history and get to know Jaxson Price better.

CHAPTER TWENTY-FOUR

Jaxson

NOW THAT I'M PLAYING TOUR GUIDE TO WILLOW, I'M excited for Saturdays to come. I still see her on Fridays at the poker game, but we hardly get to chat. Yet, she always gives me a small, knowing smile as if she's trying to tell me how excited she is for the plans for the next day.

Normally, the plan includes food.

Like today.

What can I say, I like to eat?

"So where are we off to today?" she asks. "What delicious food will I try?"

"You really do love to eat, don't you?" I chuckle.

She lightly and playfully swats at me. "No more so than you."

"I never said I didn't love to eat. Actually, I'm pretty sure I started out our friendship with the disclaimer, I love to eat."

Her lip tips up, and she bobs her head in agreement. "This is true. I'm sure that was your opening line. Oh, wait." She puckers her lips in disgust. "Nope. That wasn't your opening line. I do believe it was . . . 'like what you see?'" Her voice is low and baritone as if she is trying to impersonate me, and as she talks, she lifts her right eyebrow.

Another fit of laughs escapes my mouth. "I really did say that, didn't I?"

"Yep."

"I'm kind of a douche."

"You said it, not me." Little lines form around her eyes as she starts to laugh.

"Well, I'm happy you gave me a second chance."

"Trial basis."

She tries to keep her voice serious, but the tiny giggle she stifles gives her away.

I love seeing this side of her.

Most of the time, she's hiding behind a facade she doesn't want people to break through, but then the more I spend time with her, the walls she has up come crashing down.

I can tell she's starting to trust me, every time I see her, a piece of her disguise is missing. The feeling is everything.

We continue to walk, and with each step we take, our arms bump.

The desire to take her arm in mine is heavy on my mind, but I know I can't.

She has to be the one to make the move.

I'm not sure why she is the way she is, but I have to tread carefully. I don't want to spook her.

Also, since I don't know the skeletons in her closet, I have no idea what types of horrors she's faced, so I can't take advantage or make her feel uncomfortable. So instead of looping our hands together or touching her, we walk.

Since I know how much she loves chocolate bars, I'm planning on taking her to Dylan's Candy Bar. We are only about half a block up the road when I see a familiar face.

I lift my hand to wave, and from the corner of my eye . . . Willow turns to look at who I'm waving to. Her body tightens next to me, becoming stiff. Charles sees me and starts walking over to where we are. That's when I notice Willow's body moving closer to me, and her head looking down.

She doesn't want to meet him.

The way she presses into me, it's as if she wants to become invisible.

Instantly, my own muscles tense.

A million ways to make this easier for her run through my head, but I can't think of one that will work as he's almost upon us. That's when Willow's hand reaches up and cups her nose. Before I can say anything, she's pushing away.

"My nose . . ." she says, her hand covers her face as she starts to walk. "It's bleeding."

"Let me—"

"I'm fine, just need to find a bathroom," she hollers over her shoulder.

I shake my head in confusion, but as I'm about to take off after her, I remember Charles is heading in my direction, and I have to say hi.

I find Willow a few minutes later. She's standing in front of the candy bars, and she already has one in her mouth.

I would laugh, but I know Willow eats candy bars when she's upset. And when I see the wrapper and see it's a Kit Kat, I know she's more than upset.

She looks adorable bundled in her scarf with the chocolate in her mouth. She reminds me of a homeless puppy you want to adopt and take care of. You want to make sure they are warm and well-fed.

That's how I feel when I see her. I want to take care of her and cocoon her in a world where no one can hurt her.

The realization has me halting my steps. I've always wanted to help her, but now it's more.

At first, this started off with wanting to crack the puzzle, the code to who Willow is, but now I know, I want more.

Heading over to her, I approach her the way you would approach a caged animal. Slow and calm.

It's loud in Dylan's, but she must hear me because she turns to look over her shoulder to look at me. Her eyes don't look the same; they seem lost and hollow.

Yes, they are hidden behind the brown contacts, so that could be it, but it's more than that. I can't put my finger on what.

Maybe it's her nose.

Looking down, I don't see anything that would indicate a bleed, but I'm not a doctor, so I guess I don't know what I'm looking for.

"How's your nose?" I ask.

"Okay. It only bled a little bit, probably dry from the cold air." She turns her back to me quickly and grabs another candy bar to put in her bag.

"Oh . . . that's good. As long as you're okay."

I don't think she had a nosebleed at all. I think she didn't want to meet Charles, but the question is why.

"I'm fine." She continues to rummage, and it's obvious from the way she won't look at me that she doesn't want to talk about it anymore, but I'm still curious . . . so even though I shouldn't press, I do.

"Too bad you got the nosebleed, I would have liked to introduce you to Charles."

Still not looking at me, she stops her movements.

"Sorry." She tries to keep her voice leveled but I can hear how tight it is, giving her away.

Charles made her uncomfortable.

Is it men who make her uncomfortable? Or just him? He is a politician and a famous one at that. Maybe she doesn't like politics?

"You know he's running for the senate . . ." I say, trying to pry out of her some indication of what happened.

"Oh . . ."

"Yes. He's a business tycoon out of Michigan."

She says nothing, but I can see her jaw tighten from where I'm standing, and although she tries to hide it, her hand is shaking.

Something about the word tycoon or maybe Michigan has given her a visceral reaction . . .

I drop the conversation and start to pile my own candies in the bag Willow is holding. Once it's filled to the brim, we walk together to the register.

It doesn't take us long to pay, and before long, we are heading back out into the cold city air.

"I got it . . ." I say out of nowhere, and she halts her steps and turns back at me.

Her brows are pinched in. "Got what?"

"I know who you are." I smirk, playing it cool and funny like every time before, but really, this one is important because this one is the first time I think my guess might be close.

She lifts her brow up in a mocking way because every time before this, my guesses have been so outlandish, so she doesn't expect anything less.

"You, my dear Willow . . ." She lifts her hands to have me go on. "Are a runaway heiress who was jilted at the altar."

As the words leave my mouth, I watch her closely. I watch as her eyes widen.

She pales, and then she swallows. "Nope. Wrong again . . ." She laughs.

She laughs to cover the truth behind my words . . .

Now to figure out which part was true.

The words I said yesterday play back in my head over and over on repeat.

I had called her a jilted heiress that had run away after her fiancé left her. It isn't necessarily the words I used that had me concerned; it was the way her eyes widened that set off red flags.

It was the quiver of her jaw.

The way she momentarily worried her lip before flashing me a bright smile.

Is that it?

Is she an heiress?

Or was it the jilted at the altar part that set her off?

The involuntary movement happened so fast that I can't pinpoint what hit too close to home.

The day goes by way too slowly today, and all I want to do is get to the warehouse and look into this.

Not only did I promise myself I wouldn't look into her, but I also promised her I would do this the old-fashioned way. That and I can't get my brother's insults out of my head.

My fingers tap on the desk as I watch the clock.

It's kind of bullshit that I have to stay here.

Cocking my head to the side, I decide fuck it. I'll search here. If I do it *here,* I won't be tempted by all the high-tech shit.

I'll just search public records.

Bobbing my head up and down, I fire up my search engine. My fingers typing jilted heiress.

Nothing comes up.

Jilted heiress runs away.

Nothing.

Missing heiress.

Nope.

Runaway killer bride.

That one makes me laugh.

Obviously, it also comes back with nothing.

Maybe I was wrong.

Or maybe I'm not, and I need to go home and do an actual search. I'm sure if I were to hack into the FBI . . .

Stop.

Nope.

Not going to do it.

I like Willow.

She's unlike anyone I have ever met. She makes me feel different when I'm with her. The way she looks at me, the way she found comfort in my arms.

I felt as though I was her savior. Like she needed me, and most of all like I want to be a better man to be worthy of her one day.

I will not fuck that up by invading her privacy.

When she is ready to talk, she will.

I know she will.

I need her to see that I will not hurt her, and she can trust me.

Because I'm not willing to give her up.

Most of the women I know had every intention of trying to use me for my money or family name.

I know I'm not sexually involved with Willow, but I want to be. But it's more than that; I want to be more than that.

So even if she's concealing the truth, I'll wait.

No matter how long.

CHAPTER TWENTY-FIVE

Willow

I THOUGHT I WAS BETTER. I THOUGHT I WAS COMFORTABLE TO walk with my head held high. Ever since I've started hanging out with Jaxson these last few weeks and seeing the sights, I've been getting better. Sure, my eyes are still brown, and my hair is still dark, but I've been foregoing the hat and faux glasses. I haven't been hiding behind my own shadow.

I've felt stronger.

That was until I saw Charles.

He didn't see me, thankfully, and maybe if he had, he wouldn't have recognized me, but he was a friend of my father's . . .

I ran.

Proving that despite what I thought, I wasn't stronger.

Now I sit in Maggie's apartment, knowing what I need to do. Shay had told me to bring someone I trust.

There is only one person I completely trust. Only one person I'd feel comfortable practicing the moves with.

I have to try.

My fingers tap nervously on my lap as I stare at my phone sitting across the couch from me.

Do it.

Before I can second-guess myself, I'm stretching my arm out, grabbing my phone and hitting the call button when I see his name.

"To what do I owe this honor?" His voice rings through my ear in his typical playful voice.

I can do this.

Even though I don't know him very well, he has proved time and time again, that he won't hurt me, and that he cares.

I can do this.

"Hey." My teeth bite down on my lower lip. "I was wondering . . ." I trail off. Why is this so hard?

Because you don't want to be weak. You want to be strong.

Doing this will make you strong.

"Yes?" he asks.

"I need a partner for my self-defense class." I pause, take a deep breath, and then continue. "I don't really know many people, and I was wondering—"

"Yes."

"I haven't even finished," I say.

"But I know what you are going to ask, so I figured I'd beat you to it. I'd love to go with you."

My heart flutters rapidly in my chest. "Umm. Okay." I will my pulse to regulate.

I can't be acting like this. My heart can't beat like this at hearing his voice. With everything I'm going through right now, the least of my problems should be my sex life.

Shit.

Who said anything about a sex life?

I'm only inviting him because I need a partner, and he is the only man I know in the city.

Lies.

"Hello. Willow. Are you still there?"

"Oh. Oh, sorry," I stutter because like it or not, this man makes me act like an idiot, even when I don't want to. "Can you meet at six p.m. on Third and Eighteenth Street? There's a gym on the northeast corner."

"I'll be there."

"Thanks, Jax."

"You're welcome, Willow." The sincerity in his voice is almost my undoing. I can feel the tears collecting behind my lids as I close my eyes.

I'm not used to the amount of kindness he has shown me.

I'm a stranger . . .

A part of me wants to wonder what's the catch because in the past, there has always been a catch, but every moment I spend with him, every time I speak to him, I know in my heart there is no catch.

Jaxson Price is one of a kind.

My hands are shaking as I stand on the corner and wait for Jaxson to arrive. I came early. Nerves getting the better of me. Now, I'm standing by the front door . . . outside.

If anyone walked by, they would think my jaw is rattling from the cold. It's not that, though. It's fighting with him.

But not for the reasons I should be scared.

I'm not scared Jaxson will hurt me. Nope. I know in my bones he won't.

No. I'm scared to have him touch me for a world of other reasons. I'm scared to feel him because I'm afraid of what my heart will do.

It's not easy to tamp down my desire when Jax is around, but to spar with him . . .

I shake my head back and forth.

"Everything okay over there?" I hear, and I lift my chin and see Jaxson walking toward me.

"Yeah." I push off the wall and drop my head back down as I walk toward the door.

Once inside, I allow my head to pop back up.

I'm comfortable here. There's no need to look down.

"Thanks for coming," I say to Jax as I walk toward the room where my class is. He follows me.

I stop walking when I get to the far corner of the room. It's less crowded there.

"Are you planning on kicking my ass?" he says, his lip tugging up on the right side.

"That's the goal," I retort. Using my sarcastic humor to hide the emotions going haywire inside me.

There are few reasons that my stomach churns.

One is that every time I'm here, it reminds me of why I'm trying to get strong.

It reminds me of why I'm running.

Hiding.

Biding my time.

Two is that sometimes when I'm here, my fear gets the better of me. I don't want to be weak, and I don't want Jaxson to see me as weak.

"What's wrong?" He takes a step closer to me.

I school my features. "Nothing. I'm thinking of a way to bring you down."

But that thought makes my pulse race because bringing him down means we're touching.

"Where do you want me?" His brow lifts seductively, and now I'm sure I won't be able to do this. Because he looks too good standing in front of me.

He's wearing gray sweats, which should be illegal. No man should be allowed to wear gray sweats in public.

It makes women want to do crazy things.

His T-shirt is black, but the tee isn't much better, as it showcases his lean but apparently ripped chest.

Jeez.

I always knew he was hot, but this is beyond.

"Okay, does everyone have their sparring partners?" I hear Shay ask, and it brings me back to the here and now.

Shay fires off the moves we need to do. I punch, and Jaxson blocks. Then we work on a hammer strike. I pretend to hold my keys in my hand as I attack.

But it's not until Jaxson has to get me into a hold to practice the bear hold attack that I realize the precarious situation I'm in.

He's behind me, his front to my back, and he wraps his arms around my stomach. I'm supposed to get low and shift my weight before striking, but the feeling of him wrapped around me has the opposite effect.

Instead, butterflies start flying in my stomach, and my heart pounds in my chest. I try to ignore how my skin tingles at his touch, and I sigh in relief when I hear Shay's voice.

"Now, I want you to practice how to escape when being pinned to the ground."

Without looking at Jax, I lie on my back flat on the floor. Slowly, like a crouching tiger, he crawls up my body until his knees are on either side of me. When he leans forward, the smell of his cologne wafts up through the air. The crisp smell of citrus and wood. He smells delicious.

It's too much.

His proximity to me is too much.

My eyes close of their own accord as I try to calm the beating of my heart. Instead, it ping-pongs around inside me, rattling like the ball inside an old pinball game.

I don't have to have my eyes open to feel him, though, and I do. I feel him everywhere.

Having my eyes closed hasn't helped lessen my need and desire. Instead, without my sight, it has amplified all my other senses.

I feel him when he leans closer. When his hands lightly grip my neck.

Again, I know I should fight him. I should push him off, but instead, my eyes open.

He's staring down at me. The way he looks at me ignites a flame inside me, and the longer we stare into each other's eyes, the more on fire my body feels.

Burning me up to the core.

Ready to explode.

His hands tighten and pressure inside me builds.

Need and want.

Desperate to rise and meet his lips.

He must feel it too because his Adam's apple bobs as he leans forward, his fingers slowly caressing my skin.

Down.

Down.

Down.

His face is so close now, I can feel his breath on mine.

He might kiss me . . .

I hope he does.

"Now strike."

As if cold water is dumped on us, Shay's voice rings through the air.

Making him lift his body off mine. Making me realize what we almost just did.

That was close.

CHAPTER TWENTY-SIX

Jaxson

After I went with Willow to her self-defense class, I expected her to call me. But now, days later, here I sit in my office, and all I hear are crickets.

I'm not sure why her silence bothers me. It's not like we're fucking. It's not like we're anything.

The realization hits me. I miss hanging out with her.

I'm not sure how it happened, but in trying to get to know Willow, I grew attached to her. And as a friend I care about, I wonder what she's doing.

A tiny voice in my head says it's more.

But I shake it off.

I can't be micromanaging my thoughts on Willow because I have way too much work to do.

Like a damn spreadsheet. I'm not sure how my brother does this every day. This shit is so boring it makes watching glue dry seem entertaining.

Balancing figures and figuring out where we can cut back is my version of hell. Hell sounds better than this. I'm sure in hell, Lucifer throws a wicked party. A list of things I'd rather be doing play in my head: Get a root canal. Wait in line at the DMV. Go shopping on Black Friday. Basically, I'd rather do anything but do this. For fuck's sake, I'd rather listen to my brother bitch and complain . . . The phone on my desk rings and I pick it up.

"Jax."

"Gray."

"How is work?"

Speak of the devil.

The saying, careful what you wish for rings in my head.

"The same as it was two hours ago, and the same as it was two hours before that. Spoiler alert, it will be the same tomorrow as well."

"I wanted to check-in."

The thing is, I'm well aware that I hate this job, and I should wave the white flag and admit defeat, but I'm too stubborn and proud to do that, so instead, I pretend.

"I get that, but everything is okay here. I got this," I say.

"How are things with the—" he starts to say, but I cut him off.

"I said I got this. You don't need to go on. Everything is okay. You don't need to come home. Price Enterprise isn't going to implode," I huff out.

"It might," he deadpans.

"I promise you, Gray, and I don't know how many times I have to say this. I got this shit. Nothing is going to happen."

"I'm trusting . . ."

"Jeez, Gray. Do you ever fucking stop? After everything I've done for you and Addison. Fuck, after everything I've done for River. Leave me the fuck alone."

I hang up the phone before he says another word. As soon as the phone hits the desk, my cell phone vibrates.

"Yes," I bark out before I even check who it is.

"Down, boy," Trent says through the line.

"Whatever." I know I shouldn't be a dick to him, but I'm annoyed.

"What's got your panties in a bunch?"

I push my chair back from my desk and swivel it to look out the window. The city is gray today. A heavy fog lingers over it, threatening and ominous. Seems fitting for my mood.

"What do you think?"

"Grayson again?" he asks.

The longer I stare out the window, the more I want to jump up from my desk and stand outside and wait for the rain. Maybe that will cool me off. However, since I can't do that, I turn back and look at my computer monitor at the damn spreadsheets and close it out.

Fuck it.

I let out a long-drawn-out breath and then answer his question. "As per usual."

"Why don't you tell him to fuck off?"

"As a matter of fact, that is exactly what I did."

"Really?"

"Yep."

"Wow. I would have liked to hear that. Better yet, I would have liked to be a fly on that wall to see his reaction."

That makes me chuckle because the visual would actually be amazing.

"What's going on?" I finally ask, now that my blood has cooled, and I no longer want to kill someone. My fingers tap on my desk, waiting to hear why my friend is calling in the middle of the day.

"Happy hour today. You in?"

Normally, I would say no. But with Gray being a dick and Willow hiding, I can't think of a reason I shouldn't say yes.

"Sure. Why the fuck not?"

"Good to hear."

This is exactly what I need. A big fuck you to my brother. Hell, maybe I won't even show up for work tomorrow.

This idea holds merit. Fuck. I can't do that. If I do that, he'll hire someone, and that could make my life even more hell than it already is. It's fine, though. I'll go out, drink, then come to work. He won't be here, and no one in the office will rat me out if I'm a bit hungover.

"So where to?"

"I'm thinking Chaos."

"That's hardly a happy hour spot," I say.

"Yeah, well, when I said happy hour, I meant let's fucking go out. It's been too long, and I need to get laid."

"So do I," I groan out. "Fine. I'll meet you there," I say before hanging up. I can't even remember the last time I fucked someone. I've been way too busy with work.

And with Willow.

Too bad I can't fuck her. That would make my life easier. But as much as I want her and find her to be the sexiest woman I've ever seen, it's not going to happen.

She'd never do it. Whatever she's hiding is big, big enough that she wouldn't be open to anything with me. If only she would tell me. I'm becoming impatient to find out. If I wasn't trying to prove I have changed, I'd know already.

My fingers reach out to my keyboard and I start to search.

Within a few minutes, I'm looking at the building's security system, scrolling through footage of the lobby.

How easy it would be to run facial recognition software on her.

Do it.

No.

I'm better than that. I'm not some creeper who needs to

stalk a woman to get laid. Or, well, be friends with them.

Closing out the site, I open my email and find one from Addison. Some personal request about someone. The number of favors I do for her and her friends is becoming ridiculous. I should start charging them for my time.

But I don't because it gives me something to dangle over them if they ever give me too much shit about not working etcetera, etcetera.

I read over the email and let out a sigh.

They treat me like a trained monkey, expecting me to perform on command.

It's ridiculous that they want me to help them but don't trust me in my own company. Addison isn't as bad as Gray, but still.

I shoot her back an email, telling her I will work on it tomorrow, and then shut down the computer. Trent might have meant go out tonight, but I still want happy hour.

I don't bother saying goodbye to anyone as I head out the door. When I reach the ground level, I make my way to my favorite bar. The one I once took River to.

Funny how much time has gone by since then.

A lifetime.

Now I'm here alone, and I'm not trying to get a rise out of anyone. No, instead, I'm trying to prove I'm not that person anymore.

After I wave at the bartender, I take a seat at the bar. He knows me, so before long, I'm drinking my tequila and letting the day slip away. My thoughts drift away from my pain-in-the-ass siblings, and instead, I think about the potential of the night.

I'm sitting at the table, tequila in hand. The girls Trent invited are dancing on the banquette. Their hips sway, eyes closed, in a seductive dance. In another time, in another life, I'd be picking one to go home with me tonight, but as beautiful as they are, none of them pique my interest.

I look over at Trent, who has a smirk on his face as he watches the brunette. He must notice me watching him because he turns to face me and raises his eyebrows.

"I'm taking that one," he declares with a wave of his glass.

I nod. "Okay," I mouth back because the music is so loud, I'm not sure how I even heard him before. He was probably shouting, but he's the guy who wouldn't care if she heard him.

I'm that guy too. But as of recently . . . I don't want to be.

"Which one?" he shouts. This time, I shake my head at him. His eyes widen, and then he scoots closer to me. Now he is definitely within earshot.

"None?"

"Nope," I answer.

"Why the fuck not?"

I want to say a lot of shit, but then he'll ask questions. Luckily, for me, more people come to the table, interrupting our conversation. When I look up, though, I realize it's Bethany. Bethany is one of the many crazies I've dated. She slides into the booth next to me, leaning into me to brush her lips on my cheek. I give her a tight smile. I hooked up with her a few times, but it became obvious she cared more about my family fortune and being the next Mrs. Price than about me.

She's the polar opposite of Willow.

Willow.

I wonder what she's doing. Before I know what I'm doing, I grab my phone, and before I can stop myself, I scroll through my contacts. Looking around the table, I realize there's no way she'll be able to hear me, so I lean away from Bethany and turn back to Trent.

"Hey, let me out, man."

"Where you off to?"

"Gotta make a phone call."

He vacates the table, allowing me to pass. I can feel Bethany touch my leg as I leave, but I don't turn around. I want nothing to do with her. Nor do I want to give her any false illusion that I do.

Leaving the table, I head toward the back corridor where I know it'll be quieter. When I'm in the alcove by myself, I dial the number. It rings three times before I realize it's late. I hang up and check the time again to see how late it is. As I hit the button and see that it's ten p.m., the phone rings. Willow. I swipe the screen and answer it. "Hello."

"You called?"

"Hello to you too," I lead.

"Hi, Jax. What's going on?"

I pace the small corridor as I blurt out, "Come meet me."

"It's ten p.m."

"And you have work tomorrow?"

"I mean, no, but don't you?" she asks.

"I do. But I'm also the boss. Come meet me," I say again because I really want her to come. I'm used to being with her. Here I am at a club, desperate to have fun, but what I figured out is with her, I don't.

Not exactly sure what that means, but it's true.

You know what it means, ass. Grow a pair of balls and fucking admit you want her as more than a friend.

"Where are you?" she asks.

"Chaos lounge."

"I'm not going to a club. I just got off work."

"Another poker game?" I ask, my eyes closing as I envision the short skintight black dress that hugs all her curves that leaves nothing to the imagination.

"No. I'll talk to you later." The line goes silent, and I stare at my phone. She *hung* up on me. I laugh. This girl is nothing like any girl I've ever met before. I hit the call button again because I'm drunk enough not to care.

"What, Jax?"

"Come. I bet you're not even home yet." When she doesn't speak, I continue. "Are you?"

"No."

"Are you alone? Or are you with Maggie?"

"Maggie."

"Driving?"

"Jeez, Jax. Yes."

"Put me on speakerphone." I can hear right away when I am because even though it's loud in the main area of the club, this area is tucked away far in the back, making it easy to hear.

"Hey, Jax," I hear Maggie say through the line. I've only spoken to Maggie that one night, but still, I feel like I know her through Willow.

"I got a table and a bottle with your name on it. Bring Willow."

"Don't listen to him. I'm tired," I hear Willow say to Maggie.

"Where are you at?" Maggie asks. That makes me smile because I know I can win Maggie over, and if I win Maggie over, I win Willow over.

"Chaos. Table and free booze."

"Cool. We'll be there."

"No, we won't," Willow pipes up.

"Live a little." Maggie laughs.

"Fine."

"I'll leave your name at the door." I hang up and head to the bouncer. It only takes me a few minutes more, and then I'm back at the table, filling my glass up yet again. This is probably a bad idea, but it's been so long since I've gone out like this, and I really don't care, especially after my day. Even when I am doing my job, no one takes me seriously, so I might as well let loose, come in late to work, and have a good time.

Knowing it might take a while, I lean back, drink in hand, and I wait.

I'm done with my drink when I finally see her approach. Okay, not finished, but I'm taking the last swig when I notice her, and I choke on the sip.

Fuck.

This girl is like a wet dream. Fuck that, she's more than a wet dream. She's otherworldly. She's like a Greek goddess sent down to Earth to tempt men. Her long locks flow in waves, and this dress is even tighter than the previous ones.

She's gorgeous. And fuck me if I don't want her.

CHAPTER TWENTY-SEVEN

Willow

I CAN'T BELIEVE MAGGIE IS MAKING ME GO OUT RIGHT NOW. After a long day of working, the last thing I want to do is go to a bar and have a drink. Sure, I appreciate the phone call, but I'm tired.

"Stop pouting. It's going to be fun."

"I'm not pouting."

I am. I'm actually doing more than that. I'm having a full-blown internal meltdown over what I will do if they decide to card me.

I have no identification. I can't go.

Old Willow would have flirted with the bouncer to get in or entered with her head held high as if she owned the place.

New Willow is, apparently, a coward.

"Sure you are, but after the night I've had, I really don't care. You're coming out with me, and you're having a drink with me. We're going to have fun because as long as you've been living in my apartment in the city, we have not gone out." When she puts it like this, I feel like a big asshole. Because she's right. After all she's done for me, the least I can do is this. If they card me, I'll come up with an excuse. Yeah. That's what I'll do. *It will be fine*. Even though I tell myself this, my stomach still churns with the uncertainty.

"You're right."

"I know I am. And it will be fun."

"I'm not sure about that, but I'll try."

"Oh, my God. I'm excited. Apparently, this is the best place in the city. It's members only. Unless you're a guest, of course."

Now, I really have no desire to go. In my previous life, invite clubs were a norm. I welcome the solitude I have now. But obviously, I need to put my big girl panties on.

We take no time to get there, and before I know it, we're parked and walking inside. Lucky for me, they don't check IDs. Another reason I don't go out. I can't risk it. But seeing as we were on a list, we're escorted right in and straight to Jaxson's table.

I see him right away. Sitting at the back of the lounge, he's holding court. He's the king and these are his subjects. There are a bunch of people, men and women, trying to engage him in conversation, but he's not paying attention to any of them. No, he barely notices when the women sway their hips. His gaze is in front of him, not breaking away from what holds his attention. Me.

We are locked in a stare as I approach. Neither one of us pulls away, even when he stands and leaves the table, heading right toward me. We don't break. It's like a gravitational pull between us.

The way he looks at me is unnerving. Butterflies fly in my stomach, and when he's finally standing right in front of me, so close that our bodies almost touch and my head has to tip back so I can stare at him, I feel almost dizzy. I don't know what's happening. Who am I trying to kid? I know exactly what's happening. I'm attracted to him. I want Jaxson Price.

But I can't have him. I force my eyes to look away from him, roaming the vicinity to take in all the others now watching me.

Wondering who I am. Wondering why I am here. And most of all, wondering what I mean to Jaxson. This question haunts me too.

"You came."

"I didn't really have a choice," I reply.

"No, you didn't." He should pretend to care, but he has a smug as shit smile on his face that tells me even if he said I had a choice, I didn't, and we both know it.

"You don't fight fair."

"No. I don't," he agrees.

"Well, now that you dragged my ass out . . ." I trail off.

"What can I get you to drink?"

"What are you having?" I ask, and he lifts his brow. I have to laugh at the look he gives me. His eyes wide, as if to say, really.

"Dumb question," I remark. "Obviously, you are having tequila."

His lips tip up into his familiar smirk. The dimple in his right cheek forms a divot. That dimple is deadly, forcing me to look away. I start to walk to the table when I feel his hand on my back, guiding me. But it feels like something more. It feels like he's staking his claim. Which is ridiculous, right?

He leads us to the table, and I slide in. Maggie doesn't. Instead, she signals for him to.

"I'm gonna dance." She reaches forward and grabs the bottle of vodka, then grabs the glass. She pours it to the top, lifts it to her mouth, and takes a large swig. "But first, drink." She smiles, then takes another swig, this time bigger than the last. I want to tell her to take it easy, but to be honest, there's no point. She's right. Tonight was a rough night.

Tonight was not the typical poker night. Yes, it was at

Cyrus's house again, but the crowd was different, more handsy and seedy. I want to ask her how she knows Cyrus and how she ended up with this gig, but I don't. Maybe it's fear, or maybe I don't want to upset her when she's done so much for me. Because I owe her. She's helped me more than she knows, and I hate myself for not telling her the whole story too.

She let me in with a duffel bag on my back, no questions asked. She sat by my side as I cried and still never pried. And how do I repay her? By not telling her the truth. Because if anybody has a right to know, it's her. Every day I'm with her, giving her no choice, I'm putting her life in danger.

One day, I'll tell her. But today, I'll let her drink and have fun. Because I owe her everything.

From beside me, I see Jax reach out and pour my drink, and then he pours his own. He hands my drink to me and then lifts his.

"What are we toasting to?" he asks.

"What do you want to?"

"To finally getting you out?"

"I go out with you all the time."

"But not like this." His voice is husky and decadent like warm chocolate dripping over me. I want to reach out and grasp it, but I can't.

His innuendo makes me warm and fuzzy inside. Coming here was a bad idea, but then I look at Maggie, who has a large smile on her face, her eyes glassy, but she looks relaxed. She sees me smiling at her and waves her drink at me. I lift mine to her, then I take a sip.

The liquid is harsh against my tongue, but soon, I feel warmth pooling in my belly. I'm pretty sure the booze isn't working that fast, and it's actually my proximity to Jax making me warm, but I look down at my drink and pretend. Ignorance is bliss and whatnot.

We continue to drink, and with each sip, my inhibitions dissipate. I feel light and happy, and before long, I'm standing and dancing. Arms in the air, I face Maggie. We sway together, enjoying ourselves and letting loose.

Jax is at the table, his eyes watching me. Like a voyeur. And while it should upset me to have him gawk at me after everything I've been through, it doesn't. No. Instead, I like it.

I like the way he watches me. The way he stares. The way he undresses me with his gaze. I close my eyes so I don't hear what he's saying without words. With my vision turned off, I continue to move, I feel him. I don't need to see to know he's near.

I can smell him.

His hands touch me. His front to my back as he sways our hips together.

The way he feels behind me intoxicates me, and I can only imagine what he would feel like on top of me. I allow myself to get lost in the moment, to believe this is possible. I let the music engulf me.

I let the scent of him filter in through me, and I let myself let go completely.

The songs come and go, changing time and time again. Hours must pass, but we don't move; we continue to dance, swaying our bodies, and we don't pull apart, and neither one of us turns. We don't look at each other because we both know the moment will be lost if we do. He knows as well as I do that there's nothing for us.

At least not now. Not with so many variables up in the air. Maybe later. Maybe in the future, but right now, right here, I ignore that and let myself be.

Out of nowhere, I'm bumped from the side, and we lose the moment. I shake my head, allowing the world to rush back in. The colors and sounds hit me with a force I'm not ready for, but what I'm mostly not ready for is how he stares down at me and how I wonder what this means. Nothing. So I shake my head and smile brightly, pointing at the table.

"I'm gonna get some water."

He laughs at that, and I raise an eyebrow.

"You find that funny?"

"I find it funny that you think there's water at the table." With the lights now adjusting in my eyes, I notice there is, in fact, no water at the table, only vodka and tequila and mixers.

"Don't worry about it. Go back to the table, and I'll grab you a water."

"Do you mind?"

He smiles at that but doesn't respond. Instead, he turns on his heel and makes his way to the bar. I sit back down, but I'm not alone at the table. There's a girl I don't know, and I recognize his friend from the poker game. Maggie is still dancing, and it looks like she might've found entertainment for the night.

"Why are you here?" the girl I don't know says to me.

"Jax invited me."

"Are you fucking him?" She sneers in obvious jealousy.

"Not that it's any of your business, but we're just friends."

"Please, Jaxson Price doesn't have friends."

"Well, that is all this is, so apparently he does," I retort.

"If you say so."

I shake my head as the girl glares at me. I'm not sure who she is, but it's obvious she has a thing for Jaxson. As I'm about to open my mouth, Jaxson steps up, holding the bottle of water out to me.

"Here."

"Thanks," I respond, and I'm not just talking about the drink. I think he knows that whoever this girl is, she was giving me a hard time.

Jaxson then sits beside me and places his arm around my shoulder. I know what he's doing, but I wish he wouldn't because while he's trying to protect me, he placed a giant bull's-eye on me. If this girl could kill me with stares, I'd be dead already.

You're a minnow swimming in a pool of sharks.

CHAPTER TWENTY-EIGHT

Jaxson

WE SPEND ANOTHER HOUR DRINKING, BUT NOT DANCING anymore. The night is winding down, but I'm not ready for it to end. I know I have work tomorrow, but I don't care. The lights of the club turn on, and the music lowers. Once again, I close the bar down. It's been a while since I've done this, but I don't regret it even if I'm tired tomorrow. I turn to my left and look at Willow. She's lifting a glass of water to her mouth. She must notice me staring because she turns in my direction.

"Looks like it's time to go." When I say that, she looks around the room. She's searching for her friend, and when she spots her, her cheeks turn red. I see why. In the corner of the room, her friend Maggie is kissing one of Trent's friends.

"I'll go get her," she says, and then she slides out of the booth. I follow suit, trailing behind her until we approach Maggie. Willow lifts her hand and touches her, and her friend stops kissing the guy.

"Hey," Maggie drawls. It's obvious from the glassy appearance of her eyes and the way she speaks that she's drunk. Or at the very least tipsy.

"You ready?" Willow asks.

Maggie's eyes widen. "Well . . . I was thinking about . . ." Now it's Maggie's face that turns red. The moment gets awkward.

I step forward. "I can make sure she gets home safely," I offer.

Maggie's head turns in my direction. "Really? You would do that?"

"Sure. It would be my pleasure."

"I couldn't ask you to do that. I can just take a—" Willow starts to say, but I shake my head and cut her off.

"I insist."

"Are you going to be okay?" Willow asks Maggie, and Maggie nods. Willow turns back to me. "Okay, I'll take you up on that offer."

Together, we head toward the exit. Before we leave, I hold out my hand and help her put on her coat. Our hands touch briefly, and it feels like an electric current pulses between us. Once she's wrapped up, she puts some distance between us, probably to diminish the lingering desire that's coursed through us ever since that dance.

We step outside. If I didn't know better, I'd think we were in the dead of winter. It's so cold I'm sure if it rained it would snow.

"You really don't have to take me home. I can take a cab."

"Honestly, you're doing me a favor. I don't think I could fall asleep right now."

"Me too, actually."

I cock my head. "Do you want to grab a bite?"

"I can always eat."

"Come on. I know a great diner right up the road that's open twenty-four hours."

"How come it doesn't surprise me that you say that?"

"Probably because I love to eat."

"I feel that. Me too."

Together, we walk until we reach the small twenty-four-hour diner I always go to when I go to Chaos.

The small chime above the door rings through the air as I swing it open. I step back, and Willow walks past me. My brother might think I'm an idiot, maybe an asshole even, but I'm always a gentleman. Something my mom taught me when I was young. When Addison and Gray were traveling with Dad, and they left me home because I was so much younger, my mother taught me manners, one of them being letting a woman pass first. It's funny, but I doubt Grayson would think I would.

Thoughts of my brother and his condescending nature put a sour taste in my mouth.

I walk behind Willow until we reach a table and sit. My mood must be present on my face because when she looks at me, her forehead furrows.

"Is everything okay?"

"Yeah. I was just thinking."

"What were you thinking about?"

"My family."

She cocks her head. "What about your family? Or . . ." She raises her hands. "Forget I asked. It's none of my business."

And while I agree it's not, it doesn't sound like a bad idea. She doesn't know them, so personal prejudice will not taint her opinion. Although I rarely open up to people, I allow myself to open up to her.

"My brother treats me like I am a degenerate. Like I'm a fuckup and can't do anything right." It falls from my mouth before I can stop it, and Willow's mouth hangs open. She must think I'm crazy. Here, she won't even tell me her last name, and I'm bleeding all my drama onto her at a table at four in the morning.

When Willow is about to speak, or I'm about to apologize for the verbal diarrhea that has spewed from my mouth, the waitress comes over.

"What can I get for you two?" she asks.

"Food," I say. "Lots and lots of food. Enough food to shut me up and not make me bore you to death," I say, half laughing and half telling the truth.

"Basically, bring us one of everything," Willow jokes.

The waitress seems horrified.

I turn to her and smile. "Long night. Why don't you bring us . . ." I look down at the menu lying on the table and read off a few suggestions. Willow nods when she wants it. By the time the waitress leaves, we have ordered hash browns, scrambled eggs, chicken and waffles, and a milkshake. Anyone who will look at our table once we get our food will assume we are horribly drunk. Maybe tipsy, but we're not that drunk.

"So . . . your friends are nice . . ." she says, looking off and not making eye contact with me. I've known Willow long enough to know she's trying to ask me something but doesn't want to.

"Is that so?" I lean across the table, cocking my head. "Is there something or someone in particular you want to ask me about?" I do everything to hold back my laughter, but when her cheeks flush, I know I've hit the nail on the head.

"No. Of course not."

"She's no one," I say, and she shakes her head.

"I don't know what you're—"

"She's the past. Not the future." She looks up and our gazes lock; like lightning cracking.

Neither of us speaks as we wait for the food to arrive, but when the milkshake comes with two straws, we both reach for it, our hands touching, our fingers meeting. This moment has happened before, but this time there is no denying what is going on between us.

It's like sitting on top of a roller coaster the moment before it dips.

Invigorating.

CHAPTER TWENTY-NINE

Willow

I DIDN'T EXPECT JAX TO OPEN UP TO ME LIKE THAT. SURE, HE told me about his family before, but this was different. This was as if he cut his heart right open and allowed himself to bleed out on the table in front of me.

A part of me welcomes the trust he puts in me, but a bigger part feels like I've taken the knife and then stabbed him in the back. Hearing him speak makes me feel even worse. It makes me feel like a fraud. Here he is talking about how his brother doesn't respect him and uses him, and I'm no different. A twisting feeling starts in my stomach, weaving its way through my blood. I'm just as bad. This whole time, I've gotten to know him for the wrong reasons, and although I genuinely care about him more than I want to, and now I feel things for him I shouldn't, my motives were not pure in the beginning.

Now that I know him, I feel differently, but the motive is still there. I still need his help, and I will have to ask.

But it doesn't stop me from feeling awful. Luckily, though, the food arrives. Oh, and by the way, we ordered way too much.

The entire table has food spread across it. But everything looks amazing. The smells waft up through the air, lingering in my nostrils and making my mouth water. We both have an empty plate in front of us. That way we can share, and I'm not sure what to eat first.

"Where are you starting?" I ask.

"Chicken and waffles obviously."

"They do sound amazing."

"Amazing isn't the right word for them. You haven't lived until you've eaten chicken and waffles from here."

"Duly noted."

"So now that I divulged my whole life story to you"—he pauses—"why don't you tell me something, anything, a ridiculously mundane fact? Maybe a memory. Something you cherish."

I appreciate the fact he's not asking leading questions. Maybe to someone who doesn't know him, it would seem leading, but he's giving me room to tell a little but still protect myself. His brother really is an idiot. Jaxson Price is probably the best man I know. Although looking at some of the men I know, that doesn't mean a lot, but still.

"Anything big or small. It doesn't matter."

I look around the table and stare at the food. And then my gaze catches on the window. It faces the barren and cold city street. At this time of the night, there's no hustle and bustle, no crowds, and it's dark. Nighttime in New York is not my favorite thing because the darkness is something I don't enjoy. For me, it's not a good memory. It's a reminder of what I'm running from.

I close my eyes and try to think of something that makes me happy. It's been so long since I've been happy. I think of my mother and of my father, before, when we were still a family.

"I used to love to have picnics," I say.

Jax leans forward, his elbows hitting the table. He doesn't speak, though. Instead, he waits patiently for me to continue.

"When I was little . . ." I start, the memory of my parents playing out in my mind. My chest tightens, but as it does, I feel his warmth. I look down and see he has taken my hand in his. He gives me a little squeeze, which gives me the strength to continue. "When I was little, my mother would set up picnics. She would put a large blanket in our backyard. A big wicker basket always sat on top. To me, it was the biggest thing in the world. Almost like a Mary Poppins bag. She would keep pulling out treats. It never ended. From little sandwiches cut into shapes to chocolate-covered strawberries. I would drink lemonade from a crystal flute. She and my father would drink champagne. It was magical."

"When did you stop?" he asks, his voice low and full of curiosity.

"We stopped when my mom died." My voice cracks. That was when the magic died. The beginning of the end. I just didn't know it then.

He's quiet, and I feel the squeeze. "I'm sorry. Were you young?"

"I was eight years old. My dad raised me."

"How did she . . . ?"

I close my eyes. Behind my lids, the images flash. Glass. So much glass. The smell of burning rubber. My head shakes as if to pull myself out of the nightmare I'm stuck in. It happened so many years ago, but it's like I'm there right now. "Car accident." My eyes open, and Jax is staring at me.

"I lost my dad." His shoulders drop, his palm rubbing against his chest. I don't think he realizes he's doing it.

I can feel my heart lurch in my chest, but the words still leave my mouth. "I don't have a family." I pause to draw my bottom lip into my mouth. "Anymore."

Unspoken questions linger in his eyes, but I won't answer. I'm not ready.

"I'm sorry."

"It's okay."

Pulling my gaze away from him, I take in the spread of food. With a reach of my arm, I place my fork in the dish and pull it up. "Let's see if this is as good as you say it is."

He knows the conversation is over, and like always, he gives me exactly what I need, taking his hand off mine and grabbing his own fork. He then takes a bite too. When I place the fork in my mouth, I'm not prepared for the taste explosion. Salty and sweet all at the same time.

"Oh my God," I say with a mouth full of food. I swallow. "That is soooooo good."

"Would I steer you wrong?" His voice is cocky and confident.

"Apparently not. Because that was legit heaven."

"Wait until you take a sip of the milkshake." He winks.

I grab the glass, place the straw in my mouth, and take a sip.

It's exactly everything he says it is. And with the smirk on his face and my own moans, I sigh.

He's right.

Best thing ever.

So good it makes me savor the moment and not dwell on the pain that was holding on to my heart only a few minutes ago.

I look at him from under my lashes. "Thank you."

I'm not thanking him for the drink, and he knows it.

It's so much more than that.

Before I know it, the early morning sun is peeking through the clouds.

It's not bright, barely illuminating the black skies, but it makes me realize I'm not sure how much time has passed. I pull my phone out and check the time.

"Damn," I say.

"What's wrong?" Jax asks.

"I didn't realize how late it was."

Jax pulls his wrist up and looks at his watch. "Fuck."

"I know."

"I guess the saying is true," he mutters.

"And what's that?"

"Time flies when you're having fun."

I roll my eyes. "The lines get better and better," I quip.

"You know that's why you like me." He smirks.

"It is. Actually." At my words, his smile widens.

"We should go," he says, reaching into his pocket to grab his wallet.

"I'm not letting you pay again."

"Sure you are."

"You're impossible."

"That's the least of what I am, but you're still not paying."

"Fine," I huff, but as much as I huff, it's not real. I appreciate him doing this for me. He throws some money on the table, and I raise my eyebrow. "We don't even have a bill."

"Trust me, it's enough."

This time, I do roll my eyes at him as he stands.

"Come on, it's late. Let's get you home, and maybe I'll actually sleep an hour before work."

"Oh my God, you have to work today?"

"I do."

"How will you manage?"

"I'll be fine."

"You'll pass out at your desk," I say.

"Probably, but at least my brother won't be there."

"Well, that's good." I follow him out, pulling my coat tightly around my body.

"You're cold. Do you want—"

I shake my head. "I'm fine. Plus, you'll freeze."

"I don't get cold."

"Oh yes, I forgot. You're a superhero."

He laughs at that and then continues to walk. "My car is right there." He points up the block.

"Are you okay to drive?"

"Yeah, I'm good."

"Okay." We walk together to his car, and ever the gentleman, he opens the door. After I sit, he closes my door and walks around to the driver's side.

We both sit in the car, heat now blasting but we don't move.

"You do realize you have to tell me where you live?"

I can't help but laugh. "Shit, you're right. Stuyvesant." I can't believe I've known Jax this long and still haven't told him this. It feels like we are old friends, like I have known him forever, but he doesn't even know I'm basically homeless.

It makes me feel like an awful person. Like every word out of my mouth is a lie.

"Really?" he asks.

"Yeah. I'm crashing with Maggie."

"What do you mean you're crashing with her?"

I can feel his eyes on me.

"Not much to tell. I haven't gotten around to finding my own place. But I will. Soon."

I expect him to say something, but he doesn't. He pulls the car out of the spot and weaves his way through traffic.

We drive in silence until I have to guide him to the right

building. The thing about Stuyvesant is that you can't get close to the entrance. I'll walk fast.

Plus, the sun should be up soon.

I'm pulled from my thoughts when Jax pulls the car over and turns it off.

"What are you doing?" I ask.

"Walking you to your apartment, of course."

"You don't need to walk me up."

"Well, then I'm walking you to the building."

"Seriously, I'm a big girl, and you don't have to."

I pull my seat belt off, then fling the door open before he even knows what's happening. By the time I'm a few feet away, I'm sure he's ready to drive off, but his car is still there. I walk away when I see familiar dark eyes.

They pierce the night sky. Dark orbs. Threatening.

This can't be real.

He couldn't have found me.

Could he?

I shake my head, my pupils enlarging to take in the light. The person who passes comes into focus. Dark eyes morph to light, and bone structures change.

What the . . . it hits me. My eyes were playing tricks on me. My tired brain and lack of sleep are making me see things. Making me crazy.

Warm arms surround me. They try desperately to calm me from the panic that has consumed my body. But even though I know it's fake, my mind is having a hard time reconciling the truth.

He will find me.

It's only a matter of when.

"Shh," I hear Jax coo as his fingers trail circles on my back. I can't, though. I can't breathe.

I need to run. Go somewhere else. Go somewhere where no one will find me.

"Shh, you're okay. I have you." He doesn't know what's happening, but he's giving me exactly what I need right now.

Protection. Because even though no one has found me, and no one is hurting me, I need protection. But I need protection from myself. From my own mind.

"Take a deep breath," he says. "Inhale." I do. He counts to ten slowly. "Now, exhale." Again, I let him guide me. "That's a good girl. You're going to be okay."

I continue to breathe like that, following his cues until my body and mind reconcile that there is no threat.

Like a veil has finally lifted from my eyes, I realize I'm standing on the street with Jaxson Price's arms wrapped around me as I have a panic attack.

Again.

My cheeks warm as embarrassment sets in. I lift my hand to push back.

"No."

"Jax."

"Let me hold you for another second," he whispers against my hair. I allow it, but the longer I stand there, the more uncomfortable I become. I finally push back.

"I have to go," I say.

"Will you be okay?"

"I will."

"You know you can talk to me . . ."

I nod because I can't and finding the words to say that seems hard.

He leans down and places a kiss on my cheek. His lips are warm to the touch. A part of me wants to turn my head and let him kiss me—let his lips chase the demons away—but it wouldn't be fair.

Not until he knows the truth.

I step back.

"Good night, Jax."

"Good night, Willow."

The truth bites its way up my throat, but I swallow it and leave.

Not today.

Maybe not ever.

CHAPTER THIRTY

Jaxson

I am exhausted. In the past, a night out, or more like an all-nighter, wouldn't have fazed me, but back then, I wouldn't have had to come to the office. If I needed to work, I'd work from home.

But not now.

Nope. Here I am, with zero sleep, sitting in my office, staring blankly at my computer monitor.

I'm not sure what happened with Willow. The one thing I'm certain of is she had a massive panic attack. I tried to help her, but I don't know what set her off. The longer I know her, the more I want to find out her secret. It would be so easy.

One press of the keyboard.

But the thing is, I want something with this girl. I'm not sure if it's a relationship yet, but I like her, and I want to try.

Hacking into her life and finding out her secrets is a surefire way to fuck up any chance of being with her. So, as much as I want to delve into the black hole that will find all the answers I need, I don't. Instead, I reach for the coffee on my desk like it's a lifeline and try my best to wake up and be useful today.

I'm mid-sip when my door swings open. I pull my gaze up, and I'm met with the narrowed eyes of my brother.

"You look like shit," he grits out.

"Good to see you too, Grayson," I respond.

"I see not much has changed in my absence."

"Now, that really isn't true . . ."

He raises an eyebrow.

"In the past, I wouldn't have bothered to even come in." I swear he looks as though he could throw something, preferably at me. "Seriously, Gray, what's your problem? I'm here, and I'm working."

"And you look like shit."

"So fucking what? Why are you here? Don't you have something better to do?"

"I'm here because this is my company."

"Same, dude, so lay the fuck off. I haven't fucked up. Yes, maybe I look like shit today, and maybe I even smell, but no one is coming to my office today. And you shouldn't even be here. When you asked for my help with River, I was good enough, so why am I not good enough now? You never asked then what I was wearing or when I came home the night before. You trusted me to find out what you needed."

"It's different."

"How so? I'm damn good at what I do. I'm damn good at anything I do, including your job and my own, so get off my back."

"I can't. Not when you show up at the office looking like a homeless man."

I shake my head, then pivot in my chair to face the city. "I'm done with this conversation."

"I'm not." He holds his ground. Legs spread, arms crossed at his chest.

"Well, that seems to be a you problem."

Since he's not leaving, I stand from my chair and walk past him. Straight out of my office.

"Where are you going?"

"Well, since you're here today, and I have no work other than yours to do, I'm not needed."

I don't wait for him to respond before I push the button to the elevator.

"I need you to get info . . ."

I turn around and glare at him.

"You need me to hack someone, you mean?" Again, he just stares at me. "Funny . . . that also seems like a you problem. I'm cool. If you need info, find it out yourself." I can hear the elevator open behind me, and I step back. His mouth opens to respond, but with a smirk on my face, the elevator door closes on his.

That's the end of that conversation.

Once I'm on the basement level of the building, I walk toward my car. I need to go home and crash.

I would have sucked it up if Gray didn't come in today, but since he's here, fuck it.

Luckily for me, traffic is minimal this morning. It's still early, since after I left Willow, I came straight to the office.

It never dawned on me that my brother would show up.

But even if it did, it shouldn't matter what I look like as long as I get my shit done.

Before long, I'm parking at my loft. Then I'm lying on my bed.

My eyes close of their own accord, all the anger and animosity drifting from my body as sleep catches up to me.

With a stretch of my arms, my eyes flutter open. Light drifts in through the blinds as I try to remember what happened and why I'm still in bed.

Looking over at the clock, I see it is now noon.

Fuck, I needed to sleep.

Now what to do with my day? It's rare that I have nothing to do. It's been months. But it feels good to have a day off.

Even before, when my workload for Price Enterprise was low, I always had side jobs.

Someone always needed something from me.

And like the idiot I was, I did it, never asking for anything in return. Yet no one appreciated me.

Now, as I sit here, I wonder why I bother.

Every time I look into someone, every time I hack, I put my life on the line, and for what?

My family has no respect for me.

Done.

I'm done helping them.

Let's see how much business they can do without my area of expertise.

A smile lines my face. Yeah, this is my new game plan. There is only one person I have any interest in helping, and she's the only one who hasn't asked.

Speaking of . . .

I wonder if she's okay.

I grab my phone from beside my bed and fire off a text.

Me: Just checking in.

Willow: Hi.

Me: Are you okay?

Willow: I am. Thank you.

Me: What are you doing tonight?

Willow: Working.

That's right. Tonight is Friday, which means she's probably working the poker game at Cyrus Reed's house. I have no intention of going, but remembering she will be there, I'm reconsidering my plans for tonight.

Me: Poker?

Willow: Yep.

Me: Funny you should say that. I'll be there too.

Willow: Why does that not surprise me?

That makes me laugh.

Me: See you later.

Willow: Okay.

I close out the text and fire one off to Trent.

Me: Poker tonight.

Trent: It's on.

Even though I'm not necessarily in the mood to play, the need to be near her and watch out for her to make sure she's okay is too much to say no to.

It's odd.

I have never been this protective over anyone before. Sure, I was protective over Addison with Oliver, but this is different. She's not family. I just care about her.

Once I stop texting with Trent, I look through my missed phone calls. I'm surprised I don't have any from my brother. I also don't see one from Addison.

It appears the only person from my family who has called me is my mother. As much as I'm not in the mood to speak, I think it's safe to call her back as I'm sure Grayson didn't mention the altercation at the office.

I press her contact info and wait for her to answer.

"Hey, sweetie," my mom coos through the phone. "How's my baby boy?"

"Wow, Mom. You do realize I'm like a few years away from being thirty? That hardly makes me a baby."

"You will always be my baby boy, Jaxson Price."

"Sure. You do you." I chuckle. "What's going on? Everything okay?"

"Of course. I wanted to say hi."

"Hi," I respond.

"Always such a pain."

"Have you been talking to Gray?"

"No. Why?" she asks, her voice rising with concern.

"Nothing," I answer too fast, sending off a red flag for my mom to ask more questions.

"What's going on?"

I sigh, giving in. "The usual. Gray giving me a hard time. Gray knowing everything, Gray not taking me seriously."

"I know this isn't what you want to hear, but he means well."

"Yeah, not exactly what I wanted to hear," I agree. "I don't care if he means well. It's a pain in the ass."

"The thing about Grayson. I love my son, but he thinks he has to take care of all of us since your father died."

"Well, he doesn't. News flash. I'm twenty-eight."

"I know this, honey, but it's hard for him to turn it off."

I let out a long-drawn-out sigh. As much as I love my mother, I'm not really in the mood for this conversation.

"Mom, I have to go." I try my best to sound like I mean it, but she chuckles on the line.

"No, you don't. You just don't want to hear it."

Now it's my turn to laugh. "You're right. I don't."

"Remember I love you. I love all my kids."

"I love you too, Mom."

"Bye, sweetie."

"Bye." I shake my head as I hang up, but at least a smile lines my face now. She means well.

I spend the rest of the afternoon doing nothing. It's kind of amazing. Without my brother calling or emailing me to dig up dirt, I have nothing to do. Addison is too busy to contact me either.

So instead I watch TV.

Something I haven't done in ages.

When it's time to pick up Trent, I'm happy to be leaving my apartment. Well-rested and ready to have some fun.

"So . . ." Trent starts from beside me.

"Yes?" I say, turning my head in his direction, still keeping one eye on the road.

"What's the deal with you and Willow?"

"Are we girls?"

"Well, no. But—"

"We're just friends," I answer. Even though I want to fuck her. Hell, who am I kidding? I want to date her, which is crazy. Because I never want to date anyone.

"Really?"

"Yeah. What of it?"

"It's just I have never known you to be friends with a girl."

I shrug. "People change."

"Not that much. So, what is it? She won't fuck you?"

My fingers tighten around the steering wheel, making my knuckles turn white. "Shut up."

"Ahh. I hit the nail on the head."

"Seriously, say another word, and I'll pull over and dump your ass right on the corner."

Instead of speaking, Trent breaks out into a full belly laugh.

"Great. I'm comic relief."

"It's just funny."

"How so?"

"Every girl wants to ride your dick . . . but you fall for the one who doesn't."

"One, not every girl . . . just the ones in the tri-state area," I retort. "And two, shut the fuck up."

More laughter.

"I can't take you anywhere." I reach my hand out and raise the volume of the song on the radio, shutting him up.

It takes us no time to arrive, and as soon as we step inside, my eyes scan the room where we play cards.

I don't see her at first.

But when I do, my breath hitches.

She's fucking gorgeous. Her side profile is facing me, her skin like porcelain with red-stained lips I want on mine. She sees me watching her, and while in the past, she might have tensed, now she doesn't. No, now she rewards my stare with a heart-stopping smile.

Fuck.

What is wrong with me?

I have it bad for this woman.

She makes me act like a lovesick schoolboy.

I give her a nod, trying to pretend I'm not affected by her presence, and she nods in return, holding back her laughter.

Needing to break the haze she casts over me, I head over to the table and pick my regular chair.

I'm here for her, but I need to keep up the pretense I'm not.

Before long, cards are dealt, and the game starts. Luckily for me, poker is a game of skill, and I have more skill than these fools in spades.

Because I'm barely paying attention. And even with my attention divided, I'm still better than all of them, which is apparent in the stack of chips I've collected. From the corner of my eye, I can see her walking. Watching as her hips sway, I stare at her ass.

"She's fucking hot."

I turn toward the voice. Douchebag number one. I can't remember his name, but I've met him a million times.

"Fuck, the things I would do to her," douchebag number two says.

"To see those red lips wrapped around my dick when I choke her with my—"

Before he can go on, I slam my hands down, shutting them all up. "Do you fucking idiots mind?"

They both look at me, brows lifted, and I realize I have probably just put a huge target on her back if they figure out I like her. "I'm trying to play cards."

That's the excuse I try to use, but by the looks these fools are giving me, they don't buy it. Since, I can't leave yet to talk to her, I turn back to the cards and play. This time, my heart isn't in it, and eventually, I fold.

With that hand done, I stand. All eyes around the table are now on me. "Bathroom," I say, and they nod.

I make my way in the direction she came from. I'm still so heated from what they said that I don't notice her at first. Not until I bump right into her.

Thank fuck, her hands are empty, so she spills nothing. Because that would suck. I reach my hands out to bracket her toward me. We're so close I can feel her against my body, and I know my body will react. I push back so she doesn't feel what she does to me.

"Hey," she says, her voice low. She probably doesn't want anyone to know that she's talking to me. I don't want anybody to know I'm talking to her either. These assholes would use anything to win my money, and she doesn't need to be the target. "How is the game?"

"Winning."

"You're pretty good."

"The best," I say smugly because I am.

"And you're humble."

"I'm that too." Seeing her here makes me want to hang out with her again. I would ask her to come over after this, but I'm beat, and I'm sure she is too, so instead, I cock my head and smile.

"What are you smiling about?"

"I was wondering—"

"Never a good idea," she jokes.

"Do you have plans tomorrow?"

"Tomorrow?" she asks.

"Yes, the day that follows today."

"Cute."

"I thought so."

"As you were saying, because as much as I would love to enter into our usual sparring match, I do have to get back to work."

"Tomorrow. Dinner. My place."

"Umm, okay."

She looks tentative and a bit shy. It's cute.

"Just dinner," I say. Hands up.

"Okay. Just text me your address."

"Will do."

With nothing more to say, she turns and heads back in the direction of the tables. I, on the other hand, head toward the bathroom.

Once done, I go back to the table and play a few more hands. I don't stay much longer. Just long enough to make sure she's okay. I want to get home early to plan tomorrow.

God, I really am a girl.

The next morning comes faster than I anticipated. Somewhere before sleep, an idea for tonight's dinner popped in my head. It's pretty creative.

I know she will like it, so even though it's over the top, I set out to do it anyway.

Hours later, my apartment is set up, the food is ready, and I'm sitting on my couch with a glass of tequila in hand.

I texted her my address a little over an hour ago, and now I'm just waiting.

Midway through the glass, I hear the doorbell. First, I place the glass down, and then I head for the door.

I'm not sure how it's possible, but she looks even more beautiful today than last night. Sure, last night she was fuckable with her wavy hair, red lips, and skintight black dress, but today, in jeans and a sweater with no makeup on her face, she is the most beautiful I have seen her. She looks like the girl next door, all sweet and innocent, and it makes me want to corrupt her. Then I notice her eyes. They're blue. She's not wearing her contacts. She's no longer hiding any part of herself from me.

Shit.

I'm fucked.

CHAPTER THIRTY-ONE

Willow

When the door opens, all resolve to not jump Jaxson Price is gone. We have been dancing around this attraction for weeks, but now we are at a boiling point. There is no denying the tension between us.

I should just grab him and kiss him already. It sure would make life easier.

But I don't.

Instead, I stare with the will power of a chocolate addict in front of a cake, or in my case a Kit Kat.

"Hey," he finally says, breaking the ice.

"Hi," I respond. He steps to the side, letting me into his loft.

The place is amazing. All white, with exposed beams, and it's huge.

"Wow," slips from my mouth.

He raises a brow in question.

"Your apartment. It's amazing."

"It's home." He steps forward. "Come on, I'll give you the grand tour."

I follow him as he walks us through the foyer and past the kitchen, but when we make it to the living room, my heart lurches in my chest.

Set up in the middle of the floor, in front of large floor-to-ceiling windows that face the river, is a giant picnic blanket.

I step closer, eyes wide with disbelief.

"What is this?" I ask.

"You said you love picnics." His voice is low as if he is gauging my reaction. He isn't sure if I love it or hate it.

"I-I," I stutter. And I can feel wetness fill my eyes.

"You hate it?" he asks, and suddenly, he sounds like a little boy, unsure.

I shake my head back and forth. "No. I love it." A lone tear trails down my cheek.

He steps up closer, his finger swiping at the tear. "Then why are you crying?"

"Because no one but my mother has ever done anything like this for me." Tears come faster now.

And I don't deserve it, I want to shout.

I don't deserve this man's care. Because everything out of my mouth has been a lie. And he deserves to know the truth, and I have to tell him. I open my mouth, but I can't find my words. His hand is still on my face, his fingers brushing gently against my skin. I feel dizzy under the ministrations.

All rational thoughts leave my mind as I lift onto my tiptoes and bring my mouth to his.

His lips are softer than I imagined in my dreams, and when he opens them and sweeps his tongue with mine, I think I might die. Combust for sure.

He opens my mouth with his, pulling me tighter into his body as he guides the kiss.

I'm lost, like a passenger on a boat drifting off to sea, but he is the anchor, bringing me back.

Making me present with his touch.

The kiss doesn't last much longer, and soon, he is pulling back to gauge me with his eyes, to see if I wanted him to do that.

This is why I have fallen for Jaxson Price.

And this is why I need to tell him the truth.

Now.

I take a step back and bracket my arms around my body for protection.

"I'm married."

CHAPTER THIRTY-TWO

Jaxson

I'm sure I heard her wrong.

There is no way she just said she's married. My mouth opens and closes, yet no sound passes through my lips.

Is that her secret?

This whole time I've been falling for a girl who's married.

How could I have been so blind?

"What in the actual fuck?" I say, taking a step back and distancing myself from her. I shake my head back and forth, trying to understand what she just said.

She lifts her hand up, almost as if to soothe the news she just dropped on me.

"It's not what you think." Her hand reaches out. My first instinct is to push it away because the betrayal I feel is thick in the air.

I take another step back, but she takes another step forward.

"Let me explain." Her words sound broken, a small hiccup in her speech. That's when I finally look down and meet her eyes.

What is there breaks my heart.

She looks broken. Desperate. It looks like a world of pain hides in the depths of her blue eyes.

Pain I'd never be able to understand.

I nod and point at the couch.

The abandoned picnic looks forgotten beneath the weight of this confession.

When I sit, she follows suit. But instead of sitting beside me, she sits on the couch adjacent to mine.

She needs her distance, and truth be told, depending on what she says . . .

I need mine.

The air around us is quiet, heavy with tension. I watch as she leans forward and cradles her head in her hands, a tear falling from her eyes.

"I-I," she stutters. "I'm sorry I didn't tell you sooner, but I'm married in name only," she states.

I shake my head in confusion.

"It's hard to be married to a man who wants you dead," she whispers, and when she says the word, I feel like I'm punched in the stomach.

There is only truth in her eyes.

No lies. No deception. She truly believes this, and then like a puzzle that's been thrown on the floor, the pieces start to resemble an image that finally makes sense.

"Talk to me, Willow," I say. I keep my voice low so as not to startle her. She looks like a wounded bird and I don't want her to fly away.

"My real name is Willomena. Willomena Craft." She takes a deep breath and time stands still as I wait for the other shoe to drop. "And my husband is trying to kill me."

Thump. Thump. Thump.

It feels like my world has stopped on its axis as I listen. As I soak up each bread crumb, I've been waiting to hear this whole time.

Her husband is trying to kill her.

Never in my wildest dreams did I think those words would leave her mouth.

That's when the floodgates finally burst. The tears pour down her face like water over a dam. No longer lone tears, but now, a never-ending current flows from her.

The liquid streams down her cheeks, and without a second thought, I stand and close the distance between us, sitting beside her and pulling her into my arms. She sobs into my chest, her entire body shaking from the emotions she's held inside her.

I'm not sure how long I hold her for, but eventually, she calms. I feel her small hand on my chest as she pushes back and looks up into my eyes.

"I've never told anyone that," she whispers. "I've kept it inside all this time. I've never even said the words to myself."

I reach my hand out and stroke the tear that still glistens on her cheek.

Although I want to ask questions, need to really, I don't. I let her lead us through this maze to the truth. I let her set the pace, no matter how hard it is for me to do so.

She shakes for a minute before she sits up straight and squares her shoulders, a way to give herself strength. I take her hand in mine and squeeze, telling her without words I'm here to listen.

"I guess I should start from the beginning," she finally says, and I bob my head in agreement.

"I met Riley two years ago. It was summer, and I had just gotten home from graduate school. I was walking through town, and I bumped right into him. Literally." She closes her eyes and shivers. "Even when I first met him, something was dark about him. But he was so dashing and mysterious, attentive too. I think I fell in love with him the first day. It was a whirlwind romance; we were engaged within a month of meeting each other. The thing was, it happened so quick I didn't see the signs. None of them. He gave me the love and attention I was searching for and it didn't dawn on me to doubt it. We were married within three months. Still with my head in the clouds, I never noticed any of the signs that something was off, even when his family didn't come to the wedding. Even when I never met his friends. Even when I knew nothing about his past. Now . . . I see that all of those were a big red flag, but I spent so much of my life and adolescent years alone after my mother died. I just was hungry for love."

"But your father . . . ?"

"He was never the same after the accident. He drank . . . He always drank, before and after. It wasn't until I got married and told him he couldn't be there until he sobered up that he got clean. That's why his death was such a shock."

"I don't understand. How did your father die?"

"A few months after I married Riley, my father died from alcohol poisoning, but I swear he had stopped drinking. Riley said he was a drunk, and he had no sympathy about it. I should have known then, but still, I was blind. Maybe it was the fact I was now an orphan, or maybe it was denial, but it never made sense. After my father died, I inherited the estate. My parents were old money. A large benefactor in my town, they owned the steel plant for generations that employed everyone."

"What happened, Willow?" I ask when she pauses, and I can see she's clearly shaken.

"I couldn't stop thinking something was wrong with Dad's death. I kept telling Riley I wanted to exhume the body . . . One day, I was supposed to go to a meeting. With the company in my hands, I needed to show my face. Riley had been handling the business, but I wanted to take over. He wasn't happy, not just for my pursuit over my father's death, but also because I wanted to take my place at the helm. He stayed behind, refusing to go with me."

She trembles like a twig blowing in the wind. "Can I have a drink?"

I nod and stand, grabbing a decanter of scotch. She shakes her head. "Dad always drank that."

I place the glass down and head into the kitchen to grab ice, a shaker, and the tequila. She waits on the couch, still shaking like a leaf blowing in the wind. Once I chill the tequila, I hand her a glass.

"I shouldn't drink after everything," she mutters to herself.

"It's just one."

"It's never just one," she says. I don't understand what she is talking about, but I don't ask. She's battling enough demons without me pursuing it. "I actually never left. I had forgotten a file. He didn't know I was home. He didn't know I could hear him."

"What did you hear?" I ask.

"He was in the office on the phone. At first, I didn't know or understand what I was hearing, but then, he said it."

"What did he say?"

"It has to look like an accident, just like with her dad."

If I felt sick before, it was nothing like how I felt now hearing this.

"I was frozen in the hall, afraid he would hear me. Finally, I comprehended that I wasn't wrong, that he had killed my father . . . and that he was going to have me killed."

She buries her head in her hands. I can hear her sniffling, but when she looks up, my heart lodges in my throat. Her eyes are red-rimmed and swollen, but I expected that, what I didn't expect is how hollow they look.

Dead.

"I should have seen it." She pulls at her hair.

"Seen what?" I ask.

"All the signs. There were so many of them, and I didn't see shit. Desperate and pathetic." She's pushed away from me, but I'm not having it, as much as she pushes, I pull. I won't let her go, not like this. She needs me. "After the wedding . . ." She inhales, finding her strength. "He changed. He was no longer attentive. He worked late hours. But I never knew where he worked. That was a red flag I refused to see. His behavior changed too. He was aggressive, it's not that he hurt me, but I was afraid. He would snap. Like after the reading of the will. He screamed and shouted, but it made no sense. I mean they left me everything, why was he so upset? I never understood. Looking back, the months after we married, I walked on eggshells afraid of him, but I pushed it under a rug. I made excuses for him, but in hindsight, the signs were all there . . . I can't imagine what would have happened if I never overheard him."

I let her words sink in, and it makes me feel cold to the bone. I can't imagine a world without Willow.

"How did you get away?"

"Slowly and quietly, I made my way back outside, and I waited. I waited for him to leave, and once he was gone, I crept back into the house. I packed the cash we had under the bed, I took one picture frame of my parents and a change of clothes. My hope was that he wouldn't notice until morning. I don't know what I was thinking, but I got in the car and drove. I drove until I thought I was safe, and then I got on a bus." She takes a deep breath. "Eventually, I got to New York."

"I'm so sorry." It's a lame thing to say, but after what she just told me, I can't think of anything else to say.

"I know." She tries to give me a smile, but it comes out forced.

"So now you're in New York . . ." I lead to make her continue.

"And I don't know what the fuck I'm doing."

"What do you mean?" I ask.

She lifts her hands and buries her fingers in her hair, pulling the roots. "I don't know what to do. I'm crashing at Maggie's, but she doesn't know. You're—" Her chest rises and falls. "You're the first person I've told. I ran from home because my husband, Riley, has friends in high places, not only is he friends with the mayor, but he donates large sums of money to the police and sheriff's department. I don't know who he was working with. Hell, I don't even know why he killed my dad."

Fresh tears fall from her face when she says that. "It just doesn't make sense."

"Over the past few years, I have dealt with many shady characters . . ." I start. "Most of the time, the root of all evil stems from money."

Her eyes widen at this.

"You think he wanted to kill me for the money?"

I nod, and she looks crestfallen. "Was it all fake?" she whispers to herself.

I reach forward and take her hand in mine. "I'm not sure, but money is often a strong motivator. From what I'm understanding, your father had money, and that money passed to you."

She nibbles on her lower lip.

"By killing you, as your husband, it would go to him."

Pulling her hand away from mine, she buries her head in

her now free hands. "He-he . . ." She starts to cry again, and the sound breaks me apart.

I don't want her to feel pain.

"What am I going to do?"

"I'll help you," I say before I can even think about what that means. Because regardless of anything, this is what I do. This is what I'm good at, and unlike everyone I have helped before her, I need to do this, not just for her but for me. I couldn't live with myself if I didn't.

"What?" she asks, dropping her hands from her face.

"I want to help you."

She cries harder. "I don't deserve it. I don't deserve your help. I have lied so much."

"Stop. Not another word. This is what I do. This is what I'm good at, excel at. Let me help you. Let me keep you safe."

She hiccups. "I have something I want to say."

"Okay,"

"When I first found out about what you do, I wanted to ask you for help. I wanted to see if I could trust you, and then I realized . . ."

"What did you realize?"

"I realized who you were. And I didn't know how to ask because I didn't want you to think I didn't see the real you. Here I am, after lying to you, and I just wanted you to know. You are so much more than you let on. I don't deserve this. I don't deserve your help. I don't deserve you."

"I beg to differ. I think you deserve more."

A pregnant pause follows. I swallow and find the words inside me. "I think you deserve everything."

CHAPTER THIRTY-THREE

Willow

I MOVE CLOSER TO HIM UNTIL THERE IS NO SPACE BETWEEN us. His lips are temptation, salt water taffy wrapped in clear wax paper. Full. Sweet. Inviting. Begging to melt on my tongue.

Old Willow would have kissed him, crashed her lips on his as if she owned them.

My head rears back when I realize I can be Old Willow again. Without a word, I wrap my arms around his neck and place my mouth on his. I expect him to kiss me, but instead, I feel his hands touching my shoulders and pushing me back.

"Willow," he says, and I shake my head.

"Don't Willow me."

"I don't think—"

I lift my hand. "See, now that's your problem, Price. Thinking. Don't think."

My hand reaches out, and I place it over his heart. "I want to." I lean closer. We are only a breath away, my lips hovering over his.

"I don't want to take advantage of you." When he speaks, his breath fans my lips. "I don't want to hurt you."

"You could never hurt me, Jax. I feel safe with you."

"But—"

I press my lips to his. "Don't treat me with kid gloves. Don't hold back."

Then I feel it, his tongue sweeping against the seam of my mouth. "Well, in that case . . ." His mouth opens. The kiss is slow at first.

His lips on mine, his mouth parting mine.

Then our tongues move. It's like a slow dance. We circle each other, tease each other. We pour the pent-up emotions from our friendship into the kiss, and then we say all the things we haven't said in all the weeks; we say all the things we both feared to say. But now that the gates are open, we allow our bodies to do the talking and express all the emotions we've hidden inside, all our wants and needs.

I allow myself to become lost in the kiss. I allow it to sweep away all the past and all the hurt I have been living with. As it deepens, I bask in the warmth of his mouth on mine.

As if he knows I need more, he pulls me toward him, wrapping his arms tighter around me until there is no separation between us. I use the move to crawl up onto his lap, straddling his legs. We never break the kiss, not even when he moves his hands below my ass, not when he lifts me in his arms, and not when we stand. He holds me tight, never breaking our connection as he walks us to his bedroom. Then and only then does he set me down.

Sitting on the end of the bed, he looks down at me.

His green eyes are hooded with hunger. They devour me with promises of all the things he wants to do to me. They tell me all his wants, and I'm desperate for him to do just that.

"Are you sure?"

"Yes."

"I want you to—"

"Jax, I need this. Please. Make me forget everything. Make me feel. I have felt nothing but sadness for so long. Make me feel."

His head inclines into a nod, and I know my speech worked. He knows that there is no dissuading me. This is what I want.

I watch from where I'm perched as he undresses. Then when he's standing in only boxers, he removes my clothes.

When I'm fully naked, he lets his gaze pore over me, before he smirks. The longer he looks at me, the more on fire I become, I'm a raging inferno, reading to combust.

"I've been waiting for forever to taste you." Then Jaxson Price drops to his knees in front of me.

My heart flutters and my skin tingles. Butterflies fly in my belly as I wait. It feels like an eternity as I wait, but this moment has been brewing for weeks, and I can't wait any longer. I'm shaking all over until he finally rewards me by lowering his head and answering my secret prayer.

His lips touch my skin as he presses kisses to my knee and up my thigh until he reaches the area where I need him the most. He devours me with a frantic need, as if this is all a dream and he will wake soon. I understand his desperation because I'm desperate too.

He licks, he sucks. Then slowly, he presses a finger inside me. The movement is slow.

It's a delicious torture.

I'm quivering.

Breathless.

Needy for more.

He must feel it because soon, he is quickening his pace, driving inside me once, twice, and then I'm falling over the edge. A long and primal moan that seems to last forever escapes my mouth and goose bumps form against my skin as I come undone.

Lost in the haze of my orgasm, I don't notice him move,

but now he's standing naked before me, and I'm on the bed. I watch through hooded lids as he strokes himself before ripping a condom open and sliding it over his length.

Once it's on, I move back up the bed, and then he's crawling up my body. He frames my face with his hands and kisses me, an earth-shattering kiss that makes the world stand still. Only he and I exist in this universe. As he makes love to my mouth, I part my legs wider, pull him in closer, and then I wrap my legs around him.

"Jax," I moan as I wait for him to press inside me. I need him inside me already.

He pulls back and looks down at me. A damn grin on his face.

"Fuck me already."

He laughs then. "Like this?" he says, teasing my entrance.

Torturing me.

He gently strokes me, but he never breaches, circling so slow, I'm sure I might die.

"Please," I groan, and then as his lips part wider, he answers my pleas, slowly guiding himself deep inside me.

It feels amazing. Like heaven has come down to Earth and engulfed me.

He doesn't move for a beat, allowing me to adjust to his size, and when I finally let out the breath I'm holding, he pulls back out.

He continues this slow and steady pace.

In, out.

Slowly.

Passionately.

The feeling is too much with each press of his body within mine.

It's perfection.

Pure perfection.

An overwhelming feeling of emotions rise to the surface, a feeling of protection, that Jax will take care of me.

He must feel it too because he leans down and mutters against my lips. "I'll keep you safe."

"I know," I answer, and it's as if my complete and utter confidence in him has a primitive effect because he is no longer slow and steady. No. Now his movements pick up.

He thrusts harder and harder.

Over and over again.

He tells me with no words, I'm his. That he owns me with every move of his hips. He tells me he will make sure I'm okay.

I feel the truth in it.

And I believe him.

Our breathing accelerates as we climb to our climaxes.

Once done, he drops his frame down until his mouth is nuzzled into my neck. He peppers my skin with kisses.

Several minutes go by as we come down from our high. Then he rises and removes himself from my body.

I miss his warmth instantly as he moves from the bed and into the bathroom.

"I'll be right back. Stay here," he orders playfully.

"Where else would I go?" I laugh, and he smiles and walks away. A few seconds later, he's cleaning us off before helping me up from the bed. I excuse myself to use the bathroom.

When I'm back, I find a robe on the bed, but Jax is nowhere to be seen. I slip it on and pad my way into the living room.

I find him in the kitchen with no shirt on and low-slung sweats.

Jeez.

If I thought he was gorgeous before, seeing him again in sweats should be illegal. Or at least come with a warning label.

"Keep staring at me like that, and we will never eat."

"Eat?"

"Yes, Willow. Eat. Remember the picnic I promised?"

The picnic that started this chain of events, and as emotionally draining as it's been, I don't regret any of it.

"Let's have a picnic. I'm starved."

"Good, because I have way too much food." He leans into the fridge and pulls out a tray. I follow him as he walks us into the living room and then sets up the picnic.

I'm still shocked he's done this for me.

It's impressive.

Set up in the middle of the blanket are mini sandwiches, scones, cookies, and more treats, including chocolate-covered strawberries and Kit Kats, that makes me laugh.

Next, he grabs two wine glasses. I have never seen Jax drink anything but tequila, so watching him grab a bottle and pour us each a glass makes me feel warm inside.

I take a seat, and he hands me the glass. We each lift our glass, clinking them together.

"What are we toasting?" I ask.

"I don't know."

"Life?" I ask, and he nods.

"That works. To life."

I lift the glass to my mouth and take a sip. I'm not much of a drinker, but after today, I welcome the feeling of warmth that pools in my belly.

We both take a sip, and then I place my drink down.

"So tell me about these sandwiches?"

"What's there to tell? They are turkey and cheese."

I burst out laughing at his description. "Wow, you should write food reviews. You're very eloquent."

"I am, aren't I?"

I reach forward and grab one of the "turkey sandwiches" and take a bite.

"Well, crappy description and all, it's delicious. Did you make it yourself?"

"Yes. I placed the turkey on bread and added mayo. It was super hard."

"You have skills," I retort.

"That I do."

Cue the smirk.

"So," he starts and then stops. "Are we going to talk about the big elephant in the room?"

"The turkey sandwiches?"

"Nope."

"The fact we had sex?"

"No. Not that either."

"Oh, the fact that my deranged husband is trying to kill me?"

"Ding. Ding. Ding. That's the one."

I place my sandwich down and cock my head. "Do we have to?"

"I kind of think we have to. As I'm sure you know, I have a certain skill set, but to use it, I need to know everything."

I told him everything I knew, which, unfortunately, wasn't very much. The only thing I had to offer was my first and last name, the company's name, my husband's name, and the fact that I was from Madison Bay, Michigan. All the other details that probably would have helped were stored on my computer back home. Which, like an idiot, I left behind that fateful night.

We stayed up late even though I didn't have that much to tell, and eventually, after I'd told him all I knew, he took me home, leaving me with a soft kiss and a promise that he would call me today.

This morning, the early sunlight gleams in, making my eyes open. Although I'm tired, I feel more relaxed today than I have in a long time.

It feels like a large weight has been lifted from my shoulders. I know I have a long way to go before I feel safe, but knowing I have someone to discuss it with is comforting.

I didn't realize how hard and lonely and isolating it's been this whole time. I stretch my arms out and then stand and head to the bathroom. It's Sunday, and I'm sure Maggie is still sleeping. Tiptoeing into the bathroom, I wash my face and brush my teeth. I try to be quiet, but when I step back into the living room, I'm met with Maggie.

She's giving me a sly smile. "So . . ." she starts with a large grin on her face. "Where were you last night?"

I open my mouth to tell her, but then I shut it. I'm not sure what to say. I want to tell her the truth, but a part of me thinks I shouldn't mention it yet because she will be in danger if she knows.

Instead, I tell her enough not to send any red flags up without completely lying.

"I—" My cheeks feel warm, and I'm for sure blushing at this point.

"Oh, my God. You have to tell me!" she exclaims. "You don't even have to say anything for me to know you got some."

"Jeez, Maggie."

"Tell me."

"Fine." I laugh. "Fine. I was with Jax."

"Jaxson Price?"

"The one and only."

"Did you . . . ?" She trails off.

"Yes." And with that, Maggie jumps up and down like a lunatic.

A big, giant, excited lunatic who is having a party because her friend got laid.

"You're super strange." I giggle.

"I am. But you got some, and this is cause for a celebration."

I walk closer to where she is and cock my head to the side. "How do you figure?"

"I was starting to worry about you." Her voice sounds serious now as she nibbles her lower lip. "I didn't . . . I know you have things you haven't wanted to tell me, and I would never pry, but I'm happy to see you happy."

"Thank you."

"Come on, enough of this sappy shit. I'm hungry and want breakfast. Let's grab some food."

"Sounds good."

Maggie stands from the chair and heads into her bedroom. It doesn't take her long to reappear, but this time, she's wearing sweats and sneakers and ready to go get food.

Fifteen minutes later, we're sitting across the table from one another with two gigantic stacks of pancakes in front of us. We eat as if we don't have a care in the world, and even though we do, I still feel more at peace than I have in days. So much so, that I have none of my disguises on.

As I'm telling some PG stories of last night, the picnic, etcetera, we continue to eat.

I'm not sure what we are doing for the rest of the day, but as I'm about to ask her if she wants to go window shopping with me, my phone vibrates on the table.

Jaxson is calling.

My heart races. He's calling.

"Hello," I answer.

"Hey, Willow." Even though I have spoken to him numerous times and seen him naked once, I'm still not sure I will ever tire of hearing Jaxson Price say my name. "What are you doing today?"

"I have nothing planned," I answer, and Maggie's eyebrows rise.

"Come over. I'd like to start looking into a few angles, and I need your help."

"Okay, I'll see you soon."

When I hang up, Maggie's eyes are wide. "Was that him?"

"It was."

"And are you going to hang with him?" she asks.

"I am."

"Good." She takes another bite before placing her fork down. "Let's get the bill so you can go."

I nod and signal for the waitress to come over.

Ready to start my day and see what Jaxson has to say.

I'm still scared, but I can't hide forever.

The faster I find something on my husband, the faster I can get my life back.

I'm ready.

I show up at Jaxson's Tribeca apartment a few hours later after I freshen up and shower. He's waiting for me with a smile on his face. I, on the other hand, am blushing from head to toe, I'm sure. Because although we are supposed to be getting down to business and figuring out what to do with my estranged and very deranged husband, I'm having a hard time concentrating on anything other than Jaxson Price and all the things he did to me yesterday.

My body feels warm, my face on fire. It's funny how only a week ago, the last thing on my mind was sex, and now, since the flame has been ignited, it seems to be the only thing I can think about.

Jax must know because when that damn dimple forms on his cheek, I'm positive I will combust right there in the doorway to his apartment.

His gaze roams my body, and then he swings the door open for me to pass. A part of me wonders what we are now. Was last night a one-time thing? Emotions running high and whatnot. Will we discuss what happened or pretend it didn't? Or will we pursue a relationship? Seeing as I'm still married, in hiding, and trying to figure out my life, that option isn't ideal, but I want to kiss him again.

Even if it complicates things.

My inner turmoil is cut short when he takes me in his arms and brings his mouth to mine.

I'm caught completely off guard at first, but soon, I'm wrapping my arms around him and kissing him back.

We stay entwined for a minute, then he pushes back, looking down at me with a look I can't decipher.

Regret, maybe.

"I shouldn't have done that," he says, and I swear I feel deflated. He must notice my reaction because he holds his hand up. "Not for the reason you think. I want to kiss you. Fuck, I have thought of nothing but being with you again since last night, but first, I want to talk to you and come up with a game plan." He leans in and places a soft kiss to my lips. "Okay?"

"Okay," I mumble, our mouths still touching.

He pulls back and takes my hand in his and leads me to the couch.

Last night, this place was decorated like a park. Today, it's all business.

There is a computer sitting on the coffee table. He leads me to sit and then hands me the computer.

"What's this?"

"It's a computer," he deadpans.

"Yes, I'm not an idiot. I know it's a computer, but why are you giving this to me?"

"Last night, you said you didn't have one."

"You're giving me a computer?" I shake my head. "I can't take this."

"But can you borrow it?" He lifts his brow, and I know there is no arguing with him.

"Yes, but how is this any different from me not having one? I can't use it to find anything. That's the reason I haven't even bothered to try."

"You can. I need to show you how to reroute and hide your IP address. This computer is already fitted to do this, so once I show you, you can use it." I look at him with curiosity, not understanding what he wants me to do. "Listen, I don't want you doing any of the digging. I'll do that. But maybe you'll see something I won't. We can monitor some of your old friends and associates who worked for you. I've set up a dummy profile already. I also made the profile an employee in your company, so we have access to files, social media, and interoffice chats. There might be things you can see that I won't understand, but I don't want you searching when you're not with me." He pauses. "Just in case."

"Just in case of what?"

"In case you are being tracked. We have to be careful. But that doesn't mean you can't use this when I'm not around. Just don't sign onto the company server."

"Okay." I grab the computer and place it on my lap. "Can I use it to read gossip?"

"Seriously?" He looks shocked.

"No, not seriously. Don't you know me at all?"

"Actually, not really." His words stun me because it's true. He knows nothing about me, other than the bits and pieces I've told him these last few months, and he's still doing this for me. I know this was the goal when I first started to spend time with him, but it feels hollow now. It makes me feel like a selfish piece of shit. "But I know the important stuff. I know what makes you smile. I know that you love Kit Kats and grilled cheese sandwiches, even though you'll never admit it." His words should make me feel better, but they don't.

"Why are you doing this for me?"

"Because I can."

"That's not enough. I'm putting your life in danger, and you don't even know me. I was using you. I see that now. I was doing something selfish, and you were selfless."

"I'm used to people using me."

"I don't want to be that person. I can't let you help me."

Jax takes the computer from my lap and puts it on the table.

"Here's the thing . . . the fact you admit that means you're special. I choose this because I care about you, and I want to help. The fact you trust me and don't want me hurt shows you are worth the risk."

"I—"

"No, Willow. All my life, people have not taken me seriously, but you were never like that. Not since the moment you met me. Stop trying to convince me otherwise. You have always seen me."

"I do see you." I move closer and place my lips on his.

"I see you too." Kiss. "Now, no more objections." Kiss.

"Okay, but one thing . . ."

"Yes?"

"What are we doing? I know I'm not in the right place for a relationship . . . I don't want to lead you on."

"You aren't. Why define what we're doing? We're taking comfort in each other. For however long we need to. Let's not put titles or labels on it, okay?"

"Okay, but does that mean we can do it again?" I smirk.

"Yes."

"As much as I want?"

"Hell yes."

And then I lean up again and press my mouth to his. "Like now?"

"Fine."

And against his mouth, I laugh.

CHAPTER THIRTY-FOUR

Jaxson

I WAS FULL OF SHIT.

As much as I said I was done . . . here I am, yet again.

There is nothing worse than a Monday too. If hell was a day of the week, this is the day it would be. Still stuck in the weekend haze, the last thing I want to do is this damn report that is front and center on my desk. No. I would much prefer a naked Willow on my desk.

See. Now that would make Monday a damn good day of the week.

My fingers tap as I search through countless files on a potential buyer for our property in Moscow. Grayson had emailed me earlier this morning to do some intel on the Russian billionaire who wanted to buy an abandoned warehouse we have in the city. But as per usual, we are picky with who we sell to. So I'm looking into all known associates.

I'm typing when my cell phone vibrates on my desk. I halt my movements and check the screen.

Willow.

Seeing her name has a smile spreading across my face. I take my hand off the keyboard to answer and give Willow my full attention.

I'm about to say hello, I hear her scream in the background.

Instantly, I'm on high alert, my blood pounding in my ears as I think of the reasons she could be screaming.

"Are you okay?" I ask as I close my computer and stand from my desk.

She doesn't answer right away, but I hear a scuffle and then the sound of a plate dropping.

I'm not sure what's going on, but I think she dropped her phone. I'm out the door to my office and in the elevator before she can call me back. Thankfully, I don't get stuck in traffic as I make the trip downtown to her apartment building.

I try to call her a few more times, but it goes straight to voicemail. The worst scenarios play out in my head. Has her husband found her? Is she hurt? When the cab stops in front of the building, I throw him fifty dollars, well above what the fare is, and holler over my shoulder to keep the change. Then I'm running down the street into the building. Luckily for me, there's no security, and I'm banging on Maggie's apartment door within a minute. The door flies open and there stands a disheveled and upset Willow.

"What's going on?" I ask, pushing past her and walking into her apartment to make sure she is okay.

"Mouse," she croaks out.

"There is a mouse in your apartment?"

"Mice."

"There are mice in your apartment?" I shake my head, not understanding. That's why she freaked out, why she was screaming? A mouse?

"You don't understand."

Tears form in her eyes, and she takes my hand in hers, pulling me with her to the living room.

There on the floor in front of a pullout couch are two dead mice.

I can only imagine that when she went to step off the bed, she found them. I also now see why she didn't answer my phone calls. She must have dropped her phone when she saw them, because there lying next to the bodies is a shattered disposable cell phone.

She is shaking now and pointing down. "Do you think . . . ?"

"Do I think what?"

"I have always been scared of mice." She hiccups. "Do you think he found me?" she whispers.

And now the realization hits for why she is freaking out. She thinks this was a message. She thinks her husband found her. That he left this as proof that she is no longer safe.

I pull her toward me and lead her toward the exit.

"I'm not sure, but I'm not taking any chances. Let's go."

"But Maggie?"

"Where is she?" I ask.

"I'm not sure." She shakes.

"Come with me, and we'll call her from my phone."

"Okay," she whispers, her voice weak.

"We'll get to the bottom of this."

"Promise?"

"I do." With Willow in tow, I pull her back out of the apartment, and then we leave the building. Once on the street, I hail a cab and rattle off the address of my office.

I still have work to do, so I guess Willow will have to come with me.

After seeing the setup, I have no intention of letting her sleep on the couch again, but I don't tell her that as I lead her to my office once we arrive. Instead, I hold her close to me and take her up the elevator and into my office, then gesture for her to sit on the couch. I'm standing and about to walk to my desk when the door to my office swings open yet again, and I'm face-to-face with my brother.

"Another impromptu visit," I say.

"Yes, unfortunately, since you refused to come into work in a timely manner, Nicole called me." He grunts.

"I was here."

"Funny. When I showed up to the office, you weren't, and here you are now, with what, your—Who are you?" he says to Willow, and then he turns to me. "And what is she doing here?"

"First things first," I start to say, but Willow is standing up already, walking toward Grayson.

Gone is the scared woman from the apartment and in her place is a strong and assertive woman who isn't afraid of anything or anybody.

"Do not talk to your brother that way," she says fiercely. I look from her to Grayson and see that his eyes are wide in shock.

"And who are you?" he asks.

"It doesn't matter who I am. All that matters is you come into your brother's office and disrespect him."

"Not that I have to defend myself to you since this is none of your business."

"It is my business when I was the reason he wasn't here." That makes Grayson look at me. I'm about to speak when Willow starts up again.

"You know who I am? I'm the girl who needed your brother, and he ran to help me. If you have anyone to blame, it's me. Not him." She points at me. "Your brother deserves your respect. He is a good man. Honestly, the best man I have ever met. He's the man who will help anyone, not because he wants them to pay him back, but out of the kindness of his heart. He is the man who would help a stranger. And for what reason? Because he doesn't want to see anyone get hurt. That's the man he is. But the better question is not what type of man he is, but what type of man you are. And the only answer I can come up with is blind because only a blind man wouldn't see who he is."

I swear my mouth hangs open at her tirade, and from the look on my brother's face, so does his. He looks shell-shocked by her. I know I am.

Without another word or objection, my brother turns on his heel and leaves, but not before I see something on his face that sure appears to look like a smirk.

Once he's out the door, I turn to her.

"You are incredible."

"No, I'm not. I'm speaking the truth. It's a shame he doesn't know that."

I look at this woman. This woman lost everything, and here she is, defending me. Not even my own family will do that. Willow has no idea why my brother was mad, but it didn't matter to her. I was worth speaking up for.

"You didn't have to. What Grayson thinks doesn't matter."

"What does matter?"

"You. What you think. What I think."

"And do you see yourself the way I see you? Because I don't think you do, and you should."

"I'm starting to."

She walks back to the couch and grabs her jacket.

"Where are you going?"

"Well, you have work, and well, I have—"

"Yes?"

"Well, nothing, but I don't want to be in your hair. I've already wasted too much of your time."

"It wasn't a waste because I got to see you. Now take a seat and let me find out what was going on with the mice."

She shivers at my words, remembering how she came to be here.

"Okay," she says as she sits, and I look into the problem.

The search takes me five minutes. Maybe even less.

I close my laptop, and the sound makes her look up. "You found something already?"

"It turns out, they were bombing for rodents. You must have missed the memo, or they didn't post it. The mice must have made it into your apartment before they died."

She leans forward and buries her head in her hands.

"What's wrong?" I ask, standing and crossing the room to sit beside her.

"I feel so stupid," she groans. "You missed work and got in trouble, all because I was too dumb to know this."

"First off, stop. You didn't ask me to come. Secondly, enough. I am one hundred percent sure they didn't inform you. I'm going to dig a little deeper and see. Legally, they should have, so if that's the case—"

"Stop. I don't want to cause a problem for Maggie. She's done so much for me already and so have you."

"I can only speak for myself, but I want to. Also, I'm happy you called, and I'm happy I came. You know why?"

"No."

"'Cause now I can take you to lunch." I smile.

"Always about food with you."

"It really is. Come on, I want to take you for dim sum."

"A man after my own heart. I love dim sum."

I stand and then pull her up to follow me. I don't bother saying goodbye to the staff or Grayson. I lead her straight to the ground level and into a cab.

I have no intention of coming back today.

If Grayson is in the office, he can man the fort. Also, the job he had for me can be done from anywhere. I don't need to be here.

No. I would much rather feed my girl.

My girl?

She isn't my girl.

But as crazy as it sounds, I realize that I want her to be after what she did for me.

I want her by my side. Protected. And not just as a friend.

But more.

Now I need to convince her.

CHAPTER THIRTY-FIVE

Willow

I'M NOT SURE WHAT CAME OVER ME. ONE MOMENT, I WAS A shaking mess on the couch, and the next, I was standing up to Jaxson's brother and defending him. Every word I spoke was the truth.

Jaxson Price is the best person I know.

Hearing his brother lay into him had me going red with fury. I should have kept my mouth shut.

Seeing as I'm technically in hiding, it's probably not smart to put myself on Grayson Price's radar. I don't need anyone searching for me.

It takes me thirty minutes to cool down from my earlier sparring match. Listening to Jaxson order dim sum has helped to calm my nerves. It's an experience, that's for sure.

For a man so fit, he sure does eat.

No joke, the man ordered one of every single dish on the menu. There was not one dish left behind.

Different combinations of dumplings, bread, and something called Har Gow. Or as he so pointedly pronounced it, Ha Gow, like ow with a *g*.

Show-off.

It's like he thought we were bears going into hibernation.

I shake my head at him the moment the waitress leaves us.

"What?" He shrugs.

"Think you ordered enough?"

"Well, now that you mention it, we might need one more pork bun. I don't really feel like splitting my food with you."

"You cannot be serious."

"Dead."

"Well, it's a good thing I like you, Mr. Price."

He smiles. "What?"

"I never liked being called Mr. Price, but when you say it . . ."

I shake my head on a laugh. I'm about to tell him he's impossible, the waitress comes over with the first wicker basket of food.

Chopsticks in hand, I take the first bite.

An explosion in my mouth.

"Oh my God," I say, covering my mouth with one hand as I chew. I swallow and look up at him. "If I keep eating with you, I'm going to blow up."

"As long as I'm with you, it sounds like a good way to go."

As we continue to eat, the table goes silent. Dish after dish, we make small talk but nothing big. It's as if we know that once this meal is done, we have to talk . . . and not just talk about nothing. We need to discuss my husband.

When the check is paid, we both stand and I turn to him.

"Should I go home?" I ask, a bit uncomfortable.

"No," he responds. "I want to show you something."

"Okay." My voice is lower than normal, but I feel like the past few days have been such a clusterfuck. I'm not sure where we stand.

Are we friends? Are we more? Is he still helping me?

I'm not sure.

Together we head to the street, and I expect him to hail a cab and take me back to his office. We're downtown by Canal Street, but we walk instead. Maybe we're going back to his place.

"We'll grab a cab a few blocks up. I want to walk for a bit."

"Sure. No problem."

It's clear he's working through something in his brain and I give him the space to do it.

When we make it to Church Street, we flag down a cab. He fires off an address that I have never heard of before, and before I know it, we are weaving in and out of small streets by the river.

Eventually, we stop, but it looks like we are parked outside a warehouse. And an abandoned one at that.

For a second, I think Jaxson gave the cab driver the wrong location, but he pays him with cash, and we get out.

From there, we walk up two more blocks, and I wonder why we didn't get out closer to wherever our destination is.

Every few steps, I glance over at him. His hands are tucked into his jacket pockets, and it looks as if he's fiddling with something in it.

"Is everything okay?" I ask.

He doesn't answer, just continues to walk. Right here on this street, the world seems like a post-apocalyptic world where everyone is dead. It makes no sense why we are here and where here is.

He stops in front of a beat-up old brick building. There appears to be windows, but they are frosted with dirt, and I can't see in at all.

"What are we doing here?" I ask.

He steps up in front of the door. Then he reaches his hand out to the padlock on it.

That's when I finally see what's in his hand. Tucked away is a key on a chain.

He hands it to me, and I look down at it.

"What is this place?"

"There is a lot you don't know about me, but I'm hoping that will change. I want to start now. I've never shown this place to anyone . . . but I want to show it to you."

I'm holding the key in my hand, and he signals for me to use it.

"I want you to know you always have a safe place to go." He begs me with his eyes to trust him, so I do. I reach up and place the key in the lock and open the bolt.

"The next lock can be opened with a key or a code."

"What is the code?"

"The code is Soter, but I set up Soteria for you to use."

"What does that mean?"

"In Greek mythology, Soter is the spirit of safety, preservation, and deliverance from harm. Seeing as this is my haven, that is my passcode. That's why I've given you Soteria. Because this is your sanctuary too. If you need it. For me, it's where I am free," he says.

"And she is?" I ask.

"The goddess of safety and salvation. She's also the symbol of victory. There's actually a sanctuary made in her honor, which is one reason I chose the name for you."

"Really? Where is it?"

"Patras, a town in western Greece. It's actually an interesting story. No one was supposed to see her image, only the priests, but the part that I think you'd like is that they used to perform a ritual for her."

"And that ritual was . . ."

He turns his head toward me, and there is a large grin on it.

"They would take cakes from the district and throw them into the sea for her."

"Really? That's a huge waste of cake." I laugh.

He chuckles too. "Yep. I know. The story seemed fitting, but in your case, they would throw Kit Kats."

Still laughing, we step inside. The lights flicker on, and the room comes into focus. The large space is nothing like the decrepit outside of the building.

State-of-the-art TVs, cutting-edge computers, and contemporary furniture don the room.

In one section, there has to be a minimum of eight computer monitors.

"Are you Batman?" I say on a nervous chuckle because there isn't anything else to say.

It reminds me of the Batcave.

"Something like that." He leads me closer. "This is where I'll find your husband. This is where I'll get you your freedom. This is how I save you," he says as he sits down and powers up the computers.

The setup belongs in the Pentagon, but something tells me Jaxson could probably hack into the Pentagon.

"I can." He laughs. "And I have."

"Did I say that out loud?"

"You did. I don't blame you; it can be overwhelming."

"This is fantastic."

"It has its perks, and it has its faults. Many people use me for what I can do."

"I'm sorry."

"I'm not talking about you. I'm talking about all the times I've helped people I don't even know for reasons I don't even want to know. For you, I do this willingly."

I move to sit on his lap, and once perched, I kiss him on the lips. "Thank you."

"So where should we start?" he asks.

"Now?"

"No better time than the present." His fingers rest on the keyboard. "I'm going to start with the obvious, but often, that's the biggest dead end. What is your husband's full name?"

"Riley Smith."

He looks at me when I tell him the generic last name, and I roll my eyes.

He types furiously. Things pop up on the screen. He's in the DMV. He's hacking the fucking DMV.

My heart races as his fingers continue to move, but when they stop, my heart really thumps in my chest.

"That's not his name."

A wave of feelings run through me. Anger, fear, confusion.

"I don't understand."

"His name is not Riley Smith. Well, it could be, if he was an eighty-year-old dead man. But there is no Riley Smith who fits your husband's description."

It feels like I'm lost at sea, holding on for dear life.

Everything was a lie.

Not just my marriage, but even his name.

Was nothing true?

CHAPTER THIRTY-SIX

Jaxson

WE'VE SPENT THE PAST WEEK CAMPED OUT IN MY warehouse. The holidays have come and gone, but this year, I don't head uptown to be with my family, I spend it Willow.

It's now a new year, and that means I have to go back to work. My heart isn't there. Not at all. I would rather be helping Willow.

Unfortunately, since she's not my only priority, I've had to go into the office today. When I step off the elevator, I stop dead in my tracks. Everyone is here. Worse, they are all in the conference room. Since the conference room is all glass, they see me right away. Addison is here, which I didn't expect at all. I was sure they would be getting ready for the baby in London.

With quick steps, I make my way in. Swinging the door open and interrupting what appears to be a meeting that is in full swing.

"Nice of you to join us," Grayson says as pleasant as ever.

"I didn't know there was a meeting today." Taking two steps, I pull out the nearest chair and sit down.

My sister is beside me, and when I look over at her, she's smiling at me.

Here she is, married and happy, and Grayson is about to get married and still grumpy as can be.

"I'm back," Grayson announces.

"So am I," Addison says.

"I thought—" I look back and forth at both of them, not sure who to address first. So I pick Addison. "I thought you were going to have the baby in England."

"Logistically, it didn't work out."

I cock my head to the side for her to continue.

"Apparently, there is a good chance I'll need a C-section, and where the estate is, well, the nearest hospital is too far away, and Oliver . . ."

"Is being his normal neurotic self."

"Yes, basically. He wants doctors on call. Which left having the baby in London or here. And since everyone is here . . ."

"New York won."

"That's the gist of it." She nods.

"Well, I can't say that doesn't make me happy." It does. As much as my siblings have been a pain to me over the past years, Addison has come full circle. I'm happy I'll be able to be there for the birth of my niece or nephew.

With that settled, I turn to Grayson. "And you?" He shrugs, but I already know the answer. "You don't trust me."

"It's not that . . ."

"It is that." I take a deep breath and try to calm the emotions raging inside me. All these months when I worked my ass off to do my job on top of both their jobs, and it still wasn't enough. I tap my foot on the floor and mentally count to ten. When I hit nine, I stand. "If there isn't anything more to discuss . . ."

"Jax, it's not like that."

"It's fine. Listen, if I don't have to do your job anymore . . . I'm going to work from my satellite office. My equipment is better there for the jobs you make me do." Sucker punch. That's what it feels like, but I keep it down, not allowing anyone to see how badly I hurt.

"I understand."

"On that note." I start to walk to the door. "Text me if you need anything."

"When will you be back?"

"Not sure."

"We're having a dinner, a baby shower of sorts," Grayson mumbles. "River is throwing it." He shrugs.

"I'll send you the details," Addison chimes in and I nod before I'm out the door.

Thirty minutes later, I'm typing in the passcode and entering the warehouse. I find Willow where I left her. She's on her laptop, compiling a list of all that she remembers from her husband.

Since her husband's name was a lie, and she, unfortunately, has no pictures of him, the only thing we can count on is that maybe he told her some truth from his past that we can use to track him.

As of this morning, the answer was nothing. I'm not sure how that is possible, or maybe Willow just hasn't remembered yet.

She must hear the door because she peeks over her shoulder as I approach.

"Well, that wasn't a long day at the office."

"Nope. Not at all."

"Are you okay?"

"Fit as a fiddle," I respond, and she quirks a brow, obviously not buying what I'm selling.

"Families can suck." I lift my shoulders, but the minute it comes out of my mouth, I realize what I've said. "I'm sorry, that was insensitive."

"It's fine. At least I had my dad until recently. I wasn't completely an orphan." When she says orphan, her mouth opens wide.

"What?"

"Riley," she whispers.

"What about him?"

"I remembered something he once said in passing. Remember how I told you I never met his family? I remember he once mentioned a home. Living in a home. But the way he made it sound, I thought he was talking about a house, you know. But now . . . thinking back, what if he was talking about a group home? That would make sense since I never met his family, right?"

"It certainly is a place to start."

"Do you think we might find something?"

"We could. You never know. I'll get some parameters from you and start looking." I pause. "Willow?"

"Yes?"

"There is a good chance it might not pull anything up, though. If he lied about his name, who knows what else he lied about. He might not be as old as he says or from where he said he's from."

"I know."

"Okay, then I'll start looking." I move to my computer and turn on all the monitors to prepare my search. "I wish you had a picture of him. It would make life easier." I laugh.

"How so?"

"I have killer face recognition technology."

"Are you serious?"

"Yes." I shrug.

"Could you find me?" Her voice drops and she bites her lower lip.

"I'm sure he doesn't have what I have and can't. But yes. Because you came into my building, so if I wanted to, I could have searched."

"Show me."

"Okay."

I pull up the screen from my building to the lobby. Then scroll until I find the date and time. I remember that day with the cupcakes, so it's easy to find.

There on the screen looking right at the hidden camera is Willow.

I type, isolating the image, and then feed it to my software. Within a minute, red lines are tracing her features, scrolling through all the databases.

"Is it safe to do this?" she asks.

"Perfectly safe. Remember how I taught you to reroute your IP to a remote address if you ever used the computer I got you, when you're not here?"

She nods.

"You're fine because I have firewalls in place. If, for some reason, your husband was searching for you and hits on your name, he would track this IP address to an island in the South Pacific. I have it rerouted so many times, he'd be chasing his own tail."

Just as I'm going to explain more, her image pulls up on the computer.

She lets out a deep, audible exhale.

Willomena Craft.

"But . . . my hair. I was wearing a hat. . ." She lifts her hands to her eyes. "I didn't wear my glasses that day," she whispers to herself. "Did you ever look for me? If it was that easy . . ."

I know what she's trying to say, but I shake my head.

"As I told you before, I didn't want to learn your secrets that way."

"And how did you want to learn them?" she whispers.

"I wanted you to trust me."

She stands from her chair and crawls into my lap.

"Thank you."

"For what?"

"For allowing me to trust you. For proving to me there are good people in the world. Because that's what you are, Jax. You're a good person. No matter what anyone else thinks, know that's how I feel."

Then as the computer continues to pull up information on her, she kisses me. She shows me who she really is.

The woman I'm falling for.

The woman I think I've already fallen for.

CHAPTER THIRTY-SEVEN

Willow

THE DAY TURNED INTO A WEEK, AND I'VE SPENT EVERY minute with Jaxson. You would think I would get sick of him or bored at least. Hell, even with my husband, and even though he was lying to be the perfect husband prior to my father's death, I still needed space from him. But with Jaxson, I don't.

It's odd.

Even after spending all day in his workspace, when it's time to go home, I opt to stay with him.

It's not just because with him I have the most comfortable bed in the world—although that is a bonus—but I also like to spend time with him and get to know him.

We snuggle on his couch, watching an action blockbuster that had record-breaking sales when it released. I never saw it then, though, because my life was a shitshow when it came out.

But now, here I sit with Jaxson in front of his ridiculous TV and I couldn't be happier.

Yes, I'm still scared of what the future will bring, but for the first time in months, I feel safe. It could be the amazing security system this man has in place, or that I feel confident Jax will find exactly what we need to prove Riley killed my dad and wants to kill me.

The why is still the question. I want to know what I did to

him to earn his disdain. However, a part of me knows I might never find out the reason.

It could be as simple as the fact he wanted my money.

Jax isn't concerned about why, he only cares to keep me safe. I have never seen anyone work so hard, and it's driving him crazy that we've found nothing.

As the movie blares and I feel him wrapped around me, I let out a sigh of contentment.

"You're tired," he says from behind me.

"A bit."

"Want to go to bed?" His voice drops low, and I know he's not asking if I want to go to bed at all.

Which is fine by me.

Because if snuggling is amazing, there is only one thing I like even more.

And that is the wicked things Jaxson Price can do to my body.

Before I know what's happening, I'm undressed and his arms are pulling me into his embrace, tightening around my body, and then his mouth crashes down on mine.

We kiss hungrily.

Desperately.

As if we will never get enough of each other, and I don't think I will. I don't know if I will ever have enough of Jaxson Price.

He chases the demons away.

He makes me feel safe.

My very own Soter.

"I need you," he groans out against my mouth. The sound of his voice is enough to have me deepening the kiss.

"I'm yours."

His lips leave mine, and I hear him tearing open a condom wrapper. Then with no other warning, he's pushing inside me.

The movement is slow. Exquisite torture.

Inch by inch until he is fully seated inside me. Once he is, he lifts onto his elbows and looks down at me.

So many unspoken words are behind his gaze.

This isn't just sex.

This is so much more.

The look in his eyes, the one that tells me he's mine and that I'm his, should scare me.

But it doesn't.

Because I know *who* Jaxson is.

And I trust him with my heart.

The next morning, I wake to Jax peppering kisses to my stomach. If this is my alarm clock with him, I might never go home.

However, I have to at some point. I know I can't stay here forever.

After a few more pecks of his lips, I groan.

"What's wrong?" Jaxson speaks against my skin.

"I have to leave."

"Leave and go where?" He props up on his elbow. His eyes laced with sleep.

"To Maggie's."

"Why?"

"Because my stuff is there. Because I live there."

His head inclines to the side. "You don't live there."

"Fine. I stay there."

"You can stay here instead."

"I'm not moving in with you."

"I never said move in . . . just stay for the unforeseeable future." He laughs.

My stomach tightens. As much as I know Jax won't hurt me, the last man I moved in with did.

He must see my body tense up because he lifts his hand and touches my face.

"I'm joking, Willow. You can breathe. I'm not saying you're moving in, but you can stay here for now."

"I can't, Jax."

"I would feel better if you did. The security at Maggie's is nonexistent."

I roll my eyes at him. "Not everyone can live in Fort Knox."

"This is true, but until we have the intel we need to bring your husband down, I would feel better if you stayed with me."

"Maybe. But tonight, I'm going out with Maggie, so I'm staying there."

He lets out a huff. "Fine." He replaces his playful expression with a serious one.

"Relax. I'll be back, and everything will be okay."

"Fine. But before you leave, you're having breakfast with me."

"Depends on what you're serving." I raise an eyebrow seductively.

His lips spread into a grin. "Well, that wasn't on the original menu, but I'm happy to make substitutions."

With that, he presses me against the bed, and the blanket slips off me, leaving me bare to him.

I part my legs at him in offering because who am I to refuse? My eyelids flutter closed at the first swipe of his tongue, my hands gripping the sheets at his second, and by the sixth,

I'm writhing in pleasure, screaming his name, and vowing never to leave.

Despite my cries of passion earlier today, I have to leave. My new computer is with me, and I'm trying to figure out what the passcode could be to the server in my old house. I'm not messing around with the site myself. Instead, I'm looking over my old social media account for clues. I don't even sign in as me.

I did that the other day from Jaxson's warehouse. He could hack in and make it appear that it was someone from Russia. Even if Riley—or whatever his name is—is looking, he couldn't trace it back to me.

So now, instead of going in my account, I'm in the dummy account that Jax added to my friends' list. That way, I can look through my pictures.

Unfortunately for me, there are none of Riley.

Looking back, I realize it was odd he didn't take any pictures. He'd told me he doesn't do pictures and was adamant against posting on social media. Even on our wedding day, we only took a few pictures, but I left them in the house. I thought he was camera shy.

But now, I see it for what it was, a plan, a plot to steal my money. I'm looking through Willomena Craft's pictures, and a wave of nostalgia weaves its way through me.

I miss my family.

I miss my life.

I miss my friends.

Before I know what I'm doing, I'm switching off and opening the photo site I used as a kid.

It's an older site that no one uses now, and Riley would never think to look at it, so what harm could it do?

I tell myself it's no big deal, especially since I'm at Starbucks, just in case, so it's fine.

When I find the album I'm looking for, I spend the next twenty minutes remembering the good times. I look through the pictures before the accident. Before my life changed for the first time.

I stare at my mom, then my dad. Then I click on the pictures of me and Maggie. We were so young, probably twelve years old. It's the picture of the day she made me memorize her number. I had my dad drive me to her house. We cried and cried, and then she sat there in front of me and made me memorize her number. Saying it over and over again. Promising we would never lose touch . . .

We stayed in contact for a while through middle school, but once we started high school, the distance grew.

We were once speaking every day, then it was once a month, then less. By the time I graduated from high school, it wasn't even once a year. By the time I met Riley, it had been years.

That was why she was safe. He never knew about her, and I knew I could always count on her. Tears well in my eyes, and I close my computer. I don't want to cry at Starbucks.

Plus, after seeing this picture, I know what I need to do. I need to tell Maggie everything.

Today.

After I pack up my computer, I set off for her apartment.

It's empty when I get there.

I'm on the couch when she finally walks in. She must know right off the bat that something is wrong. Maybe it's the way I'm sitting. Or maybe it's the tears streaking down my face.

With a worried lip, she steps toward where I am and then sits on the couch next to me.

"I need to talk to you," I say.

"Okay." Her voice is low, and I know she's worried about what I'm going to say.

It's hard to find the words to say what I need to. Where does one even begin? The marriage part. The death part. Everything sounds crazy when I have to put it into words.

So instead, I lean forward and rip the Band-Aid off.

"My husband is trying to kill me."

Her eyes widen, and her mouth drops. If this wasn't such a serious matter, I would probably laugh at the ridiculous look on her face.

She resembles a fish gasping for air.

"Do you want me to start from the beginning?" I ask, and she nods because, apparently, words are still escaping her.

It takes approximately thirty minutes to explain how my life is a shitshow.

How I lost everything.

The story starts the same way most love stories do, but in my story, it ends with what I have to assume was a hit on my life.

I still don't understand it.

But I guess I never will.

Her mouth is still hanging open by the time I'm done, but she pulls me into her arms.

Her body shakes, and I think she is crying.

"Maggie," I ask tentatively. "Are you okay?"

The sound of her sobs and hiccups rings through the surrounding air. "Someone wants you dead, and you're concerned about how I feel?"

"I mean, when you put it that way . . ." That makes Maggie laugh. When she pulls away from me, red blotches stain her cheek, and her eyes have swelled.

With a lift of my hand, I take hers in mine. "I'm okay. I promise."

"What can I do?" she asks, and I bite my lip.

"Nothing. You've already done enough. I've put you in danger by staying here, and on top of that, I didn't even tell you. I don't deserve anything else."

"First off, shut up. Second, I would do it again in a heartbeat. I'm happy you thought to contact me, and that I made you memorize my number." She winks at me.

"Right," I agree. A shiver runs through my body at the thought of what would have happened to me if I didn't have Maggie.

She squeezes my hand, telling me without words that she knows what I'm thinking and that I do have her.

"What are we going to do now?"

"We," I say, "aren't going to do anything. I have it handled."

Her brow lifts. "And how do you have it handled?"

"Jax is helping me." I say nothing else. It's not my place to divulge his secrets. She nods and doesn't press. A trait in Maggie I appreciate.

"Okay, well, now that we have that out of the way, I need ice cream."

Her words make me laugh, but I'm in agreement. I'm emotionally drained, and only ice cream will do.

With Kit Kats sprinkled on top.

Nothing beats eating your emotions.

CHAPTER THIRTY-EIGHT

Jaxson

WE SPEND THE NEXT FEW DAYS CAMPED OUT WORKING. I DON'T tell Willow everything I've found because she's already too worried, but after searching encrypted texts, I could decode a conversation regarding her father's death.

If there was any question in my mind whether it was murder, I'm no longer skeptical. Unfortunately, I don't have proof that the phone used belonged to her husband. Yet.

Hopefully, I'll have the answers I need soon, but this fucker really is a ghost, and not a cute one like Willow was.

I'm also sure I have tracked him down to a boys' home. But without a picture confirmation, I'm not sure, and I don't want to get Willow's hopes up yet.

So instead, I keep searching, and I keep her as close to me as possible. Like tonight, I've invited her over under the guise of wanting to cook her dinner. Which is true, but it's also because if it were up to me, she would sleep here every night. It's safer here, and I hate the idea of her being in danger.

There isn't much food in the house, and it's way too late to do a grocery delivery, so we will have to make do with what I have in the pantry and fridge.

"What are we making for dinner?" Willow says as she enters the room. Pivoting my body, I turn to where she's leaning against the wall.

"Not we, me," I respond, and she shakes her head.

"Nope. I'm going to help you." The corner of her lip tips up slightly as she pushes off the wall and heads toward me.

"Okay, but what are you good at cooking? Because I can only make breakfast foods." I cock my head. "Plus, I only have ingredients for breakfast foods." It's my turn to smirk.

"So, I take it we are eating breakfast food for dinner," she deadpans, and I chuckle.

"Yep."

"Good, because I cook amazing eggs." She walks toward the refrigerator, and I follow her. Turning to look over her shoulder, she narrows her eyes at me.

"I'm making breakfast, so I'm not sure why you are giving me the death stare."

"Can't I do something nice for you for once?"

I open my mouth to object, but I understand where she is coming from. She's crashing at my place while I try to help her. She needs this to feel useful.

I throw my arms in the air. "Fine. The kitchen is yours." Grinning. "But don't think I won't try to distract you," I say, lifting my brows suggestively.

"You can try, but I'm not easily distracted."

"I beg to differ." I let my gaze run up her body, and she licks her lip, but she must realize she's doing it subconsciously because she starts to fake cough.

The distraction doesn't work, though. I know she hasn't even started to cook, and I have her where I want her.

"I'm going to get a drink. Do you want anything?" I walk toward the fridge and grab a bottle of wine and hold it toward her. "White goes well with eggs, right?"

"I'm sure white wine goes well with anything."

"Do you want a glass?"

"Sure," she says as she cracks the eggs in a bowl she grabbed from the cabinet.

She certainly knows her way around this kitchen. The thought should make me nervous, as a confirmed bachelor and all, but it doesn't. I care about Willow. A lot. Her in my kitchen every day holds merit.

Once I've poured our glasses, I hand her one, and then I take a sip before sitting at the barstool.

In this location, I have a perfect view of her.

As she whisks, I stare at her. She's so gorgeous; the more I watch, the more I want to forget dinner altogether and feast on her instead.

Maybe I should do that.

Who needs to eat anyway?

"Stop staring at me."

"I really can't."

She shakes her head and moves to the stove.

In my brain, I mentally calculate how long before I can have her naked on the island.

Or maybe bent over in front of the island.

Five.

That's how long it will take for the eggs to be done.

Thank fuck she isn't making bacon too.

That shit would take too long.

"What are you looking at?" she says over her shoulder as she pours the eggs in the pan and starts cooking.

"Do you want me to be honest?" I ask.

"Always."

"Your ass."

I hear the spatula hitting the countertop, and she turns toward me, her mouth hanging open. "Wow."

"What? You asked."

"Well, I didn't expect you to be that honest."

"So I guess you don't want me to tell you all the things I'm planning to do to your ass once the stove is off?"

"No."

With the eggs now on a plate, I stand from where I'm perched and stalk toward her.

"Too bad."

"What are you doing?" she says.

I signal to the plates. "Put those down."

She stares at me blankly.

"Now," I say again. This time more forceful.

The sound of the plates dropping is all I need to move in.

Before she can comprehend what I'm doing, I'm leaning down and placing my mouth on hers. She moans into the kiss, her hands looping around my neck. My hands, however, are working at ridding her of her pants instead.

I never break the kiss as I lower them, nor do our mouths separate as she steps out of them.

The next thing I know, I'm freeing myself from the confines of my pants, yet we still don't pull away. The kiss becomes more frenzied, but then my mouth leaves hers. "What are you doing?" she asks.

"Condom."

She shakes her head. "Don't. I'm clean, and I've got the shot."

"I'm clean too."

"I know." She smiles and pounces yet again, this time fusing my mouth to hers. Grabbing her from beneath her ass, I pick her up and place her on the counter, then I step in closer between her legs and align myself with her core.

With one quick thrust, I'm inside. Her mouth then and

only then slips away from mine, and a groan of displeasure escapes her as I slowly pull back out. I like to tease her, so I do.

Slowly dragging myself in and out to torture her.

I stop my movements and hover but don't breach, and she lifts her hips, pulling me deeper inside her. On a chuckle, I thrust again, and this time, I pump harder. Faster.

My movements speed up.

In. Out. In. Out.

Her breathing becomes frantic, and she pushes her hips forward as I thrust myself inside her. We keep this rhythm for a while as both of us chase our high. I'm so close, but I need her to fall over the edge first. Only then can I get my release.

Knowing she needs more, I circle my arm around her until it rests where our bodies meet, and then I press harder and firmer against her. I move my hand to meet my thrusts until she's mewling and begging for more.

She's close.

I'm closer.

I pick up the pace, and she meets my movements until we are moving in sync.

My hips rock up. My breathing accelerates. It matches the clip of my movements, of each thrust, until it builds and builds. Once the sensation in my body reaches a high, I thrust up one more time, bury my head in her neck, and when I feel her tighten around me, I know I can't hold it back anymore. My speed increases, and when she falls over the edge, I do too.

Once spent, I collapse on top of her, panting and sweating.

"Do you think the eggs are cold?"

We both laugh.

It's miserable out.

Cold.

Rainy.

Fuck, it might even be snowing.

But I don't care. Nope. Not at all. Because instead of being at work, I'm at home. With Willow.

We've spent the day in my apartment. Since the weather sucks, we've ordered pizza, put sweats on, and are watching movies.

Now that our marathon of action movies has ended, I swear the silence around us is growing awkward.

It's not that we have nothing to discuss. We have plenty, but we decided not to discuss the huge woolly mammoth in the room today, because let's be honest, a crazy homicidal husband is more than an elephant.

The easiest solution to cure our boredom is to get her naked, but that would be too easy, and what fun is that. So instead, I stand, walk over to the side table, and then come back and place a set of cards down.

"Okay, let's play." I show her the cards. "It's raining, and there is nothing better to do, so we're going to play a game of Texas Hold 'Em."

"Um. No." She rolls her eyes as I extend my arm out to help her off the couch. "Pass. Next idea please?"

"Strip poker?" I counter.

"Because that's a hell of a lot more different?" Her arms cross in front of her chest in mock defiance as she shakes her head at me. She's cute when she's being difficult.

"It is," I say with a straight face. "This requires skill."

A laugh escapes her mouth. "As opposed to?"

"Fuck if I know. Come on, live a little. Play with me." I pout.

She turns away and looks out the window, then looks at the TV. There is nothing on right now except a reality TV show, which is awful.

"Our options are limited."

An overdramatic huff echoes through the room as she begrudgingly takes my hand and stands.

Together, we walk to the table across the room. Ever the gentleman, I pull out her chair, and once she's seated, I take the seat directly across from her.

"But I don't know how to play."

"It's actually pretty straightforward." I shuffle the cards. "Basically, I deal each player two cards face down. Then five cards are dealt face up. Anyone can use them to make the best five-card hand."

She looks at the cards in my hand, contemplating whether she wants to play. Weighing out her options for the evening. A small line forms between her brows, and it's as if I'm asking her to find the cure for cancer. If I didn't want to get her naked, I'd probably make fun of her right now.

Finally, her mouth opens. "What's the best five-card hand?"

"A royal flush."

"What's that?" she asks, and if she had been following before, I'm pretty sure I've lost her.

"Ace, king, queen, jack, ten . . . all the same suit." I try to explain it as simply as I can. I'm not sure why I'm pushing this game so much, other than the fact that I really want her naked. But it's more than that . . .

Even though I'll get her naked, we'll have fun doing it. It will be something to laugh about. A memory to make outside of the drama she's going through.

"It's easy. Come on," I playfully plead, and she inclines her head down before looking back up.

I can see the need for knowledge in her eyes; they are wide and full of questions. "And after that, what's good?"

"Straight flush. Why don't we play a hand face up, and I'll teach you?" I don't wait for her to say yes before I am dealing our cards.

The first hand I deal is face up and is a five and a seven.

"Look." I point at the cards. "I have pocket tens. Now we bet?"

She lifts a brow, and I continue. "So, for example, with what I'm showing, I'd bet my shirt. And if I were you . . . I would fold."

Like a good student, she does. With that done, I shuffle and deal again, and we play another hand face up. We end up playing three more hands face up before she nods up at me. "Okay. Let's do this."

"You sure . . . ?" I ask.

"Yep."

I shuffle the cards in my hand and then deal two cards to each of us. When we both have our cards, we each look down at our hands. I see that I have an ace-king suited.

She'll be naked in no time . . .

"I'll bet my shirt," I say, and she looks at me. "Do you call?" I ask.

"What does that mean?"

"Are you betting your shirt also, or are you folding, which means you're out?"

She worries her lower lip while she studies her hand, then she nods. "I'll call." That makes me smile—only one bet away from getting her naked. I place the card underneath the bottom of the deck and flip the next three cards face up. The flop comes, I have an eight of diamonds, king of spades, three of clubs.

I have top pair. Top kicker. She's losing this hand.

"I bet my hand." I smirk.

She looks down at her cards. "So . . . I have to bet my . . . sweats?"

"Yep."

Her gaze lifts. We stare at each other, and the longer we do, the more her cheeks redden. She's flushed.

"But I'm not wearing any underwear." Her tongue juts out and licks her lower lip. I groan at the movement, the idea of all the delectable things she can do with her mouth playing out in my mind.

"That's why it's called gambling." I wink.

"Okay . . ." She trails off, eyeing her cards. "I guess I'll call."

I again place another card under the deck and flip a card face up. It's the ace of diamonds. I school my features. I am giving her a blank stare and the impression I don't have shit.

My fingers tap the table twice. "Check."

The confusion in her stare is laughable. Her eyes are wide, nose scrunched, and even if we weren't playing strip poker, I'd want to play with Willow every day, because watching her play has become my favorite pastime.

Who are you kidding? Being with Willow has become your favorite everything.

I know she has no clue what I'm talking about, so I clarify.

"You can bet, or you can check. If you check, we see the final card. And either you lose your pants, or I do." This time, I allow my lip to tip up into a smirk.

"I guess I check then." This time, I can't read her. Her face is blank. All she does is give me a shrug.

For the last time, I place one card on the bottom of the deck and turn the last card. It's the six of clubs. No way she's winning this hand.

"I'm all in."

"I guess since I have no idea what the fuck I'm doing, I'm going to have to call."

"I have two pairs of aces and kings . . ."

"Does that beat me? I have three eights . . ." She throws her cards, showing that she has the eight of hearts and eight of clubs.

Motherfucker.

My mouth hangs open as I stare down at the table and at what just happened.

When I lift my gaze, her lips are parted into what I can only call a mischievous smirk.

"Beginner's luck?"

"You are full of shit. You fucking hustled me."

"You kind of deserved it." She laughs before biting her lip and looking at me like a starved woman at a feast. "I've been working at a poker game for months. Did you really think I wasn't watching, listening, learning? PS . . . your tell, you are smug as shit, regardless of your hand, but you also look to the right when it's not that good . . ." She bats her eyelashes innocently at me. "Now strip."

Without a second thought, I lift my hips and push my pants down as she watches. Then I grab my dick in my hand.

I'm hard as a rock. Watching her hustle me was the best foreplay ever. Her eyes widen with lust as I pump myself from root to tip.

Up.

Down.

Up.

Down.

The passion in her gaze is fierce, her body quivering with need. I don't expect her to get up, but she does, and then she's on her knees in front of me.

"You won," I say.

"And you're my prize." She licks her lips.

Fuck yes. Best fucking loss ever.

Before I can say another word, her tongue sweeps against my hard flesh, licking the moisture that's collected.

It's fucking unreal.

She fucks me with her mouth, my hands pushing into her hair. With each swipe of her tongue, I get closer and closer to release. And then it happens . . .

I come undone.

I've been so wrapped in the perfect cocoon Willow and I have created for ourselves that I almost completely forgot about the party being thrown for my sister. It wasn't until an hour ago when my cell pinged with a message from Grayson that I remembered.

In his typical manner, he reminded me, and I fired back an obnoxious remark telling him I knew . . .

The thought of admitting I forgot was not going to happen. Good thing for me, Willow and I had already shopped for my present.

It's an impetuous decision to bring Willow with me, but she means something to me. Plus, she showed me she had my back when she stood up to Grayson. Since I have no choice but to go uptown for this dinner in honor of Addison, I decide to take her with me. I wouldn't have a problem honoring Addison, but I'd prefer if it was on neutral territory.

Not at my brother's apartment.

"You ready to go?" I ask her, and she looks up at me from where she's applying a thin coat of lipstick.

It's colorless but glossy, making her lips look sweet. Making me want to lick them.

"Stop looking at me like that." She gives me a stern look, but it does nothing to tamp down my need for her.

"We could stay home." The pupils of her blue eyes widen as she takes in my words. If she wants to say something about my choice of words, she doesn't. Instead, she turns back to the mirror and stares at herself.

"Are you sure I don't need them?"

She's looking at her eyes. Eyes so blue it should have been a crime to cover them. I know why she did it, and I understand, but now that she's with me, she has nothing to fear.

"We'll take my car. We'll park in his garage. We own the building. I manage the security. I can promise you; you are safe." I move to walk closer to her, and when I'm standing directly behind her, I place my hand on her shoulder. "Do you trust me?"

I expect her to think about the answer, and she surprises me when she doesn't.

"Yes."

Her words are a balm to my soul. Here is this girl who's only known me for a few months, and she trusts me implicitly with her life. And this is why I am taking her with me. Because I need her. She may not realize it, but she is the strongest woman I know, and I don't care if it makes me weak to admit I need her strength.

"Okay. No costume. No hiding. Just me."

I lean down and place a kiss on her head.

"And you are perfect."

Through the mirror, I can see her smile. It lights up the room like her.

It takes Willow a few more moments to put the finishing touches on, and then we are out the door. Like I told her, we grab my car from my basement garage and then head uptown. As I weave in and out of traffic, she holds my hand. I know what she's doing, and I welcome it.

The ride doesn't take long, or maybe it's because I'm with Willow, but before I know it, I'm pulling into Grayson's garage under his building.

I take a spot marked for me. A perk when you're a Price. Once we're parked, we then head upstairs.

Neither of us speak on the ride up. I should probably warn her, but then I think in the grand scheme of life, this is easier than half the shit she's dealt with. Plus, she's already met Grayson. Addie is pregnant and will love her, and I'm not worried about Mom. The elevator opens, and together, we step out into the apartment. I haven't been here for months, not since Willow walked into my life, and I feel like I've changed in that time.

She's changed me.

I've always been strong-willed, but watching her, I can't put my finger on exactly how she changed me, but I feel like a better man with her around.

Standing in the foyer, I reach my arm out and pull her to me. Then and only then do I walk to where my family has gathered.

Mom is the first to see us. Her face instantly turns into a smile, and with quick steps, she makes her way over. I expect her to throw her arms around me; she doesn't because my arm is around Willow.

"Jaxson," she says, voice full of love and emotion. Seeing her makes me miss Dad. Maybe that's one reason I stay away. I let my arm drop from around Willow, but I take her hand in mine.

"Mom. This is my girlfriend, Willow."

Willow drops my hand and shock plays on her face. We haven't talked about this; we haven't exactly given us a label, but that's what she is, my girlfriend, and there is no reason to pretend otherwise.

"It's so lovely to meet you, dear," my mother says to Willow. From my vantage point, I can see Willow wanting to look down. She's still wary of the attention, no matter how safe she says she feels with me. But she doesn't let it show, so no one would know. I only know because I know all her tells. But regardless of how she struggles, she holds her head high and extends her hand.

"It's so nice to meet you too, Mrs. Price."

"Please call me Annabel," my mom says as they shake.

My lip tips up as pride surges through me, but it's quickly knocked down as Willow stiffens, and I hear footsteps.

I was too busy staring at her to notice my brother approach. Turning in his direction, he furrows his brow. He's looking at Willow, probably because she looks different from the last time he saw her.

The last time he saw her, although her hair was dark, it was a mess. And although her clothes were tighter than the norm, she dressed different from now. Now she wears a sweater dress, tights, and heels. Back then, she was still in sweats.

She's come a long way. Even before we got together, she had started with the little details, such as losing the glasses and wearing fitted clothes, but here she looks regal. She looks like she belongs, and he's staring. I step up, placing my arm around her again.

"This is my girlfriend, Willow. I'm not sure if you remember her . . ."

"Oh, I remember her," he mutters before turning his attention back to her. "How could I forget her?" If my mom notices the tension, she says nothing. However, River must because she comes over quickly, throwing her arms around me and smiling at Willow.

"It's so nice to meet you," she says, and then she reaches her hand out and takes Willow's. "Any friend of Jax's is a friend of mine." Then, as if they've been friends forever, she pulls Willow and me to the table.

Oliver and Addison are already sitting, and when Oliver notices us, he stands politely, while Addison waves from her chair.

"I'd get up, but I am the size of a house and you would need a forklift," she deadpans.

"And pregnancy hasn't changed your cheerful disposition."

"Har, har, har, Jax. Talk to me when you don't sleep and have your own zip code."

That makes me laugh, and I walk over to my sister where she is, in fact, large and uncomfortably stuffed in a chair and place a kiss on her head.

"This is Willow," I introduce.

They each say hello, and before long, we all are sitting around the table celebrating the baby.

Addison is not one to have a formal baby shower. According to her, in her current state, she hates people. Oliver included.

Because of this, she insisted we celebrate with no fanfare. We drink, we eat, and then we present gifts.

I'm shocked to see Willow reach into her bag and pull out a wrapped gift. I had purchased a gift I intended to give from both of us, but once again Willow shocks me.

She's the most caring person I know.

She hands it over to Addison, whose eyes are wide.

"You didn't have to bring anything, Willow."

"It's nothing really."

Addison opens it, and inside is a dream catcher.

"I had one over my bed . . ." Her voice cracks, and I know she must be thinking of her parents.

My arm around her chair, I touch her shoulder, and she leans closer to me.

Having her move into my body makes me feel things I can't comprehend.

Important.

Strong.

Loved.

It's everything I always wanted from my family.

Ironic that sitting here in my brother's castle, I finally get it from her.

CHAPTER THIRTY-NINE

Willow

OTHER THAN THE FACT WE ARE STILL SEARCHING unsuccessfully for intel on my crazy, psychotic husband, it's been a good week.

The time I've spent with Jax, although I wish it was under different circumstances, have been the best months of my life.

It doesn't even make sense to me. How can I enjoy myself so thoroughly when I'm hiding and on the run?

But that's the thing about Jax. Every minute with him, I cherish. I don't know what the future will bring or even if we'll have a future together. It's so uncertain right now. I've chosen to live each day like it's my last because it very well may be. When most women may cry or curse their fate, I embrace it.

I allow myself to fall for a man I have only known a short time because you never know about tomorrow.

Today is all I have.

I'm back at Maggie's. She's preparing for a gig this weekend, so she isn't here. I feel bad that I haven't been around much, but it was actually Maggie's idea for me to stay at Jaxson's apartment until we resolve this.

Today, I am only back to grab a few things. The rest of my clothes, for one, and the picture of my parents. Once I throw all my stuff back into the duffel bag, I search for the picture frame. I look high and low and can't find it anywhere. I check under the couch, and then even though I know I shouldn't, I check in Maggie's room. No matter where I look, I can't find it, which is strange.

For a moment, I feel like I'm going crazy.

My hands are pounding on my head as I try to remember where I might have put it.

I've been so stressed out the past few times I've been here that it's possible I don't remember where I left it.

I feel like I'm going mad, throwing everything apart and going through every cabinet, but an hour later, there is still nothing.

Where can it be?

Did someone take it?

A chill runs up my spine, and suddenly, I feel like I'm being watched.

Did he find me?

I shake my head.

No.

There is no way.

I've been super careful. I haven't even been here. There is no way he found me.

But then . . .

My mind plays tricks on me, running through each time I thought I'd seen him.

Maybe?

No. No. No.

I haven't even gone online. How could he track me? There's no way.

Call Jax.

He will know what to do.

I shake that thought away. I cannot call him. The last time I freaked out and called him, he left work to rescue me for a dead mouse that had nothing to do with my husband. What would I say this time . . . ?

My framed picture is missing.

It sounds crazy to my own ears. Imagine how it would sound to him.

If I call now, he'll think I'm crazy. I know I'm being crazy. He'll probably tell me they should commit me.

That I have officially lost it.

Nope. It's not worth worrying anyone over.

I'm going to go back to the loft where I feel safe and wait for Jax to get home.

So now that I'm resolved that nothing more is going on, I grab my duffel and leave. I close the apartment door and head out of the building. The cold air hits my face, and my body shivers with a chill. The farther I get from the apartment, the more I should allow myself to relax.

But with each step I take, a foreboding feeling works its way deeper into my body until it has buried itself all the way in my marrow.

No matter how many times I chant to myself that everything will be fine, I know it won't.

A storm is brewing.

It's only a matter of time until it will strike.

My mind is officially playing tricks on me. If I wondered if I was crazy before now, I'm really starting to doubt my sanity. Every time I leave the apartment, I swear someone is watching me. Around every corner, I see familiar eyes. But as fast as I see them, they disappear, so I keep my fears to myself because I don't want to be the girl who cried wolf.

It's starting to weigh on me.

Each night, I fall asleep in his arms but wake to him shaking me.

Like tonight.

"Shh," he coos. "You're having a nightmare."

Nightmares plague me again, ever since the picture disappeared. I know I should say something, but I don't want to worry him for no reason. Especially since there have been no incidents. And especially since he's working so hard to figure out information.

One thing I know is that he thinks he finally caught a break. He has it narrowed down to two different boys who match my husband's description. Both were raised in a boys' home.

He's waiting for someone on both staffs to see if they can find pictures to use for confirmation. While he waits, he has opened a few sealed records from the courts.

One of the boys is a year older than I am and lived in the next town over.

His mother was a prostitute and drug addict and eventually abandoned her son.

It's heartbreaking.

I wonder if it's Riley.

Without a picture, I won't know. But hopefully soon.

The file on the other boy is sealed, and it's been harder to crack. I'm not worried, though.

I trust Jax to find out.

Still hazy from sleep, Jax rocks me in his arms, pressing kisses to my forehead and promising to keep me safe.

With each day that passes, my fears grow. I try during the day to keep them at bay, but at night, I find it impossible.

I must have fallen back asleep because when my eyes flutter

open again, it's morning. Jax is gone for the day, and I'm by myself.

Unfortunately, the next night follows in the same pattern . . . my brain racing as I close my eyes to go to bed. Will tonight be the same, or will the visions of blood on my hands find me?

My body is still shaking. It's hard for me to regulate my thoughts. I know where I am, but I still feel like I'm running.

Like he's found me.

Like I'm moments away from dying.

The air is cold, or maybe it's the sweat that has broken out on my skin. But it makes me shiver.

I feel his arms around me. They pull me tight. Rock me.

He coos quietly.

The words have no meaning now. I'm too far away. Lost in my fear. I thought I was strong enough. I deluded myself to think I was strong enough.

"You are."

Did I say that out loud? I'm so lost in my mind; I don't even realize words are slipping past my clenched jaw.

"Shh. It's okay."

His hands are on my skin. His fingers trail circles on my back.

"You're okay. I have you."

"I feel like I'm going crazy."

"I know you've been having nightmares . . . but—"

I pull back and look at him. Eyes narrowed, he's deep in thought.

"What?" I ask.

"I think you should talk to someone."

"What, why? I'm fine." I push back, but he doesn't let me go.

Instead, he wraps his hands around my biceps, his gaze searing mine. Worry is written all over his handsome features. Jaw set and a line that pinches between his brows.

"Willow."

"Jaxson," I respond, lifting a brow.

"Have you had a moment to let this sink in . . . ?"

"No. Just the few months." I roll my eyes because now that I'm wide-awake, what he's saying sounds ridiculous. It's a nightmare. It's nothing. I'm fine.

"I don't think you grieved," he says, his voice low. It's low enough that I need to clarify what he said.

"Grieve? Grieve what? My father?" I ask.

"Your husband . . ." His voice trails off, but not before it hits me in the gut.

"Why would I grieve my husband?" I shake my head in confusion. "He's trying to murder me."

Jaxson lifts his hand to stop me. "I know that, but what I also know is that before a few months ago, he was your husband. A man you thought you loved. A man you thought loved you. It couldn't be easy to find out your life is a lie. It's almost as though the man you loved died, so you still need to grieve. He was still a part of your life. I think you have things you need to discuss. Your fears, sadness . . . I think you need to talk about it."

That makes me shake my head.

"I can't."

"You can. Willow, I know we haven't known each other long, but one thing is certain."

"What's that?"

He leans down until his lips are hovering over mine. "You are the strongest person I know."

"No. Not really. I ran rather than deal with it."

"You didn't run. You regrouped. And in order to do that, you left your life behind. Most people wouldn't have been able to do that."

"I—"

"You're strong."

"I can kick someone's ass now."

"See. Mentally and also physically strong."

"I'm scared all the time."

"That may be the case, but it doesn't change it. You need to speak to someone to help you channel the fear."

"But that's another thing. I can't. I can't use my name . . ." I stop and take a deep breath. "No one can know. I can't have it tracked back to me."

Jaxson looks off to the side of the room, then smiles to himself. As if he figured out the secret to life. "I might have someone."

"Umm. Okay."

"A therapist you can talk to."

"And you trust him?"

"I do. He helped my buddy out a few years back when he was having nightmares. But it's more than that."

"Vague much . . . ?"

"Let's just say, I have helped his family out a few times."

My eyebrow raises. "Oh."

"Yeah, oh." He laughs.

"That little hobby of yours sure pays off sometimes."

"Oh, you have no idea. The number of people who owe me . . ." His lips split into a large smirk. "I'll make a few phone calls tomorrow."

"Okay."

"Now close your eyes and go back to sleep."

"I'm not sure if I can."

"Then let me help you."

"What do you have in mind?"

He doesn't answer me. Instead, he pushes me lightly back down onto the pillow and climbs on top of me.

"I'll think of something," he says as he kisses my neck.

With a smile on my face, I relax into his kisses, his touches, and just being with him and letting go.

The next morning comes, and as my eyes open, I'm met with an empty bed and a cold one at that. But I can smell the fresh-roasted coffee in the air.

I stretch my arms over my head and stretch out the last remainder of sleep still in my body.

Once I'm fully awake, I climb out of the bed and grab Jaxson's shirt from the chair. Then barefoot and sans pants, I walk to the kitchen.

I find Jax standing in sweats and no shirt.

His back is toward me, and he is holding a phone to his ear.

"Yes. I'll hold," he says as I walk up behind him and slide my hands around his middle. One of his arms reaches behind his body and touches me, before I let go and then go to move to stand in front of him.

When I do, he's lost in pouring himself a coffee before he notices me. His gaze drops and then trails up my body. He must like what he sees because his eyes seem to darken with appreciation before he steps closer to me and places a kiss on my lips.

"You busy?" I mouth.

He shakes his head.

"Hello, Preston. Yes. Thank you for agreeing to take this call," he says.

Who's Preston?

He bobs his head as he listens. "Yes, I looked into the anonymous call line you have set up, but I hacked it in under one minute." He listens more. "I know she can't be a patient, and I can't have her call in, just in case, but is there any way you can speak to her? Not as a patient but as a friend of a friend?"

Preston must say something because Jaxson paces back and forth. "No. I understand. Yes, I really appreciate it. Okay, I'll have her come to your brownstone. Thank you again."

He hangs up the phone and turns to me.

"Who was that?" I ask.

"Dr. Montgomery."

"Okay . . ." I walk around him and stand in front of the cabinet to grab a mug. I open it, reach inside, and lift onto my tiptoes. "What about him?" I ask as my fingers wrap around the porcelain.

"What?"

I turn around and see him looking at my legs, or maybe it's my ass. Probably the latter, seeing as there is drool coming out of his mouth.

"What did he say?"

"He'll see you today but at his apartment. He can't have you come to his office. Too much red tape. He also works at a hotline, where callers are anonymous, but well . . ."

"You hacked it." He nods. "You got him to see me today. Jeez, what do you have on him?"

"Nothing." He laughs. "He was cool with it. He wouldn't be your doctor. Just helping me out, I helped his brother and his sister a bit. Well, their significant others but same difference. He wanted to help."

I walk over and pour myself a cup of coffee, lifting it to my mouth and taking a sip. I don't know how I feel about seeing a therapist, even if it's not as my doctor per se.

But my main issues were getting caught.

This way, I won't. The warmth of the liquid in my mouth gives me enough time not to argue, and by the time I swallow, I know he's right.

I need to talk to someone.

"When?" I ask.

"He's expecting you in two hours."

I place my mug down. "Wait. What? That soon."

"The sooner you move on, the sooner the nightmares will stop."

"I won't move on until I have something on him."

Jax worries his lip at my words, and I instantly feel bad. He's trying. I know he's trying. It's not his fault my ex seems untraceable.

I can't even call him my ex at this point.

Are we even legally married?

Probably not. That much is for sure.

Not if he married me under false pretense.

"I'm sorry," I say, and he shakes his head.

"No. I'm the one who's sorry."

There is nothing more that either of us can say. It's a rough situation. So instead of speaking, I walk up to him and wrap my arms around his stomach and bury my head into his chest.

He kisses my head and holds me.

And even if it's only for a few seconds, everything feels right in my world.

Two hours pass by way too quickly. I raise my hand to knock on the door. I knock once before the door opens.

Standing in front of me is a man in his mid-to-late thirties, and he's handsome in a serious way. He's wearing a suit and glasses on his face, and I wonder if he's supposed to be at his office right now, and I'm the only reason he's here, or if he often takes clients at his home.

"Hello, you must be Willow," he says as he extends his hand toward me. "I'm Preston."

I go to move my hand, but it won't move. I'm cemented in place. It's as if all the nightmares have erased all the strength that I have gained through self-defense class. Touching him, someone I don't know and trust, makes me shaky.

"It's okay," he responds, pulling back his hand. I give him a small smile.

"I thought I had moved past that . . ." I say, and he nods in understanding. He steps back, allowing space for me to pass before lifting his hand and gesturing toward what must be his office.

"Would you like to talk for a bit?"

I want to say no because, at the moment, having to relive the past few months makes me ready to dash. What I want to do is bury my head in the sand and pretend I don't need to be here. But if I ever want to sleep again, I need to be here. And maybe Jaxson is right. As much as I hate my husband, there is a void still inside me from where the lie and my love used to be. Maybe I need to discuss it to fully understand why.

Or maybe I'll never know the why?

Shit. I don't know.

My head shakes back and forth as I try to clear my brain and find the strength to do this.

"It will be okay," he says.

I look back to the door and then to his office.

My foot decides for me as I stride to the open door. But not the one that leads outside, the one that leads to something scarier.

The past.

When we step through the door, I'm taken aback by the room. It's a full office with a couch and desk. It's very professional, like this man. This man, who is asking no personal questions about who I am.

"Please sit," he says as he walks over to his desk. He grabs a notebook and a pen, and I watch the movement with a steady gaze. "I know you're not my patient, but I'd like to keep notes if you're okay with it."

"I don't mind."

"I won't put your name down. It's only for me." I incline my head in agreement and then sit down on the black leather couch.

"Okay, Willow," he says as if he's collecting his thoughts of what he can and can't ask. "Let's start by me asking simple questions at first. Would that be okay?"

"Yes, it's okay," I answer.

"How long have you been having nightmares?"

That's the simple question? I want to laugh. There is nothing simple about that question. When I don't answer, he gives me a soft smile. "How about this . . . you talk, and I'll listen. Tell me anything you want. Start from the beginning or the end."

I feel so stupid starting from the end, so even though I don't want to, I start from the beginning. I tell him about my parents. About the accident that killed my mom. I tell him about my father drinking and eventually dying from supposed alcohol abuse. I tell him how I met my husband and fell madly in love, and then by the time I tell him about the phone call I heard, I'm shaking, and tears are dripping down my face.

"How can I not have known . . . ?" I finally say as my sobs settle down.

Preston leans forward in his chair.

"He lied to you, Willow. He used your weakness and preyed on you. It's not your fault."

"I don't understand. It feels like my world is a lie, and there is a big gaping hole in my heart," I admit on a sigh. "I don't miss him; I hate him, but why do I feel like the void—"

"It's hard to find out that part of your life is false. It's okay to be sad. It's okay to feel grief. You lost your mother, you lost your father, and for all intents and purposes, you lost your husband. You lost the life you thought you had. You will grieve, and you have to have realistic expectations about the amount of time required to heal from this grief. It won't happen overnight. When you left, it didn't make it go away just because you no longer saw it."

"What do I do?"

"Take one day at a time. Forgive yourself."

"I don't understand."

"You blame yourself. These nightmares, of your father's blood on your hands, mean you blame yourself for his death. For letting your husband into your life. But it's not your fault. None of it is. There is only one person to blame. Him. You need to forgive yourself. It's not your fault," he says again. His words hit me in the gut. This whole time, I was making myself physically stronger but never mentally.

I might know how to defend myself now, but I never tried to heal my heart. My brain.

Jaxson was right.

I needed this.

It might take months. Hell, it might take years, but I will rebuild what my husband took away from me. I will emerge like a phoenix. New. And stronger.

It might be a long road, but I'll get there.

I know I will.

With the weeks that have passed, Jaxson and I have become closer. I still see Preston once a week, and it helps to talk through the nightmares. I also spend my free time training. Every day, I become a little stronger. I am almost back to the way I was before my picture frame went missing.

Almost.

Today, I have a few errands to run. My hair color is growing out, and I need to buy another box to redo it. Just because months have passed and Riley hasn't found me doesn't mean I can grow complacent. I have grown more lax, no longer wearing clothes two sizes too big, and I don't wear a hat, but my hair color is the one thing I won't change back yet, even though I'm stronger, it helps me move freely around the city and still feel safe.

I hop in the shower and get ready to leave the apartment.

With my body wrapped in a towel, I reach into my duffel and go to grab a shirt.

I really need to unpack, but I don't want Jax to think I'm moving in and taking advantage of him.

I'm fishing around in the bag when my hand touches something.

My chest constricts. It feels like there is a vise around my heart, and it's tightening.

What the hell?

I wrap my palm around the item.

Its cold surface sends a chill up my spine.

I didn't pack this.

How did it get here?

A ringing in my ears grows louder and louder until it is so loud, I feel like my eardrums will burst.

My hand is now in front of me. But I'm too scared to look at what I have clutched in my hand.

It can't be.

But as much as I refuse to look, I know it.

I would know the size and shape of the item anywhere.

My ring.

My palm opens and confirming my fear, the platinum band glares at me.

My ring is in my hand.

The ring I left in my house.

The ring I left in my house when I left.

He's found me.

Jax isn't here when I arrive at the warehouse. I need to tell him what I found. I think about going to his office, but the more time that passes, I think about how crazy I sound.

There must be some reasonable explanation for why my wedding band is in my bag. The day I left, I was frantic and a mess. Could I have placed it in my bag and not realized it?

Yes.

I could have.

He hasn't found me. Again, it's paranoia having its way with me.

It's the only thing that makes sense.

If Riley was here, I'd be dead already. Why take my frame? Why leave the ring?

No. It makes no sense.

I'm being silly.

Signing on to my computer, I use the fake account to see what is happening back home. I'm not dumb enough to think Riley would post anything, seeing as he has no social media account, but I can look into what my company is up to.

When I left, Jax was able to find a comment from an employee asking for prayers for me. Apparently, I had fallen ill and was in a clinic abroad seeking medical attention.

I wondered if this was the game plan all along. Tell everyone I'm sick, so when I die overseas, no one questions it.

I can only assume Riley spun the story of a heartbroken husband who stayed behind to keep things afloat.

It makes me sick just thinking about it.

I spend the next few minutes looking at different posts, and then I see something that makes me breathe out a sigh of relief.

Riley is hosting a party tonight, or the company is, my company, but it also means that he is not in New York.

I'm going crazy.

CHAPTER FORTY

Jaxson

I'M SITTING IN MY OFFICE, BUT THERE IS NOTHING TO DO today. Or maybe there is, and I just don't want to be here anymore.

My foot taps rhythmically on the floor. It feels like time is standing still as I stare at my email.

Nothing of importance. Grayson wants background checks. Addison wants to update the company's database.

It's all things I can do in my sleep.

A puff of oxygen escapes my lungs as I push my chair away from the desk.

The metal scrapes against the floor with a jarring sound. But I don't even care who heard. I'm leaving.

Now standing, I head to the door and then step out in the hallway. I'm almost upon the elevator, but before I can press the button, I hear the creak of the office adjacent to where I stand.

Grayson's office.

Great. Just fucking great.

"Where are you going?" His gruff voice rings through the air. I know I need to turn around and look at him, but I don't want to.

The one thing in my life I don't need right now is a pissed-off Grayson looking down at me. Judging me for things he does not understand.

He wants me to run some numbers and look at mundane facts, but all I can think about is that the woman I care about is in danger and I haven't helped her yet.

I'm so close.

I can feel it.

It's hovering over me, so close I can almost see it, but I can't reach out and touch it yet. If I leave now and work, I'm sure I will.

The faster I find the connection to Willow, the faster I can find the proof that he did it, and once I have that proof, he can be gone from her life.

Right now, we don't even have anything to go to the police with, and it's frustrating as all hell.

If only I had a picture.

A fingerprint.

Something.

Still facing the elevator, I can hear Grayson's shoes hit the floor as he's coming over to me.

"I have some work I have to do at home," I respond.

"Work that is more important than being here?" he asks from behind me at this point.

I pivot my body.

Since we are about the same size and build, our eyes easily lock.

Looking at him, I wonder if Dad ever knew Grayson would try to fill his shoes. I wonder if he's peering down from the pearly gates now and shaking his head.

Dad was tough but always fair. Looking back, he always believed in me.

Even though I didn't know it until now.

He gave me my hobby, my first computer. He didn't know

it then, but that first game and that first computer changed my life.

Within minutes of starting the game he gave me, I needed to break it. I needed to win, and so I did. After spending endless hours trying to crack the code, I eventually did.

I'm good at what I do.

Too good.

It's actually a problem . . .

It's a good thing Grayson's back because I don't want to do any of his work anymore. After spending time with Willow, I realize how fleeting life is, and I've decided I'm done.

"As a matter of fact, it is."

Mind made.

"What are you working on?" he asks.

"It's personal," I respond, shutting him down.

"Are you okay?" Surprisingly, his voice drops, and I can hear real concern in it.

It's strange.

Not that I don't think he loves me beneath the grumpy exterior. No, I know Grayson does; he just doesn't have faith in me. Or at least not enough to do more than run a parlor trick for him. His jaw is tight, but it's his eyes that make me want to take a step back.

He's really concerned.

I can't tell him what is going on, but I can tell him something.

"It's not about me. I'm fine."

"That girl?" he asks.

"She's not *just* a girl. She's *the* girl."

He nods in understanding. I can see the way a line forms across his brow. He wants to ask more. Say more.

But something holds him back.

I wish it didn't.

I wish there was more to my relationship with my brother, and I could trust him with the secrets I harbor.

He only trusts me with his when he has to, when I'm the only one who can help him.

It's a shame.

Because I would really want that with him.

"I have to go."

He takes a step back, and I turn back to the elevator. I press the button, and I wait. He's still there, watching me, but it isn't until the elevator opens, and I step in that he speaks.

"Be careful, Jax."

I arrive at the warehouse, and it's empty. I'm not used to it, and I don't like it.

For the past few weeks, Willow has been here with me.

Day in and day out, we have been here together, but the thing is, even before that, we've been together almost every day for a month.

This place feels colder than normal without her curled up on the couch as I work.

Shit.

I'm not sure what I'll do once we get what we need on her husband. I'm not going to want her to leave.

What will happen?

Will she leave?

Will she stay?

Can I ask her to?

She must have a life back home that she misses.

Friends?

Maybe.

I shake off the feeling and type in my computer. I pull up my email, and what I see makes me smile.

Finally.

The names of the boys from the group home.

Now I'm getting somewhere.

It took weeks for Willow to remember that piece of data about her husband, but I wouldn't change those weeks with her for the world, especially if that means I'll be stuck here for the next twenty-four hours tracking down the leads.

I type both names into the DMV. It's encrypted and hidden behind firewalls, but it takes me no time to crack it.

Pictures pop up.

I pick up my phone and call her.

Ring.

Ring.

Ring.

Voicemail.

She doesn't answer, and it pisses me off. I know she has a life, and that she isn't at my beck and call, but I finally have a lead, and I need her.

Unfortunately, since Willow isn't here and can't tell me if either of the men is her husband, finding out is not going to happen right away.

I'll have to pick one and run with it.

Leaning back in frustration, I rub at my forehead. Beads of sweat have collected during my search. It's been at least an hour since I've started down this rabbit hole. Without her here to identify him, I'm getting nowhere.

My eyes are starting to blur. I have been at this for too long.

I pick up the phone again.

Yet again, she doesn't answer.

With no connection at all to Willow, I close the window, and then I pull up the other one.

Gregory Matthews.

Thirty years old.

I look at his height, weight, and his eyes. Not much I can tell here.

Closing out the DMV, I look into his name.

Credit history. No mortgage. Job.

Well, this is interesting. He's not paying taxes. Unless he works under the table, this guy might hold promise. I keep clicking, typing furiously as I try to find the piece of information that will tie him to her.

Thirty minutes go by and it's official—I can't find anything. Just as I think I should stop this search and start something new; I find something.

Gregory's name isn't Gregory Matthews.

His real name is Gregory Riley.

This has got to be him. Apparently, Matthews was his mother's name. He changed his name once he aged out of the home. What happened to you, Gregory Riley? Why did you go after Willow?

There is no question this is our guy. But why?

It takes me approximately thirty seconds to hack into the boys' home database. They really should fix their security, but I'm happy they haven't, and it takes me another thirty seconds for the ground to fall under me.

Holy shit.

It couldn't be.

CHAPTER FORTY-ONE

Willow

From where I'm sitting in Jax's apartment, I can hear my phone ring, but I can't find it. Standing, my feet take me around as I try to remember where I left it.

The sound of my steps echoes through the quiet, making it almost impossible to hear the ring.

I really need to make it louder if I'm going to forget where I place it.

But I'm so distracted all the time that even if it was on full blare, I'd still lose it.

It can't be in the living room, that much I'm sure of.

The bedroom?

This place is way too big.

When I'm in the bedroom, the phone is no longer ringing, so now it's pretty much a lost cause.

Five minutes pass of me undoing the bed and then remaking it. When I don't find it there, I'm on hands and knees looking under the bed.

Still nothing.

I push myself off the floor and try to retrace my steps. What did I do today? Slept, watched TV, played on the computer, ate.

Cereal.

I ate cereal this morning. Could I have left it when I was

getting food? My eyes roll of their own accord. I one hundred percent, like the scattered brain that I am, left the phone in the pantry.

That's something I would totally do. Yep. So with a nod of my head, I head in the pantry's direction to check. My gaze scans the shelves . . .

Nothing.

But my gaze goes to the fridge. The one with the milk. A long sigh passes through my lips because there it is.

Right next to the milk is my now freezing phone. I'm losing my mind, that is for sure. On the screen is a missed phone call from Jax. I wonder what he wants. He's at work, so it can't be anything too important. I'm about to call him back when a text comes through. It's from Maggie's number.

Maggie: I need you tonight to work.

I'm not scheduled to work, but I have nothing going on, so I might as well. It will keep my mind preoccupied.

Me: Okay. Where?

Maggie: The old bank on Bowery and Grand 6pm.

Shit. It's already four p.m., and I have to shower and get dressed.

Without a second to spare, I head over to the shower and turn it on and then set about getting ready for a gig I'm not mentally prepared for.

When I'm out of the shower, I blow dry my hair and then place a dusting of makeup on. Then I grab my phone, dialing Maggie to ask about the details of the party. It goes to voicemail, and I assume she's still getting ready.

Oh well, I'm sure it can't be much different from all the other parties I've worked.

Rich men drinking far too much.

It only takes me fifteen minutes to show up at the building. It's quiet outside with no valet or staff yet, but that's not uncommon at this time. I assume the party starts at seven and Maggie, being Maggie, wants me here a bit early to go over the details of the clientele.

The doors to the bank are large, ornate, and heavy to the touch. I have to use all my force to push it open.

With a bit of effort, it budges, and I step inside.

CHAPTER FORTY-TWO

Jaxson

NOW THAT I KNOW IT'S HIM, I TRY TO CALL WILLOW AGAIN. Her phone rings, but again, she doesn't answer.

It makes no sense at all.

Willow isn't one not to answer the phone, and since she's not here, she must be at my place.

Turning toward my computer, I access the security cameras.

I look through the stills, and I see an image of her walking out the door.

When was this?

I look at the time stamp. Twenty minutes ago. Okay, but where did she go?

As she walks out the door, she picks up the phone. In this image, all I can see is her face and the phone to her ear. I flip to another camera, and this time I see a full picture of her.

She's wearing a skintight black dress.

Work. Okay, she had a job. But still. Why didn't she call me back? I know I shouldn't track her, but I need to know she is okay.

Call me crazy, but I have to see with my own eyes.

I'm debating whether I should let my crazy kick in and track her when my phone rings.

It's an unknown number.

"Hello?"

"Umm," a voice I don't recognize says on the phone, "Jax?" When she says my name, I can hear the fear, and a name pops in my head.

"Maggie?" I ask.

"Is Willow with you?" Her voice is low, full of concern, and my back goes ramrod straight.

"What do you mean?" A strange feeling weaves its way through me. I know something is wrong.

"The thing is . . . I was in the shower, and when I got out . . ."

"Are you okay?"

"I'm a little rattled."

"What happened?"

She takes a deep breath. "When I got out, the door to my apartment was open. I thought maybe Willow came home and forgot to close it."

"Okay."

"Well, then . . . I opened my phone to ask her, and I saw the texts."

"What texts?"

"The ones I sent to Willow, but I didn't send them."

"What do you mean?"

"They came from my phone, but I didn't send them. Someone else did. Someone else sent the texts."

Adrenaline pumps through my veins, and I don't need her to speak to confirm my own fears, but she does . . .

"He found her."

CHAPTER FORTY-THREE

Willow

AS SOON AS I STEP INSIDE, I KNOW SOMETHING IS WRONG. I must have the wrong address.

Although the architecture is beautiful, with gold leaf ceilings and large marble pillars, the center of the room is a construction site.

It reminds me of an Egyptian tomb where they bury the living.

Yeah, I definitely got the wrong address. I pull out my phone and look down to check.

As if emerging from the shadows, I see him.

My head shakes back and forth.

He's not here.

Like the time before and the time before that, my eyes are playing tricks on me.

He steps closer, but there is no mistaking it's him.

And he's not a figment of my imagination.

Riley.

My husband.

Is standing in front of me.

Somehow, I'm no longer standing by the exit. When I was trying to call Maggie, I walked farther into the space, and that was my big mistake.

I never should have come here.

But here I am, inside a condemned building with my husband blocking the exit.

There has to be another way out. My head must turn to look because I hear a chuckle. It echoes through the air, bouncing off the marble walls. I look back to see Riley staring at me.

His eyes are black in the dim light. Almost as though they are void of emotion.

"There isn't," he says as if reading my mind.

Chills run up the back of my neck, and I know I need to leave. His plans are written all over his features.

Devious and sinister.

He will hurt me.

Kill me.

My feet move because escape is my only option, but I don't make it far before I'm tackled down to the floor.

His heavy body presses onto my back like an anchor being thrown off a ship.

Think, goddammit.

"Position your head and slam back." I hear Shay's voice, and I do just that. Arching my back, I throw the weight of my head back until it connects with his face.

The pain is unbearable, like a jackhammer drilling into me, but he lets go, so I don't think about the pain making me dizzy, making the floor sway underneath me like a boat pitching in a wake. No, instead, I sprint . . . toward the door. Toward my salvation.

Soter.

My vision blurs. I'm almost there, my hand reaching out, my fingers touching the cool surface of the door before I'm grabbed again from behind and thrown back.

I hit the concrete with a thud, my head bouncing against the floor.

A sharp pain rips across my skin, and then I feel it, warm and sticky. It ebbs and flows, pouring out of the wound he inflicted and moving down my forehead. I know it's bad. I know it should scare me.

I'm a half-dead corpse left to die.

He stands above me, menacing, blood dripping down his nose. The same black hair. The same dark eyes. The same crooked nose, broken too many times. He doesn't look like the man I married, but then again, he's not that man.

Never was.

No, that man was a figment of my imagination, and this man is a monster.

My body is twisted around as though I'm a rag doll being dragged deeper within the building. Spots dance, growing dizzier. I can feel the trail of blood I leave.

The farther he pulls me, the harder it will be to escape.

But I can't will myself to move; I'm limp and lacking life.

"What do you want?" I choke out even though I know the answer to the question.

"Why did you run away?" He takes a step farther in, pulling me along by my arm. The movement is jarring, burning, fiery death.

The arm he holds is probably dislocated. My left one. I can't feel it, but I can still fight back.

I don't bother answering his question. I'm sure he knows the reason. As the pain radiates, I find the strength to speak. "How did you find me?"

"Well, dear wife, if you are going to sign in to your photo site, hide the IP address."

"I did," I mutter under my breath. *Didn't I?*

His lips tip up into a signature smirk. "Not very well. You hid it, but you didn't reroute it. It took my IP guy ten minutes to ping you to the Starbucks. From there, it took me no time at all."

"Were you in my apartment?"

His smile broadens. It makes a chill run down my spine, and like lightning zapping through my body, I let the energy invigorate me. He looks sinister in this light, but dragons are meant to be slayed.

You can do this, Willow.

"I was."

I wasn't going crazy.

"The ring?"

"You got me."

"But why? Why do you want me dead? The money?"

"Yes, the money was a perk, but if you think that's why I want you dead, you really are an idiot."

"I don't understand."

"You want to know why?" He leans down to my crumpled body, and I know I need to move, but I can't. My legs feel heavy, my feet feel as though I'm stuck and hardened in concrete, and I'm frozen to the spot where I lie. My fingers wiggle, and I know there is still a chance I can win.

"I. Lost. Everything . . . because of him."

I don't know who him is, but I recognize his tone. And that scares me.

He is a man with nothing to lose and everything to gain by hurting me.

Without thinking, I move to get away. My legs push off the ground, my feet finding purchase on the floor, and I'm standing, ready to escape, when his arm reaches out and catches me by the bicep. His fingers grip hard, his nails biting at my skin.

"Him?" I whisper. But he doesn't have to say it for me to know. It's the only thing that makes sense.

"Your father took everything from me."

Like a freight train, it hits me. Everything I have pushed down and forced myself to forget. I can feel the car jerk. The impact. Falling forward. I can hear the screech of the tires and the screams. The smell of burning rubber. I close my eyes to run from the image in my head that I have worked so hard to forget, but it becomes crisper when I do.

The accident.

My father was driving and my mother . . . my body shakes.

"I see you're remembering now."

"My mother died." I don't recognize my own voice; it's broken.

"My whole family died!" he fires back. Words laced with venom and pain.

The other car.

And like a puzzle that has been missing the pieces, I finally have the last piece to put it together.

The other car.

There was another family.

They didn't make it.

All the hushed whispers pour into my ears. Things I had forgotten rush back.

In the other car was a family, but I never knew what happened to them. I never asked. Or pried.

"Shhh. She's too fragile," someone had said.

I remember hearing the word dead, also the word three. But I assumed they were talking about my mom.

The three of us in the car.

Liquid collects in my eyes.

"I didn't know." My body sways with my sobs, but his grip keeps me steady.

"Of course, you didn't. He made sure of that." Hatred leaks from his words. There is so much hatred. I don't understand.

"It was an accident."

"Oh, is that what they told the princess? It was no accident. Your father was drinking. But because he was rich, he didn't go to jail. He was sent to a private hospital where he was the largest donor and sat on the board. They didn't even fucking test his blood. The man couldn't walk. I saw. I was there." As he hisses in my face, I realize we are moving. Or rather he is pushing me.

The wind is knocked out of my lungs as my back hits the wall behind me.

"Everything was swept under the rug. My parents died . . ."

Still shocked from the impact, I lift my head and look at him. His feral eyes are far away and lost in a nightmare. I know he wants to kill me, but I still feel his pain. It's written on his features as if the accident just happened.

"I'm sor—"

His other arm reaches up, pinning me by the throat, his hands wrapping around my skin and cutting off my words.

"I don't want to hear you talk. I want you to listen. I want you to hear how your father ruined me. How because of him, my parents died, and I was sent to a home. The horrors I faced there. And while I was tortured, beaten"—he pauses and shakes the nightmare away of whatever else was done to him—"you were living a dream life."

"I lost my mother," I whisper.

"And I lost everything."

His arm starts to tighten. "I married you to get access to your father," he spits. "And then I killed him. He died slowly, choking on his own vomit. It was less than he deserved, and it still didn't give me what I needed. I was going to keep you around. Make your life hell, spend my whole life torturing you, the way I was tortured, but I got bored with you. So now . . . I'm going to kill you too. I'm going to ruin you, like he ruined me . . ." He trails off, his fingers wrapping tighter and tighter as the air starts to become limited.

I'm frozen in place. My mind spins as I begin to lose consciousness.

Black spots dance across my sight, marring my vision.

Soter.

Squeezing. Tighter. Tighter.

Blackness flashes again.

Soter.

The word repeats like a mantra over and over again.

Soter. Soter. Soter.

Jaxson.

I can no longer see. I can no longer feel. My mind hovers above my body.

Soteria.

The goddess of victory.

This isn't the end. The word rings in my brain. Everything Jax said to me, all the things Shay taught me.

I push past the pain, past the fear, and pull out the strength inside me. All of it. Because I won't let him win.

No.

This is where it ends.

I won't be his victim.

For months, I have run from fear. But I'm no longer afraid.

The past few months have taught me that I'm a survivor.

I don't need a man to rescue me. I can rescue my own damn self.

My arm reaches out for something to stop him. Anything.

Then I feel it.

It bites at my fingers, spilling blood with it. But through the pain, I grip the blade. I think it's a shard of glass from the construction.

I can barely see as I thrust it forward. But as I'm about to make contact, his free hand catches mine.

I thrust it forward again. The pain radiating from my hand is nothing like the pain radiating in my heart as I feel him grab it too and thrust.

I take my last breath as the shard finds its location.

The warmth of the blood caressing my skin.

The room turns black.

CHAPTER FORTY-FOUR

Jaxson

With the text that Maggie found on her phone, I'm able to figure out where she is. I'm out the door before I can even hang up on Maggie.

Luckily, the location is close.

The wind batters me with each step I make, but before long, I'm walking up to the old bank.

Throwing the door open, I'm running into the building. My eyes scan the room, and then my stomach drops. I see his body first. He's lying on top of Willow.

I run closer.

Her face is tucked under his, so I can't tell if she's alive.

But what I do see makes me dry heave.

There is so much blood. Too much blood.

Neither of them are moving.

I'm too late.

I shake the thought away as I bend to lift him off her.

Pulling her out from underneath him takes all my strength. He's dead weight.

When he's finally off her, she's curled in a ball. Blood covers her body. But I can't tell if it's her blood.

"Please be okay." I lean in and place my hands on her gently, trying to find her wounds. With my other hand, I swipe my phone, pressing the SOS button.

"This is nine-one-one. What's the emergency?"

"My girlfriend was attacked. There are two bodies . . ." I fire off the address and set the phone down, touching along her neck to see if there is a pulse.

"Please, baby, wake up."

She doesn't move, but beneath her skin, I can feel the signs of life. She needs to wake up because a world without Willow is a world I don't want to know.

"Please." I place my lips on her skin. "Please wake up. I can't be without you. I didn't know what love was before I met you. You showed me what it means. You showed me the man I want to be, so open your eyes, because I want to tell you I love you."

"Say it again," I hear, and I pull back and see her eyes fluttering.

"You're awake! Are you okay?"

She lets out a groan. "I hurt."

"The blood . . ."

"Not mine. Well, at least not all of it. My hands."

I look down at where her hands are on the floor, and I see crimson streaks. But nothing life-threatening. She goes to move, but I shake my head.

"Don't. Not yet. The ambulance is on the way."

She nods, and I pull her into my arms. As I hold her, we wait.

The police are here a few minutes later and the ambulance too. They usher Willow away to the hospital, and I ride along with her.

It's cut and dry that it's self-defense. But I have the files just in case they need proof.

Things fly from there. Doctors come in and out to check her. They reset her shoulder and observe her for a mild concussion.

She has some bruising on her neck and cuts on her hands, but she's going to be okay.

When we are finally alone in the hospital room, I take her hand in mine.

"That was the scariest shit ever . . . seeing you like that."

"I'm sorry," she whispers. "I was stupid. I led him right to me."

I lift her hand and place kisses on each bandage covering her skin. "You weren't stupid."

"Then what am I?"

"Brave as fuck. The bravest person I ever knew, and I was wrong."

"About what?"

"You were never the damsel in distress. You didn't need me to storm the castle. You picked up the sword and saved yourself."

Willow makes space for me on her hospital bed and I slide in next to her, never looking away.

"I love you."

Liquid pools in her blue eyes. "I love you too."

We both stare at each other for a while, but neither of us speak.

"Now what?" she eventually whispers.

"Whatever you want," I respond. I know there is a chance she'll go home. I hope she doesn't. I hope she chooses me.

"I don't know where this leaves me. The company . . ." she starts, and I know what she is saying. She has to go home. She has to go back to Madison Bay, Michigan. It feels like my heart is going to explode as I wait for my fate.

"Whatever you decide, I'll support you. But I love you, and I don't want to lose you. If that means coming with you, I will."

"You would do that for me?"

I lean down and place my lips on her. "Don't you know by now? I'd do anything for you."

"I guess home we go." She kisses me back. "Maybe not forever, but until I figure out what to do. I know I want you with me."

"Then I'll be there."

Willow was allowed to go home, so I took her to my place, tucked her in, left her with Maggie to babysit, and then made the trek uptown.

I didn't announce my arrival. Instead, I just showed up. The truth is, showing up unannounced runs the risk they won't be there, but I'm so eager to let what I need to say out that it didn't even dawn on me to call until I was walking to the doorman.

He picks up the phone and calls up.

"Mr. Price, your brother is here to see you," he says over the phone, and then he nods, signaling to me that I can head over to the elevator.

I ride quietly until the elevator arrives on the top floor.

When the doors open, I see that Grayson is waiting for me. Concern is laced on his face.

"Are you okay?" he starts, and I nod. I see him staring at my shirt. That's when I realize that in the rush to get here and say what I needed to say, I forgot that I have blood on me.

"It's not my blood."

"Talk to me." He points at the couch, and I follow him to where he sits. "You want a drink?"

I'm surprised by this. Usually, Grayson doesn't push booze on me at this time of day. It's only ten a.m.

"You know what . . . I will." After the day I had yesterday, and the fact I still haven't slept, I could use it.

He fixes us two glasses, and I'm shocked to see he's poured us both tequila. Maybe there is hope for us yet.

"What's going on, Jax, and why do you have blood on you?"

I think of how to say what I need to say, but I decide to cut to the chase. "I'm taking a leave of absence."

His eyes go wide.

"You don't need me. My job has always been a smokescreen for what I really do."

"That's not true."

"It is. And you know what I realized? I don't care. I have no passion to do what you do. And I don't need to. I'm not you. And that's okay. I don't want to be."

I expect him to object, to say something, but instead, he only stares at me. "I appreciate the opportunity, but I'm not going to pretend to be someone I'm not anymore. And I'm going to need you to appreciate me for who I am."

"I do," he finally says.

"Then why do you push me to be you?"

A line forms between his brows, and his jaw tightens. "I never meant to. I thought . . ." He lifts his hands and buries his head in them. "I didn't mean to make you feel that way. I thought that if I treated you the way Dad treated me . . ." He trails off. "For the longest time . . . it might sound crazy to you, but I was jealous."

"Of me?" Shock is evident in my voice. I lean forward in my chair because I couldn't possibly have heard him right.

"Yes, of you." He inhales deeply. "I always thought I'd be like Dad. I never thought I had a long life ahead of me. I was always envious of how you lived. You didn't live like me with a feeling of impending doom hovering over you. No, you just lived, and I hated you for that. You lived, and I was jealous. I'm so sorry.

When I met River, I realized how precious life is, and I promised myself I would change, but I couldn't. Not then. I wanted to help you grow, but the only way I knew how was to act like Dad did with me."

"You're not my dad."

"I know."

"And I'm not you."

"I see that now, and I'm sorry. I am, truly. I don't want to lose you. I can't lose you."

I don't speak as I take in his words, as I watch him for any tells.

There are none.

All I see is love. All I see is pride.

All I see is truth.

My leg jerks when I realize I've made the same mistake with Willow. I thought I needed to save her, but she was strong enough to save herself.

"I do appreciate you. Everything you've done, for me, the company, for River . . . we need you."

"And I'll always be there for you."

He stands unexpectedly, and I'm not sure what to make of it, and then he does something completely unexpected. He hugs me.

It doesn't last long, but it does its job.

It mends the last broken piece and makes me whole.

"I can work remotely on certain projects," I say to break the silence that has now fallen as he sits back down. He knows I'm talking about my side gig.

"Can I conv—"

"No. I have to go."

"Where are you going?"

From where I'm sitting, drink in hand, I fill him in on all that's happened to Willow. Her husband. The attempted murder. When I'm finally up to this morning and leaving Willow in bed, he blinks.

"Wow."

"I know."

"She sounds like a strong woman."

"The strongest."

"I'd like to meet her again," he says. His voice sounds sad. He did meet her, but he never got to know her.

I incline my head. "You will. Soon. I'll be taking her home to figure out what she wants to do with her parents' company. If she decides to stay, I'm staying. I'll work on whatever you need from there."

"Jax—"

I lift my hand to stop him.

"Don't try to object. She's it for me. She's my River . . . I would do and be anything she needs me to be."

I watch as he looks off toward the opposite side of the room. I follow his stare and see his eyes land on a picture of him and River. Then he looks back.

"I'm happy for you. If you need anything . . ."

"One thing . . . use of the company plane."

And with that, he laughs, and I know everything will be okay.

EPILOGUE

Jaxson

SHE HAS NO IDEA WHAT I HAVE PLANNED, AND THAT thought alone has me smiling broadly. She thinks we're here to help Addison look at a piece of property, and while yes, we are here to look at property, this piece of property has nothing to do with Price Enterprise.

As we get off the private jet, and I usher her to the waiting car, she doesn't say anything, but once the car door closes, and she is sitting beside me, tucked into the nook of my arm, I feel her head move.

I look down at her, and she's looking up at me.

"This is some job perk. Private planes. Greece."

"Addy's job, not mine. Remember, my job is in the office behind a computer."

She lifts an eyebrow. "As if you mind being stuck behind a computer all day. That's like your happy place."

Leaning down, I place a kiss on her temple. "You're my happy place," I say against her skin.

Together, we stare out the windows as we drive to our destination. Through narrow, winding streets, and overgrown trees, we continue our trek up the mountain.

Fifteen minutes later, we pull off the road. The clearing opens, and there set amongst the rocky cliffs is the house I had built.

"What is this?" she whispers. "I thought you said that this was land to build on."

"I might have lied."

"Why would you do that . . . ?"

"All in good time." I kiss her again. "You don't want to ruin the surprise."

"Surprise?" Her voice cracks, and with my lips still on her skin, I smirk.

"Yep."

The car pulls over by the front door. Once it is completely stopped and parked, I open the door, step out, and stretch my hand out for Willow.

She lets me help her out before the two of us walk hand in hand over to the front door.

It's hard to see the view from where we're standing, but I'm excited to show her.

"Come on," I say, and I place my finger to the keypad next to the door. "Actually . . ." I take her finger and place it on the pad, and the sound of a clicking rings through the air.

"What did you do?"

"Not me. You. And what you just did was unlock the door."

"The door to what?"

"Let me show you." I laugh as I push the now unlocked door open.

As she steps inside, she lets out a long audible breath.

I did the same thing when I came here after the construction was done, so I understand her reaction.

Still holding her arm, I lead her through the house until we are standing in front of the floor-to-ceiling windows that overlook the cliffs and the water.

From where we stand, you can see the docks below and anchored to the wood is a boat.

"What is this place? And why does my finger work to open it?"

"This place . . . This is our sanctuary. Remember that story I told you?" She nods. "This is that place. We are in Patras." Her eyes are wide in shock. I figure while I'm shocking her, I might as well tell her the real reason we are here, and with that, I drop to my knees.

At my movement, her jaw starts to shake.

"What are you doing?"

I take her hand in mine, and then with my other hand, I reach into my back pocket and pull out the box.

How she didn't realize I slipped it in there before we got out of the car is beyond me.

"Willow."

Tears start to roll down her face.

"I love you, and I want to spend my whole life loving you. Not just today or tomorrow. I want to love you past forever. Will you marry me?"

"Yes," she says as she throws her arms around me.

Her lips find mine, and as my tongue delves into her mouth, claps erupt all around us.

She pulls back and sees that we aren't alone here. My family and Maggie are here.

"You're all here."

"They are."

"For our engagement."

"About that . . ." I trail off.

"What's going on?"

"I love you, and you know how I said that I wanted to love

you until forever?" Her head bobs. "Well, how about if forever starts today?"

She shakes her head in confusion. "What do you mean?"

"I want to marry you today. Everyone who means anything to us is here . . . so what do you say?"

"We just got engaged."

"Good thing you said yes."

"Who's going to marry us?"

I hear a cough and look up to see Trent walking over. "I actually can do that for you." He laughs.

"Seriously?" Willow's eyes are wide.

"Yeah, I was bored and maybe a little drunk. Don't ask."

"Oh, I won't." Willow laughs. "And what about a dress?"

Addison walks forward. "I got you covered. My friend Madeline works for a couture clothing line, Valentina Fisher. She made you a one-of-a-kind couture gown."

I step up to her and place my hands on her jaw. "We don't have to do it like this if you don't want. We can go back to New York. We can throw a bi—"

"No. This is what I want. Like this. Everyone I care about is here, but even if they weren't." She looks me in the eyes. "You are. And that's all that matters. Being with you. Being your wife."

I lean forward and kiss her mouth. "Let's get married."

Willow

My arm is being tugged, and I'm in so much shock, I allow River to pull me down the hall and into a bedroom.

The sound of the door closing has me shaking my head and remembering what we are doing.

"First, hair and makeup and then the dress," River says, and that's when I notice that standing next to Jaxson's mom is a woman I have never met before.

"Hi," she says, stepping closer to me. "I'm Krista, and I'll be doing your hair and makeup for the big day."

"He really did think of everything," I say as I extend my hand and shake hers. "I'm Willow, but I have to assume you know this already."

She lets out a soft laugh and nods. "I do. I also know you don't really wear makeup and that you like to wear your hair down with loose curls."

"Wow. I didn't realize he noticed that much."

"That was actually my input," Maggie says from across the room. When she's standing in front of me, I tilt my head and bite my lip.

"Thanks for being here," I whisper.

"As if I'd miss your wedding." She laughs, and then I start to laugh because this is really crazy. Here I thought we were going on a business trip, not my wedding. "Now, let's get you ready." She grabs my hand and leads me to where the makeup woman has set up.

An hour later, my strawberry blond hair is styled in loose waves, and makeup adorns my cheeks and eyes.

When I step into my one-of-a-kind couture dress, my breath leaves my body.

I feel like a princess.

The dress is perfect. Every last detail. With tulle and hand-sewn beadwork, it's divine.

When the veil is placed on my head, Jaxson's mom walks over to me. Her eyes are filled with tears.

"You are beautiful."

"Thank you," I say, my own tears gathering.

"I'm so happy you'll be my daughter."

Fresh moisture trails down my cheek, and she starts to shake her head. "No. None of that. Jaxson will kill me." She laughs, and I wipe away the lone tear.

In the distance, I can hear the creak of the door, and I look up to see Grayson walking into the room.

"Can I come in?" he asks, and I nod. When he's standing in front of me, butterflies start to flutter in my stomach from nerves. "Willow," he starts. "I know your father isn't here . . ." He stops and lifts his right arm up and runs it through his hair. "I'm doing this wrong." His Adam's apple bobs. "I love my brother," he starts again. "But in the past, I didn't understand him. I wasn't there for him. I wasn't the big brother I should have been. But having you in his life . . . you gave me my brother back. Through you, and his relationship with you, I was able to see the man he was, and how wrong I was. Thank you, Willow." Tears well in my eyes. "What I wanted to say to you is that it would be a great honor to me if you would let me walk you down the aisle."

I need to inhale deeply and stare up at the ceiling to calm the tears of joy threatening to spill from me.

It's hard to find my words, but I know that I need this. Jax needs this, and Grayson needs this.

The Price boys have had their differences but allowing Grayson to give me away will help bridge the gap to the future.

"I'd love that."

He beams at my words. "Then it's time."

My heart feels full as I follow him out the door and into the hallway. I'm not sure of the location or what to expect, so when we step outside and see the grounds facing the water set up for a ceremony, my breath leaves my body.

Seats have been set up with flowers and candles on either side of an aisle that runs up to the edge of the cliff, and at the end stands Jaxson. He's not in a tux or a suit. But it wouldn't be Jax if he was. No, he's wearing white linen pants and a light blue button-down. His hair is unruly like always, but this time, it's not from running his fingers through it. This time, it's from the breeze coming across the water.

"You ready?"

I nod, and Grayson and I start to walk. As soon as I step on the path that will bring me to my soon-to-be husband, violins start to play in the background. I don't even know where it's coming from, but the sound makes this feel real.

Jaxson has thought of everything.

Each step I take brings me closer to my future until I'm standing in front of him, and he's staring down at me.

Taking my hands in his, he speaks.

"The very first time I saw you, I knew you were different. I knew you were someone I wanted to know. I love you, Willow. I love you now. Tomorrow. I love you forever. Every part of you. No matter what."

"I love you too." I hiccup through my tears, and he smiles, pulls me to him, and seals his mouth to mine.

I'm sure Trent says something else, but I'm lost in Jax's lips and what the future will hold.

Four Years Later . . .

My gaze scans the distance ahead of me, and I can't believe this is my life. After everything I have been through, I find I still want to pinch myself sometimes. How did I get so lucky? Yes, there are days I miss my mother and father terribly. Even today, as I stare across the field at my daughter running toward the bouncy house, I know Mom would have loved to be here. But as I look at all the faces around me, everyone here celebrating my daughter's second birthday, I know I'm blessed.

I take a few steps closer to where the cake is to light the candle, and then I lift my arm in the air to signal for Jax to come over.

He's standing with his brother. They look deep in conversation, but now I know that even though their faces are serious, they aren't fighting. No, they stopped fighting years ago. Right after Jax left Price Enterprise to start his own consulting firm, things changed between them. Of course, Jax's biggest client is his brother, but it took most of the pressure off them.

The change didn't happen overnight, but each day, they got closer and closer. Grayson still made the ritual phone call every morning, but instead of harping about the endless tasks he thought Jax should be accomplishing, he would call just to talk. Now years later, I know it's one of Jax's favorite parts of the day.

It makes me happy to know he has that.

As for me, I've been busy being a mom. But that's not all my life has become. I actually went back home to Madison Bay, and after a few weeks, I placed my father's company on the market. Being home, I realized there was nothing left for me other than painful memories. The happy memories I carry in my heart, and it doesn't matter where I am, my mom and dad are always with me.

I took the money I made and opened a haven of my own.

This time for women and children of abuse. Shay is now my business partner. We provide all the resources a woman would need to start over and find her strength.

It feels good to help. I was lucky enough to have Jax and Maggie; not everyone is as lucky as I was.

I smile to myself as I watch my husband smirk at Grayson, and I follow where they are looking.

That's when I see that my daughter, Penelope, is playing with Grayson's daughter, Skylar. The leaders of the pack are Addison and Oliver's kids, Charlie and Sophie.

They are taking turns going down the large inflatable slide.

Once Jax makes sure everyone is playing nicely, he pats his brother on the back and walks over to me.

When he is standing in front of me, he leans down, kisses my temple, and then places his hand on my stomach.

"How's he doing?" he says.

I place my hand on his, covering the bump that houses our baby boy. "He's good. Kicking like crazy."

"He probably wants to join the fun."

"I'm sure. But not for three more months." I laugh.

"At least," he agrees. "I love you."

"I love you too." I lift to my tiptoes and place a kiss on his lips. "Thank you," I say against his mouth.

"For what?"

"For this. For all of this." I motion around me.

"Anything for you. You are my world, Willow."

"And you are mine."

I'm safe. Protected. Loved and cherished.

I have a family again.

It's not the family I was born with, but it's mine.

ACKNOWLEDGMENTS

I want to thank my entire family. I love you all so much.

Thank you to my husband and my kids for always loving me. You guys are my heart!

Thank you to my Mom, Dad, Liz and Ralph for always believing in me, encouraging me and loving me!

Thank you to my in-laws for everything they do for me!

Thank you to all of my brothers and sisters!

Thank you to everyone that helped with Conceal

Lawrence Editing

Jenny Sims

Gemma Woolley

My Brother's Editor

Marla Esposito

Champagne Formats

Lori Jackson

Hang Le

Thank you to Chad Johansson for the most perfect image of Jaxson EVER!

Thank you to Zachary Webber, Andi Arndt, Kim Gilmour and Lyric for bringing Conceal to life on audio.

Thank you to my AMAZING ARC TEAM! You guys rock!

Thank you to my beta/test team.

Gemma! Thank you for dropping everything to read!

Livia: Thank you for always listening and helping!

Parker: You didn't help at all! Just Kidding! Thank you for everything you do for me.

Leigh: Thank you for always being there and always making time to read and talk.

Sarah: Your input and feedback is always amazing! Thank you!

Kelly: Thank you for all your input and proofing my audio.

Jessica and Lulu. Thank you for your wonderful and extremely helpful feedback.

Jill: Thank you for all your help.

Melissa: Thank you for everything.

Harloe: Thanks for always being there.

Mia: Thanks for always talking shop ie plots.

I want to thank ALL my friends for putting up with me while I wrote this book. Thank you!

To all of my author friends who listen to me complain and let me ask for advice, thank you!

To the ladies in the Ava Harrison Support Group, I couldn't have done this without your support!

Please consider joining my Facebook reader group Ava Harrison Support Group

Thanks to all the bloggers! Thanks for your excitement and love of books!

Last but certainly not least . . .

Thank you to the readers!
Thank you so much for taking this journey with me.

ABOUT THE AUTHOR

Ava Harrison is a *USA Today* and Amazon bestselling author. When she's not journaling her life, you can find her window shopping, cooking dinner for her family, or curled up on her couch reading a book.

Connect with Ava

Newsletter Sign Up: bit.ly/2fnQQ1n

Book + Main:
bookandmainbites.com/avaharrison

Facebook Author Page:
www.facebook.com/avaharrisonauthor

Facebook Reader Group: bit.ly/2e67NYi

Goodreads Author Page
www.goodreads.com/author/show/13857011.Ava_Harrison

Instagram:
www.instagram.com/avaharrisonauthor

BookBub:
www.bookbub.com/authors/ava-harrison

Amazon Author Page
amzn.to/2fnVJHFF

Made in the USA
Columbia, SC
23 March 2023